THE CASE OF THE LONELY HEIRESS

THE CASE OF THE LONELY HEIRESS

A PERRY MASON MYSTERY

ERLE STANLEY GARDNER

MYSTERIOUSPRESS.COM

INTEGRATED MEDIA

· NEW YORK

Copyright © 1948 by Erle Stanley Gardner

Cover design by Ian Koviak

ISBN: 978-1-5040-6133-9

This edition published in 2020 by MysteriousPress.com/Open Road Integrated Media, Inc.
180 Maiden Lane
New York, NY 10038
www.mysteriouspress.com
www.openroadmedia.com

CAST OF CHARACTERS

PERRY MASON—crack criminal lawyer, whose methods of solving cases might be termed "a little unorthodox"

DELLA STREET—Mason's Gal Friday—and all the other days of the week

ROBERT CADDO—publisher of "Lonely Hearts Are Calling"—self-styled psychologist who capitalizes on the diffidence of friendless people

PAUL DRAKE—head of Drake Detective Agency-long-time, long-suffering friend of Perry Mason

MARILYN MARLOW—an heiress with no flair for it—her ad in Caddo's magazine brings some startling results

ROSE KEELING ETHEL FURLONG—the nurses who witnessed the signing of the late George Endicott's will

KENNETH BARSTOW—one of Drake's most attractive operatives—especially adept at portraying young men fresh from the farm

DOLORES CADDO—Robert Caddo's outraged wife, who vents her wrath on the other woman in her husband's life

LIEUTENANT TRAGG—of Homicide—who has devised new and ingenious methods of producing mental anguish

RALPH ENDICOTT—brother of the late George P. Endicott—his thumbprint stars in a major role

PALMER ENDICOTT—who seems unduly suspicious of brother Ralph

LORRAINE ENDICOTT PARSONS—frosty sister, full of family feelings (including avarice) and fear of publicity

PADDINGTON C. NILES—the Endicotts' lawyer, eager to help his clients contest their brother's will and dismayed to find them way ahead of him

SERGEANT HOLCOMB—of the police—suspects find it a sheer delight to have nothing whatever to do with him

DEPUTY DISTRICT ATTORNEY HANOVER—skillful prosecutor, and more than a match for Mason

THE CASE OF THE LONELY HEIRESS

CHAPTER 1

Perry Mason extended his hand for the oblong business card which Della Street was carrying as she entered the lawyer's private office.

"Who is it, Della?"

"Robert Caddo."

Perry Mason studied the card, then smiled. "LONELY LOVERS PUBLICATIONS, INC.," he read. "And what seems to be Mr. Caddo's troubles, Della?"

She said laughingly, "They are what he described as 'complications' arising from an ad which he has been running."

She handed Mason a copy of a cheaply printed magazine entitled *Lonely Hearts Are Calling*.

"It looks like a cheap edition of a mail-order catalogue," Mason said.

"That's what it is."

Mason raised his eyebrows.

"At any rate, that's *almost* what it is," Della qualified. "You see, there are stories in the front part, and then in the back there are classified ads, and there is a blank on the back inside cover that can be torn along the perforated lines and turned into a mailing envelope with a message folded on the inside."

Mason nodded.

"I gather from Mr. Caddo that all such messages received at the office, properly addressed, will be forwarded to the advertiser to whose box they are addressed."

"Very interesting," Mason said.

"For instance," Della went on, opening the magazine at random, "here's Box Number 256. Would you perhaps like to communicate with Box 256, Mr. Mason? All you have to do is to tear off the back cover, cut it along the perforated lines, write your message, then fold it, place a seal on it, and deliver it by any means you may select to the office of Lonely Lovers Publications, Inc."

"Tell me more about Box 256," Mason grinned. "I think we're going to enjoy Mr. Caddo."

Della Street read the classified ad:

Refined woman of forty, with rural background, wishes to contact man who is fond of animals.

Mason threw back his head and laughed. Then suddenly he quit laughing.

"What's the matter, Chief?"

"After all," Mason said, "it's ludicrous and yet it's tragic. An unmarried woman of forty, with rural background, finds herself in the city with no friends. She probably has a cat or two. And she . . . What does Caddo look like?"

"He's about thirty-eight, high cheekbones, big ears, large blue eyes, partially bald, big Adam's apple, tall, has big feet, and sits rigidly erect in the chair. He won't lean back and relax. He makes me nervous just watching him."

"And his trouble?"

"He said he could only tell me that it was due to peculiar complications which he'd have to explain to you personally."

"Let's have a look at him," Mason said.

Della Street said, "Don't throw the magazine away. Big-hearted Gertie out at the switchboard is all worked up about it. She wants to write letters to all of them and cheer 'em up."

Mason thumbed through the pages of the magazine, musing half to himself.

"Looks like a racket," he muttered. "Take this first story—'A Kiss in the Dark,' by Arthur Ansell Ashland—'Never Too Late for Cupid,' by George Cartright Dawson. . . . Let's have a look at our friend Caddo, Della. He *may* be someone we want to take apart."

Della Street nodded, slipped back through the door into the outer office, and returned with a man who was tall in a gangling, loose-jointed way, with a static, vacuous grin seeming to betoken a continuous attempt to placate and mollify a world which somehow kept him on the defensive.

"Good morning, Mr. Caddo," Mason said.

"You're Perry Mason, the lawyer?"

Mason nodded.

Caddo's thick, sinewy fingers squeezed the lawyer's hand. "I'm mighty glad to meet you, Mr. Mason."

"Sit down," Mason invited. "My secretary says you're publishing this magazine." He indicated the magazine on the desk.

Caddo's head nodded in eager assent. "That's right, Mr. Mason, that's very true."

The light from the window glinted on the smooth, shiny expanse of his high forehead as he bowed. The big ears seemed to dominate the face. One almost looked for them to flap in accord, much as the reflex wagging of a dog's tail helps to communicate his emotions.

"Just what is the object of the magazine?" Mason asked.

"It's a means of communication, a means by which lonely people are brought together, Mr. Mason."

"It has a newsstand circulation?"

"Not exactly. It's sold through certain outlets. And then I have a small subscription list. You see, Mr. Mason, nothing is quite as cruel and impersonal as the solitude of a big city."

"I believe the theme has been the subject of poetic expression," Mason said dryly.

Caddo flashed him a quick glance from his big eyes, then grinned vaguely. "Yes, I suppose so."

"We were talking about the magazine," Mason prompted.

"Well, you see, this has the sort of stories that appeal to people who are hungry for companionship, people who are alone in the city, alone in life. We cater largely to women who have arrived at an age when they are afraid love may be about to pass them by permanently, an age of loneliness, an age of panic."

And Caddo's head once more embarked upon a series of regular, rhythmic nods, as though some inner clockwork mechanism had started him mechanically agreeing with himself.

Mason opened the magazine, said, "Your stories seem rather romantic, at least the titles."

"They are."

Mason skimmed through the story entitled "A Kiss in the Dark."

"Don't read that stuff," Caddo said.

"I just wanted to see what sort of stories you were publishing. Who's Arthur Ansell Ashland? I can't remember ever having heard of him."

"Oh, you wouldn't ever have heard of anyone whose stuff appears in *my* magazine, Mr. Mason."

"Why not?"

Caddo coughed deprecatingly. "Occasionally one finds it necessary, almost imperative, in fact, to do considerable detail work in order to be certain that there will be an ample supply of stories carrying out the general theme of the magazine."

"You mean you write them yourself?" Mason asked.

"Arthur Ansell Ashland is a house name," Caddo admitted modestly.

"What do you mean by that?"

"The magazine owns the name. We can publish anything we want to under the name of that author, using that by-line as a tag."

"Who wrote this story?"

Caddo's big teeth showed in a grin. "I did," he said, and once more started nodding a steady rhythm of affirmation.

"And how about this next one, by George Cartright Dawson?"

The nodding continued without the slightest change in tempo.

"You mean you wrote that one too?"

"That's right, Mr. Mason."

Mason watched the light glinting from the high forehead as the head continued to nod.

"And the next story?" he asked.

There was no slightest change in the tempo of the nodding.

"For the love of Mike," Mason said, "do you write the *whole* magazine?"

"Usually. Sometimes I find a story I can buy at my regular space rates of one-quarter of a cent a word."

"All right," Mason said crisply. "What are your troubles?"

"My troubles!" Caddo exclaimed. "I have them by the thousand! I . . . Oh, you mean why did I come to see you?"

"That's right."

Caddo opened the magazine which Della Street had placed on Mason's desk. With a practiced hand, he thumbed the pages and stopped at Ad 96. "Here we have it in a nutshell," he said.

He passed the ad across to Mason.

Mason read:

I am a girl of twenty-three, with good face and figure. I am the type the wolves all say should be in Hollywood, although Hollywood doesn't seem to think so. I am an heiress with a comfortable fortune coming to me. I am tired of the people who know who I am and are quite obviously making love to me for my money. I would like very much to form a new circle of acquaintances. Will some personable young man between the ages of 23 and 40 write to tell me he knows how I feel. Also, when you write, tell me something about your background. Enclose a picture if possible. Communicate with me at Box 96, care of this magazine.

Mason frowned.

"What's the matter?" Caddo asked.

"Quite obviously this is a fake," Mason said acidly. "No intelligent heiress would even read your magazine. A good-looking heiress would be far too busy and far too intelligent to waste her time reading such tripe, let alone sending in an advertisement for you to publish. This is the cheapest type of exploitation."

"Oh, I'm *so* sorry," Caddo said.

"You should be."

"I mean I'm sorry that you can't understand."

"I think I do understand. I would say that this ad was the result of a collaboration by Arthur Ansell Ashland and George Cartright Dawson."

"No! No! No, Mr. Mason! Please don't," Caddo said, holding an uplifted hand with the palm toward Mason, as though he were a traffic cop restraining an impatient pedestrian.

"You mean you *didn't* write that yourself?"

"No, definitely not."

"Then you had someone do it," Mason charged.

"But Mr. Mason, really I didn't. That's what I came to see you about."

"All right, tell me about it."

The lawyer's cynical eyes, boring into his, caused Caddo to shift uneasily. "I wish you would believe me, Mr. Mason."

"Give me the facts."

"In this business, you understand, as in any other business, once a person blazes a trail there are others who will follow it—in other words, I have imitators, and these imitators are my bitter rivals."

"Go ahead."

"One of these imitators has complained to the authorities that I am boosting the circulation of my magazine by resorting to false advertising."

"What do the authorities say?"

"They've advised me either to withdraw this issue from circulation or prove to them that the ad is genuine. And I can't do either."

"Why not?"

"In the first place, this is not really a magazine, in the usual sense of the word. It's sort of a pamphlet. We print a large number and keep them in circulation until they're sold out or until the freshness has so worn off that our advertising returns cease. To call in all the magazines and print others would be out of the question. Oh, I suppose it *could* be done, but it would be expensive and annoying and would necessitate a *lot* of work."

"If the ad is genuine, why can't you prove it's genuine?"

Caddo stroked his big jaw with long, powerful fingers. "Now there's the rub," he said.

"Meaning no pun, I take it," Mason observed with a swift glance at Della Street.

"I beg your pardon?"

"Nothing. Go on."

"Well," Caddo said, still rubbing his chin, "perhaps I'd better explain to you a little something about how we work, Mr. Mason."

"Go ahead."

"The only way a reader can communicate with one of the persons who has seen fit to insert an ad in my magazine is by purchasing a copy of the magazine at twenty-five cents, writing a message on the back page, and seeing that that page reaches the office of the magazine, properly addressed to the box with which he wishes to communicate. We then take the responsibility of seeing that the message is placed in the proper box. That's all. If the message is sent to us through the mails it's done by the subscriber at his own risk. In fact, we suggest that it be delivered personally, but if a subscriber lives out of town, of course, he usually has to mail his message."

"Go ahead."

"Now, a person who wants a pen-pal will be quite apt to communicate with several different advertisers. In other words, a person will often write ten or fifteen letters."

"All at the expense of buying a magazine for each letter at twenty-five cents a copy?"

"That's right."

"And then what?"

"He will probably receive an answer to every letter he writes."

"So that he then ceases to be lonely and therefore ceases to be a customer."

Caddo smiled. "It hardly works out that way."

"No?"

"No. A person who is truly lonely," Caddo said, "is very apt to be so because of some facet of his own character, not because of his environment. In other words, Mr. Mason, you take a mixer, a person who is going to be popular, and put him down in a strange city where he doesn't know a soul, and within a couple of weeks he'll have quite a circle of friends. Of course, with a woman it's a little more difficult, but they always manage some way. Now, the people who use my columns are, for the most part, mature people, who have something within themselves that keeps them from mixing, from making friends. A normal girl is married by the time she's thirty. One who passes that age, still unmarried, and not from choice, is quite apt to have a personality that will doom her to a solitary life. In other words, she has erected a barrier between herself and her emotions, between herself and the world; yet she's yearning to have someone smash that barrier. She herself lacks the power to remove it.

"Anyhow, without going into a lot of details about the psychology of lonely people—and I can assure you, Mr. Mason, I've made quite a study of that psychology—the fact remains that my customers are, as nearly as I can tell, more or less steady. For instance, we'll take the case of a hypothetical Miss X. Miss X is perhaps a spinster of forty-two or forty-three. She is wistful, lonely and essentially romantic. There are, however, certain mental inhibitions which keep her from letting herself go, so that only in the privacy of her own mind does she have these romantically gregarious thoughts.

"She's probably been someone's old-maid aunt who has perhaps lived with her married sister, helped take care of the children until the children grew up, and then found either that her welcome was wearing thin or that she was being used more and more as a servant. So she starts out for herself and she's completely lost. While she lived with her married sister she had a vicarious sort of life, a man around the house, children to care for, a feeling she was doing something. When she struck out for herself, she became an isolated piece of flotsam on a sea of cold faces."

"You certainly talk the way Arthur Ansell Ashland writes," Mason interpolated, "but go on with your story."

"Someone tells our hypothetical Miss X about my magazine,"

Caddo continued. "She puts an ad in, a very diffident ad, using the same old clichés about an unmarried woman of refinement, in the thirties, wishing to correspond with some gentleman whom she will find congenial.

"Now, the gentleman she has in mind is an ideal that exists only in her own mind. He certainly isn't going to be one who is answering the ads in my magazine."

"What about the men who answer the ads?"

"There aren't as many of the men as there are women. There really aren't enough to go around. Of course, we get lots of answers, but some of them are from practical jokers. It's quite the thing for pranksters to buy copies of the magazine, write that they're lonely widowers with large fortunes and good automobiles and things of that sort, and build up a correspondence with some of these women, simply for the purpose of a practical joke. It is, of course, cruel."

"But each letter nets you twenty-five cents."

Caddo nodded and said, without enthusiasm, "However, I would like to have the practice discontinued. It's cruel and it's bad for my business, but there's nothing I can do about it."

"Tell me something about the men who aren't practical jokers," Mason said.

"The men are mostly crusty old bachelors who are in love with the dream of a childhood sweetheart who is dead or married to someone else. There are, of course, a sprinkling of glib-tongued adventurers who are interested only in the small savings the women may have put by for a rainy day. In short, Mr. Mason, the men who advertise are all too frequently somewhat spurious. There is, however, one class, and that's the green-as-grass young swains from the country who are awkward, diffident, and shy. They want to get acquainted and don't know just how to go about it."

"And they all build circulation."

"It all helps."

"So eventually your hypothetical Miss X will come back to put other ads in your pamphlet?"

"That's right. I hold her as a steady reader by the stories I run, stories that deal with women who have been misunderstood, who finally meet and marry a man who would be able to sweep a movie queen off her feet."

"And you charge for those ads?"

"Oh, yes."

"How much?"

"Ten cents a word, and that includes box rental."

"You seem to have quite a few of these ads."

"The business is profitable; in fact, lucrative, quite lucrative!"

"Publication is at irregular intervals, you say?"

"Yes, depending on the number of ads that come in, the return on the ads, and our stock."

"Why can't you find out who this heiress is, if she's genuine?"

"Everyone who puts an ad in the magazine is given a number, and that number represents the box in which messages are placed. These are something like the boxes in a post office. Each one is opened with a key. An advertiser is charged for the ad. Then the box is given to that advertiser for a period of thirty days, with a renewal for sixty or ninety days on the payment of an additional fee. Any person who has the key has access to the box during the period for which the rental is paid. After the rental has expired, the box is closed and the person can either make new arrangements with the office or surrender the box. Letters to out-of-town advertisers, of course, go by mail.

"Now, in the case of this mysterious woman who placed the ad in the paper, the situation is somewhat complicated. As soon as I realized that it was necessary for me to communicate with her, I wrote a letter to her stating the facts of the case and asking her to give me some evidence of her identity and the sincerity of her ad."

Caddo fished in his pocket and said, "I received rather a sharp letter in reply."

He handed this letter over to Mason.

It read:

Dear Sir:

I placed an ad with you in good faith. I paid for it and I rented a box for thirty days. I am receiving replies. I chose to make my contacts in this way because I preferred to remain anonymous. I see no reason why I should sacrifice my privacy for your convenience. I can assure you that every statement contained in the ad is true and on that score you have nothing to worry about.

The letter was signed simply: "Miss Box 96."

"But she comes to the box for replies?" Mason asked.

"She does not. She sends a tight-lipped, hatchet-faced woman who certainly knows her way around."

"You're certain this isn't the one who is posing as the heiress?"

"I think not. I tried to follow her on two occasions. I suppose I was rather amateurish. She certainly told me that I was. She stopped both times, until I had no alternative but to saunter up to her immediate vicinity. Then she gave me a veritable tongue-lashing, told me that I was falling all over my feet. She said she had, in times past, been shadowed by experts and that I was hopelessly inept. It was a blistering bawl-out."

"How about writing mash letters in answer to her ad?" Mason asked.

"I've tried that. The woman seems absolutely uncanny in her ability to spot a phony letter. I have written a dozen different letters, telling her how much I wanted to meet a young woman of her type, that the fact she was an heiress meant nothing to me. I was interested only in her charming personality."

"And what happened?"

"I got no answers."

"I take it this young woman is getting quite a lot of letters?"

"Letters!" Caddo exclaimed, moving his hand in a sweeping gesture. "The box is simply jammed with letters! Replies are pouring in."

"And as far as you know, she treats them all the same?"

"Yes. If my own experience is any criterion, she isn't answering *any* letters."

"Then why did she put the ad in the magazine?"

"That is something I simply can't explain. But she definitely isn't answering letters. I've sent her over a dozen."

"What do you want me to do?" Mason asked.

"Get me off the spot with these authorities who are demanding that I either produce the woman or recall the magazine."

Mason thought for a minute and said, "It would probably be cheaper for you to recall the magazine."

"I don't want to do it unless I have to. It's expensive and. . . ."

"It would be less expensive than coming to me."

"It would also be an admission of guilt," Caddo said, "and there's another angle. Suppose this woman is a real heiress? I've made an agreement to publish her ad. I recall the magazine. She sues me. Then what?"

Mason said, "Bring me up a dozen copies of your magazine and a check for five hundred dollars. I'll see what I can do. It will take a little detective work."

"I'd want some sort of a guarantee," Caddo said, his eyes narrowing.

"What do you mean?"

"I'd want you to guarantee me something in return for the five hundred dollars."

"That's right," Mason grinned. "I'll guarantee to give you a receipt for the money and I'll guarantee to give you an itemized account of the money that is spent for detective services. And if, as I rather suspect, you're trying to use me as a cat's-paw to front for you on a come-on scheme you've adopted to increase your circulation, I'll send you a bill for five thousand dollars and see that you pay it!"

Caddo stroked his chin. "That's putting it rather crudely."

"I tried to put it that way."

"Please believe me, Mr. Mason! I'm in good faith. . . . Why did you want the magazines?"

"I just want to look them over," Mason said.

Caddo smiled. "You have one magazine," he said, "and, in case your idea was to bait this heiress by writing letters, I have here a large number of back pages, torn from the magazine, which you can use at your convenience."

And Caddo opened his brief case and took out some two dozen back covers which had been cut from the magazines.

"Give Miss Street your check for five hundred dollars," Mason said, "and I'll see what can be done."

Caddo sighed and took out his checkbook. "You're right," he said, "it's going to prove expensive."

When he had gone, Mason picked up the magazine, thumbed through it. "Listen to this," he said to Della Street, and read aloud from the story by Arthur Ansell Ashland:

"Once more Dorothy stood before the mirror where she had so frequently surveyed herself. Now there had been a magic transformation. The face that looked back at her was no longer wan, drab, lined with care. Love had waved its wand and the reflected features were those of a transformed woman, mature, to be sure, but radiant, feminine, in every way desirable.

"Another reflection formed behind the face in the mirror, the face of George Crisholm who had quietly entered the room and was now standing behind her.

"'My darling' he exclaimed. 'Don't waste your sweet beauty on that cold glass. Turn and look at me.'

"She turned, and strong arms crushed her in an embrace. Hot, eager lips were searching the pent-up recesses of her soul, releasing floods of desire that were all the more potent for having been so long denied."

Della Street whistled.

Mason said, "In a way, the thing is a crime. In another way, it probably brings solace to lonely hearts. If our friend Mr. Caddo is on the square we'll play ball. If he isn't—God help him."

CHAPTER 2

Perry Mason continued to thumb through the magazine, pausing occasionally to read other bits aloud to Della Street. Abruptly he closed the magazine and dropped it on his desk. "Della," he said, "we are now about to compose a love letter."

Della Street, nodding, held her pencil poised over a shorthand book.

"We'll block it out in rough form on the typewriter," Mason said. "Then I'll copy it in pen and ink on the back page of the magazine and send it to the magazine office to be put in the box."

Della smiled. "One would say that the surroundings were hardly conducive to a letter of passion."

Mason said thoughtfully, "I'm not at all satisfied that she wants a letter of passion."

"What *does* she want?"

"Let's consider that question, Della. It's highly pertinent. She has advertised in a lonely-hearts magazine. She announces that she is an heiress. She says she is fed up with the class of people she has been meeting. Observe, Della, that quite obviously the woman is not *lonely*. She only wants a *change*."

"Don't you suppose she has it by this time?"

"That's a chance we have to take," Mason said. "But after all, she's only human and she's going to read the letters that come in. If we can work out something that catches her fancy, we'll get a reply."

"Robert Caddo's letters didn't rate a reply."

Mason said, "We're going to profit by his mistakes. Caddo must have gone about it in the wrong way."

"His reply sounded all right to me."

Mason shook his head. "Observe that in every one of his replies he stressed the fact that he wasn't after her for her money."

"What's wrong with that?" Della asked. "Surely a girl would hardly be flattered by a man who wrote and said, 'Dear Miss Box 96: I am interested in you because you are an heiress.'"

"I'm not so certain," Mason said musingly.

"Why, Chief, what do you mean? Certainly she . . ."

"She took particular pains to mention that she was an heiress," Mason interrupted. "If she didn't want people to take that into consideration, why did she set it forth?"

Della Street frowned and said thoughtfully, "Yes, of course, she *did* mention that she was an heiress, but that was just to arouse interest."

"Then a man who wrote her that he was not interested in her because she was an heiress branded himself at once as being a damn hypocrite."

"Yes, I suppose so."

Mason said, "Let's try her with two letters. We'll start with this one:

"'Dear Miss Box 96:

"'I am a poor young man, and since you are an heiress I don't suppose there is any possibility that you would be interested in me. But, nevertheless, I am writing to tell you that I would like to meet you and would do anything to get your friendship. I think we have some things in common.'"

"That's all of it?" Della Street asked.

"That's all of it."

"Why, what a vague letter!"

"Exactly," Mason said. "I want it vague. I think perhaps Caddo's letters didn't get to first base because he was too specific.

"Let's suppose, Della, that this heiress is playing a pretty shrewd game. Perhaps she isn't lonely at all. Perhaps she just wants to contact someone whom she can use for some particular purpose."

"What purpose?"

"I don't know. We'll have to find that out."

"Then why not use more regular channels, if that were the case?"

"Because she's not interested in the sort of person she'd get through regular channels. Remember, Caddo said some of his readers were young men, chaps who came mostly from the country."

"Young men from the country know plenty these days," Della Street said.

"Most of them do," Mason admitted, "but there are some who are young and impressionable and haven't been around too much. Suppose, for instance, our heiress is really trying to get hold of someone who is green as grass?"

"I would say there wasn't much chance," Della Street said.

"I'm not so certain. Let's try her with this sort of a letter:

"'Dear Miss Box 96:

"'An heiress, gee! I've always wanted to meet an heiress. I haven't been in the city very long and I guess I've got no business writing you, but, golly, I certainly would like to meet up with a real, honest-to-goodness heiress, just to see what she looks like. I'm good and strong and husky and can handle just about any kind of farm work there is. I know a little something about cattle and am not afraid to pitch right in. Maybe if you'd like to meet a man like me, you could give me a break.'"

Della Street said, "You don't tell her what you look like, how old you are, or anything about yourself."

"That's right," Mason said.

"A woman who is looking for a boy friend would want to know those things first off," Della suggested.

Mason nodded. "I'm acting on the assumption she isn't looking for a boy friend, but is looking for something else."

"What else?"

"I'm darned if I know."

"What names do you want to use on the letters?"

Mason said, "The second one is easy. I'll sign it 'Irvin B. Green.' The initials, you'll notice, make it read I B Green."

"And the first one?"

Mason grinned. "The first one will have been written by a man named Black. We'll see what color she wants, black or green. Tell you what to do, Della. We'll need two different types of handwriting. Go down the hall to Paul Drake's office and get Paul to write out the one to be signed by Mr. Black and I'll write the one by Mr. Green. Paul Drake keeps a couple of post-office boxes that he can use for mail when he doesn't want to give a business address. Assign one of those box numbers to Black and the other one to Green. Then see that the letters go to Caddo's office."

"Do you want Caddo to know that these are your letters?"

Mason shook his head. "Let them be handled in the usual routine manner. From now on the less Caddo knows about what I'm doing, the better I'll like it. We'll give him a report on results, not on the means we use to get those results."

CHAPTER 3

Paul Drake tapped on the door of Mason's private office, a loud knock followed by four quick, gentle knocks, then two more loud knocks.

"That's Drake's code knock," Mason said to Della Street. "Let him in, Della."

Della Street unlocked the corridor door and the tall detective grinned fraternally at her. "Hi, Della, what's new?"

"Whatever you have in your hand," Della Street said, smiling at the letter Drake was holding.

Drake moved on in, nodded to the lawyer. "Well, Perry, we got an answer."

"An answer to what?" Mason asked, looking up from the brief he was studying.

"Remember the letters you had me mail day before yesterday?"

"Oh, those. Who got the answer?"

"Mr. Green got the answer," Drake said. "Mr. Black seems to have drawn a blank."

Mason narrowed his eyes thoughtfully. "Now, that's something!" he said. "She's looking for someone who's green as grass, an impressionable, gullible young chap. Let's see what she says."

Mason took the letter Paul Drake handed him, slit open the envelope, shook out a sheet of paper that had the crested initials MM. He raised the paper to his nostrils, caught the scent of perfume, grinned, and said, "The heiress speaks."

"What does she say?" Della Street asked. "I'm burning with curiosity."

Mason read the letter aloud:

"Dear Mr. Green:

"I was so thrilled to receive your letter. I only i wish I could tell you how much it has meant to me to hear from a man like you.

"I get so bored with the playboy type with whom I am forced to spend so much of my time that a letter like yours is like a breath of fresh country air in a stuffy room.

"I gather that you are big and strong and young and are from the country, that you haven't been in the city long, and that you have but few friends. Am I right?

"Perhaps if you would go to the Union Depot and stand at the desk marked 'Information' between six o'clock and six-fifteen tonight, I might be able to get away and meet you. Don't be too disappointed if I can't make it, because I'm going to have to try to break a date, but I can promise you that I will try to be there.

"You might wear a white carnation in your right lapel so I can recognize you.

"And if I can possibly make it, I'll come up and speak to you. Don't be too surprised to see just an ordinary looking girl. After all, heiresses are no different from other people except that they have money.

"Until tonight, then.

"Yours, MM."

"What the heck is this all about?" Paul Drake asked.

Mason grinned. "It's a job for you, Paul. I want a detective about twenty-four or twenty-five, a great big raw-boned hunk of manhood who can appear awkward and self-conscious and all that goes with it. I want him to dress up in one of his older suits, one that's perhaps a little tight or a little short in the arms and legs. He won't have any model to go by because we want him to make up as something that no longer exists, a terribly green country kid."

"What makes you think they don't exist any more, Perry?"

"Three things," Mason said, grinning. "The radio, the automobile and the movies."

Drake thought that over and then said, "Yes, I guess so."

"It always comes as a surprise to the city dweller," Mason said, "to tell him that people who live in the country may not be quite as blasé and cynical as he is, but that they know the answers about as well. I think our mysterious MM is a confirmed city dweller who doesn't know too much about life in the country."

"And she wants a hick?" Drake asked.

"Quite definitely she wants a hick. Can you get a man to take the part, Paul?"

Drake made a mental canvass of the operatives who were available for work of that type and finally said, "Yes, I guess I can. I have a chap who answers the description. He came from the country. He's done quite a bit of farm work."

"That's fine," Mason said. "She may try to trap him by asking questions about the farm, but I don't think the answers will mean much to her. Now I'll want three or four more operatives, Paul."

"What for?"

Mason said, "She may never go near this man at the information desk, but she'll be sizing him up. She'll think that he's too green to know what her game is or to spot her, but I want men sprinkled around who can spot her and who will follow her in case she doesn't make contact with our plant."

"Just what do you want?"

Mason said, "For the present, I want to find out who MM is. I want her name, her address, and I want to find out something about her background."

"Okay," Drake said, "it should be easy. If she doesn't go up and speak to my man, it's a cinch she'll be wandering around where she can size him up and my boys can pick her up."

"Okay," Mason said. He turned to Della Street and said, "Ring up Robert Caddo and tell him I think we'll have an answer to his question some time tomorrow. Make an appointment with him for tomorrow at ten o'clock, Della."

She nodded, jotting down the time in her appointment book.

Paul Drake weighed the letter thoughtfully. "Perry, do you suppose there's any chance this is on the up-and-up?"

"Of course there's a chance," Mason said indulgently.

"How much of a chance?"

Mason grinned. "Offhand, I'd say just exactly one in a million, Paul."

CHAPTER 4

Perry Mason and Della Street entered the big terminal depot, Mason carrying an empty suitcase and a small traveling bag, Della Street equipped with an overnight bag and carrying a coat over her arm. The hour was five minutes to six.

"How are we doing?" Mason asked.

"Fine," she said. "There are two seats over there to the left."

Mason followed Della Street over to the two vacant seats, placed his bags in front of his feet and ostentatiously displayed a timetable which he studied with frowning concentration.

Della Street, with an attitude of assumed travel weariness, kept Mason posted on developments.

"If Paul Drake has men scattered around here," she said, "I'm so dumb I can't spot them."

"Of course not," Mason said over his timetable. "A detective who could be spotted as a detective wouldn't be worth a hoot to Paul Drake."

"Aren't people who are intelligent supposed to be able to pick out a detective?" Della Street asked.

"They're supposed to," Mason said, "but they can't."

"Well, here comes the bait," Della said. "Gosh, he's a good-looking boy."

Mason glanced up over his timetable.

A tall, awkward lad, about twenty-four or twenty-five, wearing an expression of open-eyed credulity, attired in a suit which somehow seemed just a little too small for him, walked diffidently up to the information desk. There was a white carnation in his right lapel, and his face was darkened with what appeared to be a deep tan.

"Gosh," Della Street whispered, "he's perfect."

"We'll see if he gets the heiress," Mason said. "Have you spotted her?"

"Gosh, no, and I'm looking all around, too."

"Don't overdo it," Mason said.

"I'm not, I'm just a weary housewife who has had to go through all of the strain of packing and hurrying to get away to go to San Francisco and visit Aunt Matilda. I'm pretty tired, but I'm still interested in the people around me and keyed up with anticipation for the trip."

"That's the idea," Mason said, "only don't take too much interest in the people around you."

Mason folded the timetable, got up and took one of his bags over to the parcel-checking locker, placed the bag in the locker, took out the key after depositing his dime, then returned to his seat beside Della Street. He unfolded an evening newspaper. "All right," he said, "keep me posted," and forthwith apparently became engrossed in the news of the horse races.

The activity of the terminal depot flowed past them in an unceasing stream. People walked aimlessly toward the train gates, only to turn and walk aimlessly back, waiting for arrivals and departures. Other people plodded wearily to seats, apparently waiting between trains. There were others who seemed anxiously awaiting trains where they were to meet friends or relatives. Here and there businessmen and seasoned travelers bustled about, sending telegrams, placing last-minute calls in the telephone booths, putting hand baggage into the custody of redcaps before boarding trains. In contrast to these crisply energetic travelers were the tired ones who waited, slumped down on the hard benches, wrapped in weary lethargy.

"Oh, oh!" Della Street suddenly whispered. "Wait a minute! I think I have her spotted. The brunette in the plaid skirt. Take a look at her, Chief."

"Just a minute," Mason said. "Get your eyes off of her, Della, so that I can look up casually over the top of the newspaper. She may be suspicious."

Della Street said, "She's directly in line with the parcel-checking window. Look a little over your left shoulder, Chief."

Mason slightly lowered the newspaper, opened his mouth in a prodigious yawn, threw his head back, and, as he was yawning, studied the girl Della Street had indicated.

As Mason was watching her, she reached a decision, suddenly walked up to the man at the information desk, touched him on the arm and smiled sweetly at him.

Paul Drake's operative raised a big, awkward hand to his hat, pulled it off and grinned with pleased embarrassment.

The pair talked for a moment, then the girl glanced swiftly around, said something to the man, and they left the terminal, turning toward the big doors through which people were streaming in and out.

Della Street, watching them in dismay, said, "Chief, they're leaving!"

"Uh huh."

"But no one's following them."

"How do you know?"

"No one's paying the slightest attention to them. Drake's men must have fallen down on the job."

"Don't worry," Mason said, "they'll be on the job, all right."

"Shouldn't we try to see where they . . ."

"Definitely not," Mason said, and stretched out once more to yawn wearily. Then he devoted himself to his newspaper.

"You're the most exasperating person in the world at times!" Della Street said. "I'm burning with curiosity."

"So I gathered."

"And we don't know anything more about who she is than we did before."

"We've had a look at her," Mason said. "That's mainly what I wanted."

"Just a glance," she said. "You couldn't possibly tell anything about her."

"I can jump at conclusions," Mason grinned. "They may be wide of the mark, but in any event they're conclusions."

"Such as what?"

"In the first place," Mason said, "I don't think she's an adventuress. I have an idea she's on the up-and-up. In the second place, she's frightened about something. This meeting meant a lot more to her than might have been supposed. There was a look of relief on her face when she realized that this man was just the type she was looking for."

Della Street thought that over, then said, "Yes, I guess there was, come to think of it. . . . I can tell you something about her clothes. They're simple clothes that really cost money. I wonder what sort of a car she's driving."

"Nine chances out of ten it's a taxicab," Mason said. "She wouldn't take a chance on letting anyone get the license number of her car until after she'd had an opportunity to talk and size him up. Well, Della, I guess the show's over. How about eating?"

"Now you're really talking."

A travel-weary woman, who had elicited Della Street's sympathy, patiently pushed back the four-year-old boy who had been clinging to her knees. The man who was with her said, "I guess the train's late. I'll get Junior his ice cream cone." He plodded away dispiritedly and returned in a moment with the ice cream cone. Then suddenly he veered over toward Perry Mason and Della Street.

"I'm supposed to make my report direct to Paul Drake," he said, "but they've gone away in a taxicab. Since the contacting operative is with her, we followed instructions and didn't make any attempt to tag along. I guess that's what you want to know, isn't it?"

Mason smiled at Della Street.

"That is what Miss Street particularly wanted to know," he said.

5P1.55

Mason said, "come in and sit down, Mr. Caddo."

Caddo's manner seemed nervous. "You have a report for me?" he asked.

"That's right. I think I can set your mind at ease on the matter concerning which you consulted me."

"So soon?"

Mason nodded.

Caddo seated himself and almost immediately began stroking his chin nervously with his long, powerful fingers.

"Your lonely heiress in Box 96," Mason said, "is Miss Marilyn Marlow. She inherited approximately three hundred and fifty thousand dollars from her mother under rather peculiar circumstances. Her mother was a special nurse who attended a George P. Endicott during his last illness. Endicott made a will, leaving a large, old fashioned, rambling mansion where he had been living to his two brothers and a sister. He also devised and bequeathed to each the sum of ten thousand dollars. All the rest, residue and remainder of his estate he left to Eleanore Marlow, Marilyn's mother. The will also contained a proviso that if any of the heirs should question the validity of gifts he had made to Eleanore Marlow in his lifetime—some cash and a collection of gems that were family heirlooms—such heir would forfeit all right to take any property under the will.

"Eleanore Marlow was killed in an automobile accident shortly after Endicott died. Marilyn is her only daughter. She is worth somewhere in the neighborhood of three hundred thousand dollars—perhaps more. She certainly comes within the definition of an heiress. In fact, her mother's estate has not as yet been closed and the Endicott Estate has not been closed. There are some properties in Oklahoma which are potentially oil-bearing.

"The will was admitted to probate, but the brothers and the sister plan to contest it. The witnesses to Endicott's will were two nurses, a Rose Keeling, and Ethel Furlong. The contest may be pretty hot. At the time the will was executed, Endicott was partially paralyzed. He signed with his left hand."

Caddo heaved an enormous sigh of relief. "Mr. Mason, I can't begin to tell you how grateful I am. I can't even begin to tell you what a load you've taken off my mind."

Mason nodded.

"But why in the world," Caddo went on, "would a woman like that—young and attractive and wealthy—want to use my magazine for the purpose of making new friends?"

"I believe the ad says that she is weary of the type of people with whom she comes in contact," Mason said dryly. "Fortune hunters and people of that sort."

"But if I understand you correctly," Caddo said, "she must have old friends, friends whom she knew before she ever inherited the money. After all, this is rather a recent development, isn't it, Mason, this wealth of hers?"

Mason nodded.

"Then she *must* have had friends whom she knew before. . . . How long has she lived here, Mason?"

"Apparently about five years."

"I don't understand it," Caddo said.

"Do you have to?"

"What do you mean?"

"As I understand your position, you are being accused of endeavoring to build the circulation of your magazine by a false advertisement."

"That's right."

"What's false about the advertisement?"

Caddo rubbed his chin. "Nothing, I guess."

"Exactly," Mason said.

A slow grin suffused Caddo's features. "I guess, Mr. Mason, thanks to you, I'm sitting pretty." Mason nodded.

"And the replies," Caddo went on, "keep rolling in. Good heavens! The mail that girl is getting! I had enough of the magazines printed to last me two months, and stocks are getting low already."

"Then you'll have to put out a new issue of the magazine?" Mason said.

"Don't be silly," Caddo said. "I'll simply reprint. With that ad pulling the way it is, I'll keep on selling those magazines until the cows come home. Boy-oh-boy, what a sweet spot to be in! She's getting a hundred replies a day right now."

Caddo got up out of his chair, then paused. "Are we all square, Mr. Mason?"

"All square," Mason said. "I've had some expenses, but I'll pay them out of the five hundred dollars and still have enough left to cover my fee."

"That's splendid! Would you mind telling me how you pulled this particular rabbit out of the hat, Mr. Mason?"

"It took a little head work and a little leg work, that's all."

"I presume, of course, you hired someone to do the leg work."

Mason said, "I try to get results, Caddo. I believe I got them."

"That's right," Caddo said, "you certainly did."

He shook hands with Mason, beamed at Della Street, and then, halfway to the door, said, "By the way, I'd better get all the dope on this Marilyn Marlow. What's her address?"

Mason consulted a card and said, "The address is 798 Nestler Avenue, at the Rapahoe Apartments. Any details you need about the rest of the layout, in case you do need them, you can secure from the office of the Probate Clerk, Matter of the Estate of George P. Endicott, deceased."

Caddo pulled a fountain pen from his pocket, scribbled a note on the back of an envelope, smiled beamingly once more, and went out.

Mason said to Della Street, "Well, let's forget the heiress, Della, and get to work on this brief. It seems terribly prosaic now. Hang it, why *did* Marilyn Marlow put that ad in? Oh, well, we have work to do."

Mason went to lunch, returned at two o'clock, worked until three, and then Paul Drake telephoned.

"Perry," the detective said, "do you want to talk with Kenneth Barstow?"

"Who's Barstow, Paul?"

"The operative who was on that Marilyn Marlow case."

"Shucks, no, that case is closed."

"I had an idea you might like to get the low-down from Barstow. Something's a little strange there. He thought she might be looking for something."

"So what?" Mason asked.

"I mean she may be wanting him to do something specific, something that was a little bit shady."

"Where is he?"

"In the office here. He's been talking to me and I thought you might like to ask him a question or two, just to complete your files in case anything else turns up."

Mason glanced at his watch and said, "Oh, bring him in, Paul. Let's hear the story."

Drake said, "We'll be in right away."

Mason nodded to Della Street. "Open the door for Paul, Della. He's bringing in the operative who made the pickup with Marilyn Marlow."

"Some sheik," Della observed. "And you were going to put him out of my life, just like that?"

Mason laughed. "I don't know why I should waste any more time on it. The client has been satisfied; we've got a fee. But let's hear his story. I'm curious."

Della Street opened the door and a moment later Drake and

his operative entered the office. "This is Kenneth Barstow," Drake said by way of introduction. "Sit down, Kenneth. You've seen Perry Mason, I guess, and this is Miss Street, his secretary. Tell them your story."

Barstow was no longer the awkward-appearing young man from the country. He wore a double-breasted suit that fitted his slim-waisted figure to advantage. His thick, wavy black hair was combed back from his forehead, and his blue eyes dwelt appreciatively for a moment on Della Street, then shifted back to Perry Mason.

"I made contact with the subject at seven minutes past six," he said. "We went in a taxicab to a restaurant. She bought the dinner and did most of the talking. I put on an act of being bashful and tongue-tied. She cross-examined me some about the country and life on the farm. She didn't know too much about life in the country and I did, so it was duck soup. We walked from the restaurant over to a parking station. She had her car there. I got the license number and knew then that I was getting to first base. She drove around the city, got up in the park and stopped to show me the lights, and we did a little necking."

"How much?" Drake asked.

Barstow glanced apologetically at Della Street and said, "All of the preliminaries."

"Then what?"

"Then I drove home with her and saw her to her apartment. She bought me a drink, and that was the end of the evening."

"No more necking?" Drake asked.

"Not after we got to her apartment. She was businesslike then. She said she might have a job for me. She wanted to see me again right after lunch, this afternoon. I told her I wasn't working at present, because I thought it would be a lot easier to stand by that than to tell her I had a job and have her check on it and find I was wrong. You see," Barstow went on, "I didn't know whether this was going to be just a one-time contact job or whether it was going to run along for several days."

Mason nodded.

"I went back about one-thirty, as she had suggested. We were going to play some tennis. I told her I wasn't too good at it, but she wanted to play a couple of sets. She said she had to watch her figure."

"Did you play?"

"No."

"What happened?"

"I got in bad."

"How?"

"That's the thing I don't understand. I went up to her apartment and she bought me a drink and chatted along a while, then she went in the bedroom to change her clothes. The phone rang a couple of times and she talked on the calls."

"Any necking?" Drake asked.

"Yes, there was a little necking," Barstow said, "and to tell you the truth I wondered just what she had in mind. And then after the second call I made a halfway pass at her and got my face slapped so hard my ears were ringing. The first thing I knew, I found myself out on the street, and boy, did I get a bawling out! She said I was just like everyone else, all I thought of was making passes; that she thought I'd been a sweet, unspoiled country boy, and I turned out to be an amateur wolf, and she wanted me to understand that the wolf act was strictly amateurish."

"Perhaps you went too fast too soon," Mason said.

"Or too slow too late," Della Street supplemented.

Barstow smiled at Della, then frowned. "After the way the thing started out last night I know I wasn't exceeding the speed limits. I was getting along swell. Then something happened. I'd swear she egged me on to the face-slapping point just so she could throw me out. It's some place where I didn't put my act across the way I should. I think she found out I was phony, and it worries me. My technique shouldn't be that bad."

Drake said, "Well, as soon as you phoned in and gave me the license number and her address we double-checked on her, so we have everything we want. Does she know where she can get in touch with you?"

"Yeah, I gave her a phone number. It's a friend. She *could* reach me there."

"Think she'll call up?" Drake asked.

"I'd bet a hundred to one she doesn't. She sure was mad when she put me out"

Drake said, "Sounds to me as though she gave you a pass to first and you tried to steal second."

Mason said somewhat impatiently, "Oh, well, it's all right. It's all over now. Forget it."

"I hate to think I've muffed a play," Barstow said.

"We all do once in a while," Drake reassured him and then said apologetically to Perry Mason, "I thought you'd like to know all the details, Perry."

Mason said, "Okay, thanks, Paul. That's fine, Barstow. You did a good job. We got the information we wanted."

Barstow arose somewhat reluctantly, glanced again at Della Street and said, "I don't ordinarily fall all over myself that way. I still would like to know what I did wrong."

They left the office, and Della Street said to Perry Mason, "What do you make of it, Chief?"

Mason glanced up from the brief which had once more claimed his attention. "Make of what?"

"That Barstow incident."

"I don't know," Mason said. "The guy probably misunderstood the signals and made the wrong play."

"I don't think so."

"He must have done something," Mason said. "She turned against him all at once, and it wasn't for nothing."

"I don't think it was anything he did," Della Street said. "I'm just checking my impressions on Marilyn Marlow and giving it to you from a woman's angle. Remember, this Marlow person used an ad in a lonely-hearts magazine. She met this chap and started giving him a rush act. She sized him up at a restaurant and then certainly encouraged him to throw a forward pass."

Mason pushed the brief to one side. "All right, Della, what are you getting at?"

She said, "I think it was the telephone call."

Mason frowned, then whistled and said, "Perhaps you've got something there."

"A telephone call," Della went on positively, "that tipped Marilyn Marlow off to the fact she was playing with dynamite. Now, who could have placed that call?"

Mason let his eyes narrow in thoughtful speculation. "Wait a minute," he said, "let's get the time element on this thing." He motioned to the telephone and said, "Get Drake's office. See if Barstow has left. Ask him what time he got the gate."

Della Street put through the call, turned to Mason and said, "About one-fifty."

The lawyer started drumming with his fingers on the edge of the desk. He was frowning and thoughtful.

"Do you," Della Street asked, "know more than I do?"

"I'm simply putting two and two together," Mason said. "The answer?" Della Street asked. Mason said, "I guess I've been a little too easy-going, Della."

"How come?"

Mason said, "If I'd thought it was that sort of a play I'd have charged him another thousand."

"You mean Robert Caddo?"

"Robert Caddo," Mason said.

"Good grief! Do you think it was Caddo? What would have been the idea?"

"I think it was Caddo," Mason said. "And the idea is that our friend, Robert Caddo, intends to cut himself a piece of cake, and he evidently wants to be certain he gets the right piece—the one with all the frosting."

CHAPTER 6

At five o'clock, Gertie the receptionist and the two typists went home. At five-ten, Jackson, the law clerk, thrust an apologetic head into Mason's private office. "If there's nothing else, Mr. Mason, I think I'll leave early tonight."

Mason smiled, glanced at his watch and said, "It's ten minutes late now."

"Early for me," Jackson said. "I just can't seem to get caught up with things."

He was so deadly serious that Mason merely smiled and nodded.

At five-twenty, Mason pushed the law books and the brief back on his desk, said to Della Street, "Let's call it a day, Della, and get a cocktail. I'll drive you to your apartment, or, if you haven't a date, I'll buy you a cocktail and also a dinner."

"You've sold a dinner," Della Street told him. "Let's have a cocktail down at that little place in the Spanish Quarter and then go over to the restaurant that's run by your Chinese friend for dinner. I feel like spareribs sweet and sour, fried prawns and some pork noodles."

"Simply ravenous, in other words," Mason said, smiling.

"I have to keep my strength up to hold my nose on the grind-stone—particularly with all these heiresses bobbing in and out of our lives."

"*Out* is right," Mason said.

They closed up the office, drove in Mason's car down to the Spanish Quarter and sipped a Bacardi while they toyed with thin sheets of fried corn-flavored delicacies.

Della Street said, "You have your car here, and the depot's only a couple of blocks away. Let's drive around and pick up that bag you left in the parcel-checking locker last night. We were so worked up over the heiress, we drove away and left it."

"Good idea," Mason said. "I guess we're all finished with those stage props. Hang it, I hate to be double-crossed by a client."

"Of course you aren't *certain* it was Caddo."

"There was only one person," Mason said, "who knew that Barstow was a detective and who also knew Marilyn Marlow's address. That person was our esteemed contemporary, Robert Caddo. You can see what he did. He got Marilyn Marlow's name and address. He left my office, took an hour or two to get details, then hatched a plan, called her up and told her that a detective was on her trail."

"But the detective had indirectly been employed by *him!*"

"Naturally," Mason said, "he didn't tell her that. He posed as an unselfish friend who had taken a fatherly interest in her because the ad had appeared in his magazine."

"I suppose it must have been Caddo," Della said.

"Caddo," Mason went on, "is just one of those things. His whole magazine business is a racket. I'm kicking myself I didn't realize that right at the start. However, he enlisted my sympathy with his hard-luck story. I'm always a pushover for a client's tale of woe. . . . What time is it, Della?"

"Six o'clock."

"Well, it's a little early to eat, but—let's go over and pick up the bag. Then we'll have a Chinese dinner and by that time we can probably find a show we haven't seen."

Mason left two silver dollars on the table, escorted Della Street out of the cocktail lounge and into his car. They drove to the terminal, and Mason parked the car.

"I like to watch people around a depot," he said. "It's fascinating. You can see so much of human nature that way. People aren't on their guard when they're dead-weary or when they're completely removed from their usual environment. A person who lives here in the city feels he's on his own home ground, no matter what part of the city he's in, unless it's the depot. But the minute he walks into the depot he's started, so to speak, on a complete change of environment and he lets his guard down. He . . . Della, *do you see what I see?*"

"What?"

"Over there at the information desk," Mason said.

"I don't see anything. I . . . Oh . . . ! He has a white carnation."

"In his *right* lapel," Mason pointed out.

"Do you suppose he's *another* candidate?"

"Evidently so," Mason said. "She must make a habit of it—and, after all, why not? Having picked the best place for her to size up her prospective boy friends, there's no particular reason why she should change it from night to night. If this is the *best* place for her purpose, any other place would be inferior, and . . . Let's get that bag and then move over here and sit down where we can watch proceedings, Della."

They found a couple of seats three rows back, but in such a position that they had a good view of what was going on at the information booth.

Della Street regarded the young man who was standing somewhat self-consciously in front of the information-booth barrier, and said, "He's nowhere near as attractive as Kenneth Barstow."

"Seems to be an upstanding young chap," Mason said.

"But not attractive in the way that Barstow is. Tell me, Chief, have you known Barstow before?"

Mason shook his head. "Just one of Drake's operatives. They come and go. That young fellow probably was in the war and hasn't been back with Drake more than six months or so. I just haven't had occasion to meet him, so I can't answer your question."

"What question?" Della Street asked, frowning.

"As to whether he's married."

She smiled. "I hadn't asked it"

"I merely told you I couldn't answer it."

They waited for a moment in silence, then Mason said, "I wonder if she'll pass this one up. She's probably sizing him up from some other part of the station, but I don't want to try rubbering around. It'll make us too conspicuous. Wait a minute, here she is, coming out from that telephone booth. That's a good place for her. She can sit in there and size up the one she lines up."

"She's certainly going to a lot of trouble to get the perfect mate," Della Street said.

"I'm afraid she's not looking for a mate," Mason observed thoughtfully.

"For what, then?"

Mason shrugged his shoulders and said, "For someone to commit a murder, for all I know."

Marilyn Marlow glanced quickly around the depot, then walked up toward the information desk.

"Certainly has a snaky figure," Mason said.

"And how well she knows it," Della Street said acidly. "She certainly dresses for it, and . . . well, here we go again."

Marilyn Marlow walked up to the young man at the information desk. By this time that individual was rather absorbed in his own thoughts and it was necessary for her to touch his arm before, with a sudden quick jump, he whirled and smiled down at her, removing his hat in a single quick gesture of easy grace.

"That's no boy from the country," Della Street said. "That chap knows his way around. I'd like to know what he told her in his letter."

"Something that got a response," Mason said, "and from what we know, that isn't an easy thing to do. A hundred candidates a day! That's quite a handicap—one chance in a hundred!"

The couple chatted for a moment, the man smiling affably and easily.

For a moment the girl seemed somewhat dubious. Her large dark eyes sized him up from head to foot in critical appraisal, then, apparently reaching a decision, she smiled an invitation to accompany her, and the two left the depot.

"Well, that's that," Della Street said. "I suppose it's another taxicab and . . ."

Mason was crisply businesslike as he said, "We'll make certain of that, Della."

He arose and started for the exit.

"Want me with you?" Della Street asked.

"Uh huh, it'll make it seem less conspicuous. When we get to the door, you pull back and argue with me to put through a telephone call to Aunt Myrtle. I won't want to do it. That'll give us an excuse to stand there without seeming to be gawking."

She nodded and at Mason's side walked out to the cement apron in front of the depot.

Marilyn Marlow and the young man were standing there, not saying anything at the moment.

"Come on," Della Street pleaded in a loud voice, "you simply *have* to call Aunt Myrtle. She'll never forgive us if she knows we went through town without calling her."

"Oh, forget it," Mason said. "Then we'd have to go out and spend all our time between trains sitting in a stuffy parlor and talking a lot of family stuff. Let's look the city over and see what it's like. It's the first time we've ever been here."

"No, we *must* call Aunt Myrtle. Perhaps we can go out after that."

They were still arguing when a car pulled over to one side.

"Shucks," Della Street said under her breath, "they can't get a taxicab here. What are they waiting for? The taxicabs are around at the other end and . . ."

Abruptly Mason said, "All right, let's go telephone Aunt Myrtle," and putting his arm around Della Street swept her back toward the depot.

"What is it?" Della asked quickly.

"You might try looking back over your shoulder," Mason said.

Della Street looked back. A car had driven up and stopped at the curb. Marilyn Marlow swept imperiously toward it and the young man, quickly reaching past her, opened the door and assisted her in, then climbed in beside her. The door slammed and the car moved away.

"Get a look at the chauffeur?" Mason asked.

"Good heavens, yes!" Della Street exclaimed. "It was Robert Caddo! And he was all dolled up in a chauffeur's cap and a suit of livery!"

CHAPTER 7

Mason regarded Della Street's practically untouched plate.

"Not hungry, Della?"

She shook her head.

"I suppose you're thinking of the same thing I am," he said.

She nodded.

"I hate to be double-crossed by a client," Mason went on, "but let's try and get it off our minds while we're eating. How about a dance?"

She nodded, and Mason swept her out on the dance floor.

But neither of them could enjoy the dance. There was a certain tension about Della Street, and Mason's jaw had a determined set to it.

"Of course," Mason said at length, "it's none of *our* business what she wants the chap for, but it certainly looks as though she wants to get some green-as-grass chap she can twist right around her fingers. I wonder if there's something phony about that will, Della."

Della Street laughed. "You're not only reading my mind, but you're getting it all churned up."

"Okay," Mason said, "let's get out of here and take another look at Drake's report."

Mason called the waiter, paid their check, retrieved his car from the parking lot and drove to his office building.

The night janitor who operated the elevator grinned at Mason as the lawyer signed the night register. "You seen Paul Drake, Mr. Mason?"

"Not recently."

"He's looking for you. He said that if you came in, to be sure to have you call him on the phone before you did anything else."

Mason said, "Okay, I'll stop in and see him."

The elevator cage shot upward.

"What was that message again?" Della Street asked.

"Said for Mr. Mason to call him on the phone before he did anything else."

"Mr. Drake is home, then?"

"Nope," the janitor said. "He's in his office."

Della Street exchanged glances with Mason.

"The perfect secretary," Mason said. "I'd missed that one, Della."

"How's that?" the janitor asked, as he brought the cage to a stop.

"Nothing," Mason said.

They walked past the lighted offices which bore the sign, DRAKE DETECTIVE AGENCY, on the door, down the long corridor, around the bend, and Mason unlocked the door of his private office.

Della Street was at the phone, dialing Drake's number almost before Mason had the lights on.

"Mr. Drake there?" she asked. "Mr. Mason's office calling."

A moment later she said, "Hello, Paul. The Chief wants to talk with you. . . . How's that . . . ? Yes, down in our office. . . . All right, I'll tell him."

She hung up the phone and said, "Paul's on his way down here."

Mason said, "Must be something important or Paul wouldn't have acted this way. I overlooked the significance of Paul's message, Della. I'll have to hand you one for that. There must be someone waiting in his office and . . ."

The steps of Paul Drake in the corridor sounded through the night silence of the big office building. Della Street opened the door of the private office.

Paul Drake entered the room, a slow smile twisting his features.
"Hi, folks!"

"Hi, Paul."

"Did you get my message, Perry?"

"Yes. Why did you want me to telephone? Someone in your office?"

"That's right," Drake said, settling himself in the big, leather client's chair, and hitched himself around so that the small of his back rested against one rounded arm of the chair while his long legs dangled over the other. "What kind of a client did you have on this job I used Kenneth Barstow on?"

"That's what's bothering me," Mason said. "I think he may have been trying to cut himself a piece of cake."

"With a chisel," Drake said.

"How come?" Mason asked.

"The heiress is in my office."

Mason whistled. "What does *she* want?"

"I don't know what she *did* want. I think she wanted Kenneth Barstow, but what she wants now is you."

"And she's waiting?"

"Yes, I told her I could get in touch with you sooner or later, that I'd leave word in case you happened to come to your office, and I'd keep working on your apartment."

"Is it that important?" Mason asked.

"I think it is," Drake said. "As I get the story, it's quite a yarn. You want to talk with her, Perry?"

Mason nodded.

"The hell of it is," Drake went on, "you may find yourself in an adverse position to your client."

"Which client?"

"The one that was trying to find out about her."

"The relation of attorney and client in that matter is entirely separate, and it has been completed. He wanted me to do certain things and I did them. I charged him a fee and he paid it. That's the end of it as far as I'm concerned. I don't like to be double-crossed by a client and I don't like chiselers."

"Okay," Drake said, "I'll bring her in."

Mason nodded.

Della Street's eyes were sparkling. "I knew she'd fallen for Kenneth Barstow. That one she met tonight couldn't hold a candle to Barstow, not as far as appearance or anything else. And I'll tell you something else. He wasn't the greenie he was trying to appear, either. That boy knew his way around. I wouldn't trust him any farther than I could toss that safe over there with one finger."

Mason settled himself at his office desk, took a cigarette from the humidor, and said, "This man Caddo is beginning to get on my nerves."

He smoked in silence for a few seconds. Then Drake's steps sounded once more in the corridor. The pound of his heels was accompanied by the quick tapping of high heels as the woman at his side tried to keep up with Drake's long strides.

Drake pushed the door open for Marilyn Marlow to enter the office and said, "Miss Marlow, Mr. Mason, and Miss Street, his secretary. Go on in."

Drake followed her into the room.

Marilyn Marlow bowed acknowledgment of the introduction. There was no cordiality in her snapping black eyes.

"Well," she said to Perry Mason, "you've got me in a sweet mess. Now suppose you try getting me out."

Mason smiled. "Suppose you sit down and relax while you tell me about it."

She sat down in a straight-backed chair across from Mason's desk while Paul Drake slid once more into his favorite sprawling position in the client's chair.

"Well?" Mason asked.

She said, "You framed that letter to me, and I answered it, like a fool, and then you ran that detective in on me."

"You're making statements," Mason said.

"You've messed everything up for me!"

"And why did you want to see me now?"

She smiled. "I want you to un-mess things."

"If you're calling on me as a lawyer and want me to do something for you, I think it's only fair to warn you that I may not be free to accept you as a client. However, so we can quit beating around the bush, we may as well get certain facts straight.

"Your mother was the special nurse who attended George P. Endicott in his last illness. Endicott had been in poor health for a long time and your mother had quite a hard job of it. Apparently, she did her work well. When Endicott died, he left a will by which he left your mother the bulk of his estate. His brothers, Ralph Endicott and Palmer E. Endicott, and his sister, Lorraine Endicott Parsons, inherited the house and a relatively small bequest. The will has already been submitted to probate. The amount of the estate is appraised at approximately three hundred and seventy-five thousand dollars, and it is indicated that the brothers and sisters are going to file a contest after probate, claiming fraud, undue influence and all the rest of it. Your mother was killed in an automobile accident. You inherit all of her property. Now then, you . . ."

"Have you been approached by any one of the Endicotts?" she interrupted.

"No."

"Someone connected with Rose Keeling?"

"Rose Keeling?" Mason repeated the name, then shook his head. "I don't place her. . . . Oh, yes, Rose Keeling was one of the subscribing witnesses to the Endicott will."

"You don't know her? You've never met her?"

"No."

"And you don't know the Endicotts?"

"No."

Marilyn Marlow seemed debating some move in her own mind. Then she said suddenly and impulsively, "Will you help me?"

"Let's keep to generalities for a time," Mason said. "I may not be in a position to help you. I may be disqualified. Generally, what do you want?"

"I'm virtually certain the Endicotts are offering Rose Keeling a big bribe to sell out. I think she's considering the offer. I've tried every way I know to get a line on the thing and I'm stumped. If she sells put, it leaves me out on a limb. I'm licked."

"Why did you advertise in that magazine?"

"I wanted a man of a certain type."

"Why?"

"Rose Keeling is romantic. She falls fast and hard. I wanted a man I could control, one of the type I could know all about who wouldn't double-cross me. I wanted to have him get friendly with Rose, but report to me."

"Did you think you could pick up a man who would be so fascinating to Miss Keeling that she'd confide in him and tell him that . . ."

"I feel certain I can. I know her pretty well. I know just the type she falls for. She'll be suspicious of anyone who has a city background. But a tall man with a country background, a man who is shy but has plenty of latent oomph can knock her for a loop. I'd make the build-up myself, of course. I'd see that he met her under just the right circumstances."

"You are personally friendly?"

"Oh, yes. She's friendly enough, all right, but she's got her handout. She's been hinting lately that Mother told her that after the estate had been distributed she could count on something in the nature of a reward."

"Do you think your mother told her that?"

"I know she didn't," Marilyn Marlow flamed. "Mother was a square-shooter and a hard worker. All she called these other two nurses in for was to act as witnesses. She could have picked out any one of a half-dozen nurses on the floor. That attitude of Rose Keeling's makes it look as though there was something crooked about the whole business. And there wasn't. It was all square shooting."

"How do you know?"

"I . . . well, I just know!"

"It's necessary to have proof."

"But we've had the proof. Rose Keeling went on the stand and swore to exactly what happened."

"And now she wants to change her testimony?"

"She would if she thought she could get away with it and get some money out of it. I understand she's being asked to say she had stepped out of the room just before the will was signed."

"But after she returned, Endicott acknowledged to her that he had signed the will?"

Marilyn Marlow said impatiently, "You're a lawyer. Do I have to draw a diagram for you? She'd change her testimony just enough to make the will invalid. That's what she'd be paid for. Naturally the Endicotts wouldn't pay her a cent unless the will was knocked out."

"And do you think the Endicotts would suborn perjury?"

Marilyn Marlow hesitated a minute and then said, "The Endicotts feel that my mother was an adventuress who took advantage of their brother. They'd do almost anything to upset that will because they think it would only be justice, after all, to have the will knocked out."

Mason said, "Suppose you tell me a little more about what you have in mind, Miss Marlow, what you are trying to do, why you put this ad in that magazine."

"All right, I'll tell you. I'll put my cards on the table. I knew that Rose Keeling had her hand out. For a while I thought that *I* might offer her something, but then I realized that I'd simply be bidding against the Endicotts, and there are two witnesses to that will. If I started paying one, I'd have to pay the other. I need *two* witnesses to make it stand up. The Endicotts only need *one* to tear it down. And I was opposed to doing anything crooked like that. I knew that Mother had been a square-shooter. She wouldn't have paid anyone a nickel. I didn't want to cheapen her memory."

"Go ahead."

"So I tried to get close to Rose Keeling. I thought perhaps she'd confide in me and tell me exactly what the score was; that the Endicotts had offered her money. She was too smart for that. She intimated and that's all."

"So you wanted to get hold of a man?"

"That's right. I wanted a man of a certain type. Rose Keeling is very peculiar. She's suspicious of every woman friend she ever had. But when she falls for a man, she falls hard and tells him everything.

"I knew exactly the type of man she would fall for. I happen to know she's going through a period of heartbreak right now, and she'd be a pushover for the right man. But, of course, I had to be certain of my man first. I wanted to get one who would fall for me, but who would make a play for Rose Keeling and get her to confide in him as a service to *me*. I couldn't afford to get one who would perhaps fall for Rose Keeling and tune me out. Before I introduced him to Rose, I had to make him . . . well, make him fall for me. See?"

Mason nodded.

She said, "In order to do that, I wanted a man of just a certain type. I didn't want one who knew too much. I didn't want one who thought he was too smart. I wanted one who would be honest. I wanted a man who really had something to him. And, of course, I had to work pretty fast. I had to know a good deal about this man— how far he'd go and—well, a lot about him."

Mason encouraged her to go on, with another sympathetic nod of his head.

She said, "I put that ad in the magazine. I said right out in it that I was an heiress. . . . I knew that that would help me get replies. I knew that anyone who said he wasn't interested in my money, after reading that ad, would be a hypocrite and a liar. I wanted a man who was frank—and truthful."

"You've had lots of replies?"

"Hundreds of them. I've been meeting men every night for the last week. Then one I met last night was the one I wanted, and then he turned out to be a detective!"

"How did you know he was a detective?"

"The publisher of the magazine rang me up and told me about it. He said he was sorry that the ad had attracted the attention of undesirable parties, but that he felt it was his duty as publisher of the magazine to warn me that such was the case."

"How did he know where you were, your name and address?"

"I don't know. He said the magazine had a way of finding out those things. I don't understand that, because the woman I had calling for replies at the magazine office was *plenty* smart. She carried the replies around with her for a ways and then dropped them in a branch post office, addressed to me, wrapping the whole day's mail in a package that was sent to me first-class mail, special delivery. I'd get it in about two hours from the time she deposited it in the post office. In that way, it was impossible for anyone to follow her or to locate me through her."

Mason nodded.

"However," she said, "this publisher did ring me up and warn me about this man. I liked him. He'd signed the letter 'Irvin Green,' but the publisher said he was a detective and that *you* had employed him."

Mason glanced significantly at Della Street. "And then what did the publisher do?"

"He offered to do anything he could to help me. He wanted me to confide in him. I wasn't ready to do that quite yet. I wanted to see something of him first. He offered to put his car at my disposal, in case I didn't want to use my car, because of having the license number traced. He said he would drive his car as a chauffeur, and actually rented himself a chauffeur's livery so he could make it convincing."

"Then how about the boy you met tonight?" Mason asked.

She made a little grimace of disgust and said, "He was terrible! I didn't like him in the first place. He wrote a nice letter, but when I sized him up he didn't look like the sort I wanted. I almost didn't speak to him, but finally I went up to him and we went out to dinner. I gave him the gate almost immediately. He was two-faced. He would have sold me out to Rose Keeling and—well, there was something repulsive about him. He was just promoting whatever he could get for himself."

"The one last night you liked?"

"Yes."

"And that's why you're here?"

She met his eyes and said, "Frankly, Mr. Mason, that's why I'm here. That man who gave me the name of Green was exactly the type Rose Keeling would fall for, and I had a feeling that he'd be—well, he'd be loyal to me. I think I could hold him. I think he liked me—a lot."

"You liked him a lot?"

"Yes."

"And then what happened?"

"When the publisher telephoned me and told me he was a detective who had been planted to get something on me, I was furious. I let him get in such a position that I could sever all connection with him without arousing suspicion, and I went ahead and did that—fast."

"Then what?"

"Then I got to thinking things over. After all, Mr. Mason, the fact that the man is a detective is nothing against him. It might be something in his favor. The more I got to thinking the thing over, the more I realized what a ninny I'd been, trying to play detective. It would be much better for me to have put my affairs in the hands of someone who knew all the ropes on that sort of stuff and knew how to go about it."

"And you thought that I controlled this man whom you knew as Green and that in order to get him, you'd have to play ball with me?"

"Well, something like that."

"What did you do next?"

"Then I got rid of Mr. Caddo, the publisher, and came up to your office. I asked the janitor who runs the elevator at night if you were in your office or if he thought you might be in. He said Mr. Paul Drake sometimes knew where you were, that Drake ran a detective agency on the same floor and—well, I put two and two together and assumed that this Mr. Green was Mr. Drake's man. As soon as I talked with Mr. Drake, he said he couldn't do anything until he got in touch with you, but that he'd try to reach you."

"You have a lawyer representing you?" Mason asked.

"No, there's a lawyer probating Mother's estate, but that's all. He's not really representing me, just handling the estate."

"And what did you want me to do?"

"Frankly, I want to put things in your hands. I want you to go ahead and do anything that needs to be done. I felt this detective I met last night was just the type. I thought that I could talk with him frankly and tell him what I wanted and he'd be loyal to me. He'd make a nice one to get in touch with Rose Keeling."

"Just how did you intend to go about doing something like that?"

She said, "Rose loves to play tennis. I would fix up a foursome and get her to play. And she's something of a pirate. She likes to steal other people's—no, I won't put it that way; but if she sees that someone is particularly devoted to me, it flatters her vanity if she can lure him away from me."

"Sort of a love pirate?"

"It's not that exactly, although that's what I started to say. It's just a complex she has. She likes to make passes at my men. If she doesn't get anywhere, she's furious. But if she can arouse their interest, it makes her feel better because she thinks that . . . anyhow, it gives her a lift."

"And this man Caddo doesn't know you've come to me?"

"Oh, no. I just used him to help me out. I haven't told *him* anything about this, but I've told him about the other."

"All right," Mason said, "take my advice. Don't tell him anything more; clam up on that man."

"He's most anxious to help me, says he'll do anything that he can to be of any assistance, because he feels I deserve it. He feels that . . . oh, I don't know, I guess he's just—you know."

"Making passes?" Mason asked.

"He is the sort who paws a girl," she said. "He's always putting his hand on your shoulder and then letting it slide down the arm, and things like that. He can't keep his hands off. I suppose he's just like all the rest."

Mason nodded.

"Can you do it?" she asked.

Mason said, "I'll let you know tomorrow. Give me a number where I can call you. I'll think it over. I don't think I'm disqualified because of any clients I've had so far. Frankly, my interest in you was simply to find out something about the ad."

"Who retained you, Mr. Mason? Who was your client?"

Mason smiled and shook his head. "I can't tell you that."

"I can't imagine who would be interested."

"I certainly can't tell you."

She said abruptly, "I don't think I care too much for Mr. Caddo."

"But he cares for you?"

"He wants to—I don't know just *what* he wants. He wants to paw me, but there's something that he has in his mind, something more specific than that."

"He knows about your inheritance?"

"Yes. I told him a lot when I first met him."

"He wants to help you collect it?"

"He hasn't said so in so many words."

Mason said, "In the event that I should act as attorney for you, in case Mr. Caddo approaches you and wants anything, suggest that he come to me."

She nodded.

"However," Mason went on, "Caddo is the least of our worries right at the moment. You feel certain Rose Keeling is on the point of selling out?"

"Yes."

Mason said, "There are, of course, two ways of handling that. One of them is to keep her from selling out. The other is to get the proof that she has sold out and confront her with it at the proper time."

"Yes. I hadn't thought of that last."

Mason said, "I'm not certain but what I should go and have a talk with her. After all, she's already gone on the stand and testified at the time the will was first admitted to probate."

"That's what Mr. Caddo told me," Marilyn said. "He told me that since she's done that, she'd have a hard time changing her testimony; that the thing for me to do is to see if I can't get her to leave the country or something of that sort. And then, when the will was contested, her testimony could be read right into the record, the testimony she had given at the time the will was probated."

"Caddo told you that?"

"Yes. He said that, under the circumstances, the parties to the controversy having been the same, I could simply read her testimony, on showing that she was out of the country and wasn't available. He seemed to think I should get her out of the country."

"I see," Mason commented.

She said, "Mr. Caddo keeps asking questions about Rose Keeling. I don't know just where *he* fits into the picture."

"Perhaps he wants to be the frame," Mason suggested.

She puckered her forehead. "Now, just what do you mean by that?"

"A frame always has a very advantageous position, so far as the picture is concerned. However, let me think it over. I'll give you a ring tomorrow morning."

"Could I have this man Green work for me?"

Mason said with a smile, "That's one of the things I was thinking of, young lady. I think that perhaps it might be better for you to retain the Drake Detective Agency and get Green to work with you as a detective, than to bother with my legal advice."

"But, Mr. Mason, I'd love to have *you*. I've heard a lot about you and I think that you know a lot about the case, and if you'll just tell me frankly that you weren't representing anyone . . ."

"I'm not representing anyone connected with the will case," Mason said. "I'm not representing anyone who has any interest in the estate or in any part of it. The person I was representing was interested only because he wanted to find out something about that ad."

"But why would anyone hire a lawyer to—my God!"

"What is it?" Mason asked as she stopped abruptly.

"Why, there's only one person it *could* have been," she said. "So *that's* how he knew that the man I was talking with was a detective!

Mr. Mason, do you mean to say that Mr. Caddo would have hired you, and then have warned me?"

Mason said dryly, "I not only don't *mean* to say anything about Mr. Caddo, I'm not *saying* anything about Mr. Caddo."

The dark eyes showed startled understanding.

"So," Mason said, turning to Drake, "I guess there's no reason why Miss Marlow can't have your operative working for her. His name, by the way, is Kenneth Barstow, not Irvin B. Green."

"Oh, I *like* that name," Marilyn Marlow said.

"I thought perhaps you would," Mason said, smiling at Drake.

She scribbled a telephone number on a card, pushed it across the desk to Mason. "You'll call me in the morning?"

"In the morning," Mason said, "I'll let you know."

CHAPTER 8

Mason, entering his office shortly after ten o'clock the next morning, found Della Street waiting in the private office, her finger to her lips.

"Hi, Della. What's up?" Mason said, keeping his voice low in response to her signal.

"There's someone in the outer office you don't want to see."

"Man or woman?" Mason asked cheerfully.

"Woman."

"What's the pitch?"

"Mrs. Robert Caddo."

Mason threw back his head and laughed. "*Why* don't I want to see her, Della?"

"She's on the warpath."

"What about?"

"She wouldn't tell me."

"This Caddo family is becoming a nuisance."

"I told her you might not be in all day, that you saw people only by appointment, and that you wouldn't see anyone unless I was able to give you a general idea of the nature of the business."

"So what?"

"So she plunked herself down in a chair, clamped her lips together and said, 'I'll see him if it takes all week.'"

"How long's she been there?"

"Over an hour. She was waiting in the corridor when Gertie opened the office and as soon as I came in, I went out and talked with her."

Mason laughed good-naturedly. "What sort of woman is she, Della?"

"She's younger than he is, not bad looking. But right now she's not exuding any charm and she isn't bothering with sex appeal. All she needs is a rolling pin to be perfectly typical."

Mason elevated one hip on the corner of his big desk, lit a cigarette and regarded Della Street with amused eyes. "What the devil do you suppose she wants here?"

"I suppose Caddo is trying to use you as an alibi."

"Exactly," Mason said, "and the alibi will be for his association with Marilyn Marlow. Hang it, Della, I'm going to talk with her!"

"I warn you. She's on the warpath."

"Irate women are all part of the day's work in a law office. Let's have a look at her, Della."

"Well, get over in your chair," Della said. "Rumple up your hair, pull some law books around. Look busy and dignified. You try to meet this woman informally and you'll have me calling a doctor to pull pieces of rolling pin out of your head."

Mason laughed, seated himself at the desk, opened some law books and held a fountain pen poised in his hand over a pad of paper. "How does this look, Della?"

She surveyed him with critical eyes and said, "It looks staged. There's no writing on the paper."

"Right you are," Mason said, and immediately scrawled on the pad of yellow foolscap: *Now is the time for all good men to come to the aid of their party.*

Della Street walked around to place a hand on his shoulder and peer over at what he had written.

"How's that?" he asked.

"That is perfectly swell. I'll tell Mrs. Caddo that you're very busy working on an important matter, but that you'll give her five or ten minutes."

"Shoot the works," Mason told Della Street.

Della left Mason's private office, returned after a few seconds with Mrs. Caddo in tow.

Mason heard Della Street say, "He's absorbed in looking up a law point. Don't interrupt him."

Following that cue, Mason started to scribble meaningless words on the sheet of foolscap.

Mrs. Caddo pushed Della Street to one side and said in a high, shrill voice, "Well, *I've* got a problem for him to concentrate on. What does he mean by sending my husband out, chasing after some little hussy! If I had my way, a lawyer who does that would be made to pay damages. The idea of breaking up a home!"

Mason glanced up, said somewhat absentmindedly, "Caddo . . . Caddo? You're Mrs. Caddo? Where have I heard that name before, Della?"

"*You* know where you've heard it!" Mrs. Caddo screamed at him. "You advised my husband. You told him to go out and cultivate this hussy, and then he tells me, '*My lawyer will know all about it!* A business matter,' he says. He didn't think I'd ever find out who his lawyer was but I fooled him. I looked in his checkbook and there it was, big as day, a check stub showing Perry Mason had nicked the family bankroll for five hundred bucks. For what? For sending my husband out fawning around on a snaky-hipped brunette, that's what for!"

Mason said, "Oh, yes, Robert Caddo, the publisher of the magazine. Sit down, Mrs. Caddo, and tell me what's bothering you."

"You know perfectly well what's bothering me. A *publisher!* Robert Caddo is running a racket."

"Indeed," Mason said, raising his eyebrows.

"And I'll tell you something else," she went on, moving toward Mason belligerently. "Such as he is, he's mine! I've got my brand on him and I don't intend to let him get away. I've put up with enough to turn my hair white. I've got too much of an investment in him to let him go. Do you understand?"

"Perfectly," Mason said.

"If I had it to do all over again, I wouldn't marry him for a million dollars, but he had a good line and after he'd talked me into it, I kept tagging along, thinking we'd work it out all right some way."

"How long have you been married?"

"Seven years. And it doesn't seem long at all when you look back on it—not over a hundred and fifty or two hundred."

Mason threw back his head and laughed.

"Go ahead and laugh," she said savagely. "I suppose it strikes *you* as funny. I wasn't bad looking in those days and Robert had a little money. I wasn't in love with him but I didn't think he was going to turn out to be a complete heel. So we tied up for better or worse, and I really and truly tried to make a go of it.

"I've put up with a lot since then. A couple of times I thought I'd pull out. But I stuck, and gradually, bit by bit, Bob has been getting a little property together. Now he's getting to the age when he strays off the reservation now and then, and I don't like it."

Mason said, "You're young yet, Mrs. Caddo. You certainly are far from being unattractive. If you think your life has been ruined . . ."

"I didn't say my life had been ruined. I'm not one of these women to come wailing around that they've given a man the best years of their lives. Bob Caddo never had the *best* years of my life, although he may think he had. But what gets my nanny goat is to have him go traipsing around after this brunette and pull the line that he's merely following his lawyer's advice."

"That would bother me too," Mason said. "Suppose you sit down and tell me about it."

"I'm too mad to sit down."

Mason said, "Stand up and tell me about it, then."

She said, "Who's Marilyn Marlow?"

"What about her?" Mason asked.

"Bob has gone for her, head over heels. She's got some property. Bob thinks he can sink his grub hooks in that property and throw me overboard."

"You're certain?"

"Just as certain as I need to be. He's been gallivanting around lately and I wasn't born yesterday. I'm not so dumb, even if I am a big blonde. I tailed along and found out where he was going. Then I gave him a piece of my mind when he finally got back home with the old story about being out on business. He tried to back it up and told me that it *was* business, that this Marlow girl had been using his magazine and that there were some legal difficulties and he had retained 'a prominent lawyer' to advise him and that the lawyer told him that he had better stick close to her and try to work out some sort of a settlement."

"Your husband told you that?"

"That's right."

"You're certain there's no opportunity for a misunderstanding?"

"None whatever."

Mason sighed, and said, "Mrs. Caddo, none of us is perfect. We all of us have our little faults. These are imperfections in character which range from the trivial to the serious, and none of us is free from them, but in addition to what other minor imperfections he may have, your husband is a liar and I would appreciate it if you'd tell him I said so."

"Humph!" she said, quite evidently surprised at Mason's frankness.

"And you are free to quote me on that," Mason went on. "Tell your husband to come in and see me in case he feels aggrieved."

She regarded Mason quizzically. "Say, I believe you're regular. I came in here to throw inkwells, but you seem to be on the up-and-up. Who's Rose Keeling?"

"Are there *two* women?"

"I don't get the sketch," she admitted. "I caught Bob off first base. I snitched a little red notebook he carries in his inside pocket. When he finds that's gone, he'll have a fit. He had two names in there, this Marilyn Marlow and Rose Keeling. This isn't the first time and it isn't going to be the last time. I know that I have to put up with a certain amount of that stuff, but believe you me, Mr. Mason, once I catch up with him I see that there isn't any great amount of pleasure left in it for him. I'm a wildcat when I get started."

Mason said, "Sit down and let's discuss the matter. Do you think that being a wildcat, as you term it, buys you anything?"

Mrs. Caddo sank down in the big client's chair and grinned at Perry Mason. "I know very well it does. That's the way to handle Bob."

"Of course," Mason said, "all of these tirades, these fits of temper, gradually leave an indelible mark upon *your* character."

"Oh, I suppose so," she said wearily, "but just between you and me and the guidepost, Mr. Mason, I go through these tantrums just to protect my vested interests. They aren't fits of temper. They're an act.

"You see, Bob has piled up quite a little money in this racket of his. He's smart enough to keep it where I can't get my hands on it. I don't mind too much if he philanders around a little, but I don't want to have some little siren come along and then walk off with my share of the money. So whenever I think anything is getting serious, I raise Cain with Bob, then I find out who the woman is, and I certainly do put on an act with those women! And believe me, I'm good at that."

"I daresay you are," Mason said.

She said, "Well, I'm not going to take up any more of your time, Mr. Mason. It was nice of you to see me. You've been perfectly splendid about this. I came up here to make a scene and raise a rumpus in general, but somehow I don't think it would have impressed you too much anyway. That's the only thing that will hold Bob in line. He knows that about the time he gets to the gooey stage I'm going to come tearing along behind like a tornado and make everyone dig for the cyclone cellar. I knew this Marilyn Marlow wasn't business, but it isn't just a philandering proposition either. There's something back of it all that I don't like. I think Bob would like to pull a fast one there. Anyhow, I'm going to pay my respects to Marilyn Marlow and I'm going to call on Rose Keeling, and when I get done with *those* two women they'll realize that crime doesn't pay."

Mason said, "I think, Mrs. Caddo, that perhaps this time it might be better just to work on your husband a little. . . ."

"Nope," she said determinedly, "it's a system I'm playing, Mr. Mason. I don't ever dare to vary it. The last time Bob did any philandering, I went up to the woman's apartment, and I really wrecked the place. I tore her clothes off, blacked her eyes, smashed a mirror, just to give her bad luck for seven long years, and threw a few dishes around. The landlady came up and threatened to call the police and I told her to go ahead and call them and let it get put in the papers the sort of place she was running and the kind of tenants she had and the goings on that had been taking place there. Believe me, that put *her* in *her* place.

"After that I had the field all to myself and when I left, the landlady canceled the lease on the little tramp and I understand now she's living in a dirty little bedroom and paying five times what it's worth.

"Bob is a funny chap. He likes to play the wolf, but he hates a scene, and if I make enough of a scene it's just like spanking a small kid. He shudders every time he thinks of the punishment. . . . You've been perfectly grand, Mr. Mason. I'm glad now I didn't slam the inkwells around. I was just going to sit out in the other office until I was certain you were in, and then I was going to push past that receptionist out there, march on in here and spread a little gloom around the place. I knew that would get back to Bob and I figured you'd make him pay for it. Well, thanks for seeing me, Mr. Mason. You're a good sport."

"I would respectfully suggest," Mason said, "that in this particular instance you curtail your righteous indignation and refrain from calling on the two women whose names you have . . ."

"I'm sorry, Mr. Mason. I'm afraid you're like Bob. I guess you don't like a scene."

"On the contrary," Mason said, "I love them."

"Boy, I'd like to have you along on this one," Mrs. Caddo said. "It's going to be a humdinger. Well, good-by. I guess I can get out this door all right. . . . No, don't get up. And do me one favor, Mr.

Mason—if Bob asks if I was here, tell him I raised a row in the office and that you expect him to pay for the damages. Will you do that for me? No, I suppose you won't. You're truthful. But anyhow you're nice and I know you'll protect my confidence. Good morning."

The door banged shut behind her.

Mason glanced at Della Street and said, "The joys of matrimony!"

"I don't blame her a bit," Della Street said. "You can take a look at Bob Caddo and see what he is. One of these old wolves that run around pawing girls and trying to cut corners. She's absolutely right. That's the only way of holding him, and . . ."

"Get Marilyn Marlow on the phone," Mason said wearily, "and I guess you'd better tell her to warn her friend, Rose Keeling, that I think a cyclone is on the way and it might be just as well if they weren't available. I guess we owe that much to a client."

"She's going to be a client? You were to call her this morning."

"That's right. We'll kill two birds with one phone call. I'll tell her I'll try to handle Rose Keeling for her and that an irate wife is on the warpath. I . . ."

The office door pushed open. Gertie, the receptionist, white-faced, said, "Gee, Mr. Mason, I heard her go out. Her husband's out there and he's worried sick. Gosh, it was just luck he didn't walk in while she was out there. If he had, I'd have been in the middle of a real domestic battle."

Mason grinned. "He knows how near he came to getting caught, Gertie?"

"Evidently not. He wanted to know if his wife had been here. I told him that he'd have to ask you about that, and he's out there pacing the floor like a caged lion."

"I take it that he's disturbed at the idea his wife may have been talking with me," Mason said.

"*Disturbed!*" Gertie said. "Oh, Mr. Mason, you do use the mildest language! I tell you, the man's having kittens!"

Mason winked at Della Street, said, "I'll go out and see him. Hand me that inkwell, Della."

While Gertie watched with fascinated eyes, Mason dipped his finger in the inkwell, rubbed one smear across the side of his cheek, said, "Now your lipstick, Della, just a faint line that will look like the aftermath of a scratch down from the forehead, across the nose—that's right. Now I think, Gertie, we're in a position to add to Mr. Caddo's discomfiture. After all, I hate a client who's a chiseler."

Mason followed behind Gertie, out to the outer office. "Good morning, Mr. Caddo," he said sternly.

"Oh, my God," Caddo said, "my wife's been here!"

"Your wife has been here," Mason said.

"Now look, Mr. Mason, I'm not responsible for my wife. Honestly, it's one of those things with her. She is subject to jealousy that amounts almost to insanity. I'm sorry this has happened, but, after all, you can't blame it on me."

"Why not?" Mason asked. "Isn't there any community property?"

"Good heavens, you're not going to sue a woman for a little fit of temper, are you?"

"A little fit of temper?" Mason asked, raising his brows.

"Now look here, Mason, I'll do the right thing. I'll be fair about this. I thought perhaps you were cheating yourself a little bit on that fee you fixed the other day. After all, there's no reason why you and I can't get along on this. I want to be fair. I want to do what's right."

"Was that the reason you rang up Marilyn Marlow and told her that the man with whom she was about to play tennis was a detective employed by me?"

"Now, Mr. Mason. Mr. Mason, *please!*"

"Please what?"

"I can explain."

"Well, go ahead and start explaining."

"It's something I prefer not to go into here, not at the present time. Not while you're in your present frame of mind. I . . . I'd like to see you later, Mr. Mason, when you've had an opportunity to regain your composure and get your office cleaned up. I—I'm sorry this happened, but Dolores *will* throw inkwells when she gets worked up. Mr. Mason, you didn't tell her anything about Marilyn Marlow, did you? No, you couldn't have. You're a lawyer. You have to preserve the confidences of a client."

"Certainly," Mason said.

Caddo's face showed relief. "I knew I could count on you, Mr. Mason. I'm going to come in and see you in a day or two. You get things straightened out and cleaned up, and we'll assess the damages and . . ."

"I didn't *tell* her about Marilyn Marlow," Mason said, "and I didn't tell her about Rose Keeling. I didn't need to."

"What do you mean?"

"I mean that since you had so thoughtfully placed their names and addresses in the little red book you habitually carry in your inside breast pocket, and since your wife had taken possession of that book, she knew. . . ."

Caddo clapped a hand to the breast of his coat, then plunged the other hand down into the pocket. An expression of almost ludicrous panic twisted his features.

"She has that book?"

"She has it," Mason said.

"Oh, my God!" Caddo said, and, turning on his heel, dashed out of the office.

Gertie, inclined to avoirdupois, good nature, and a highly developed sense of humor, pushed a handkerchief into her mouth, making inarticulate sounds of merriment.

Mason returned to his private office, washed the ink and lipstick from his face, grinned at Della Street and said, "I think now we're beginning to get even with Mr. Robert Caddo. We don't have Rose Keeling's address, do we, Della?"

She shook her head.

"Well, see if we can get Marilyn Marlow on the phone and warn her of what is due to happen."

Della Street found Marilyn Marlow's number, called half a dozen times without getting an answer, then finally said, "Here she is on the line, Chief."

Mason said, "Good morning, Miss Marlow. I'm afraid I have bad news for you."

"What is it?"

Mason said, "It seems that your friend, the responsible business-man who has been giving you such fatherly advice in such a disinterested manner, is a married man. His wife apparently is named Dolores and she has a passion for throwing inkwells. Her husband, it seems, has what might be classified as a philandering complex, and the wife has a nasty little habit of throwing tantrums and ink all over the recipients of his affections and . . ."

"Mr. Mason, are you kidding me?"

"I'm kidding you on the square," Mason said. "Mrs. Caddo left my office a half or three-quarters of an hour ago and she was very much on the warpath. It seems that your friend, the magazine publisher, had very carelessly made some notes in a leather-backed memo book he carries, jotting down names and addresses, not in alphabetical, but in chronological order. Therefore, when Mrs. Caddo made an informal and surreptitious search, the last names in the book were those of Marilyn Marlow and Rose Keeling, in that order. And I believe your esteemed friend had placed the addresses opposite the names."

"Good heavens!" Marilyn Marlow said. "She mustn't, she simply *mustn't* call on Rose Keeling! *That* would be the last straw."

"When last seen," Mason said, "she was looking for new worlds to conquer."

"And Rose Keeling's name would have been the last in the book," Marilyn Marlow said in dismay. "That means she'd go to Rose Keeling first."

Mason said, "I don't have Rose Keeling's address or telephone number. I thought perhaps it would be advisable for you to let her know."

"I can't do that. I can't tell her anything like that."

"Then you'd better get her out of the way for a while," Mason said.

"I'll have to do that. I'll go to her at once and make some excuse to get her out of the way. We'll play tennis, I guess."

"By the way," Mason said, "you never did give me her address. Perhaps I should have it, since I'm going to be involved in this, both directly and indirectly. I've decided to represent you, since you manage to stir up such pleasant asides to vary the routine of a law practice that might otherwise become monotonous."

"You mean you'll help me?"

"Yes."

"Oh, that's fine! I'm so glad."

"When things quiet down a bit to the point of stability on the domestic front," Mason said, "I'm going out to see Rose Keeling and have a heart-to-heart talk with her. If she's attempting to sell her testimony to the highest bidder, I may dampen her enthusiasm for a sell-out. What's her address?"

"2240 Nantucket Drive. The telephone is Westland 6-3928."

"Will you telephone her about Mrs. Caddo?"

"I—I think I'd better run over there, Mr. Mason. I'll invite her to run out for some tennis."

"You may not have time," Perry Mason said; "better telephone her to meet you some place."

"I'll . . . all right, I'll work out *something*. Thanks for calling, Mr. Mason."

"Remember," Mason said, "that there's a certain method in Mrs. Caddo's madness. It's not merely the indignation of an outraged wife; it's a method she uses. Her system is to make such a terrific scene every time she catches her husband in a philandering expedition that . . ."

"But this wasn't philandering."

"I think that Mrs. Caddo resorts to disciplinary measures purely for the purpose of keeping her husband in line," Mason said. "It isn't so much what he has done, as it is a means of keeping his feet on the straight and narrow path in the future."

"All right, I'll get in touch with Rose. Thanks for calling, Mr.

Mason. Of all the goofy women! Why in the world did I ever let that man Caddo horn in on my business?"

"I've wondered that, myself," Mason said. "And you will doubtless have occasion to ask yourself the question again and again in the near future. Good-by, Miss Marlow."

"Good-by," she said, and slammed down the telephone.

Mason glanced at his watch, then frowned. "The trouble with these divertissements," he said to Della Street, "is that they are so fascinating they take my mind off the other problems that should be uppermost. What about that brief in the Miller case, Della?"

"I have the citations you gave me all arranged in order, and the points you wanted to raise all blocked out."

"All right," Mason said, "I'll take a look at it."

For a half hour he busied himself with the brief, then abruptly pushing his swivel chair away from the desk said irritably, "I can't get that woman out of my mind."

"Marilyn Marlow?" Della Street asked.

Mason shook his head. "Not Marilyn Marlow, Della; Dolores Caddo. There's a lusty, two-fisted woman for you. She's teamed up with a heel but she doesn't intend to have anyone impair the value of her investments in him. She has her own unique methods—and there's something about her that impresses one."

"She certainly leaves her mark wherever she goes," Della Street said.

"Yes. With an inkwell," Mason commented dryly. "Let's give Rose Keeling a ring and get acquainted with her over the telephone. Tell you what you do, Della, ring her phone and ask if Marilyn Marlow is there. You can do the talking. Don't say who you are—simply that you're a friend of Marilyn's."

Della Street consulted the office memo she had made and said, "All right, I have the number—Westland 6-3928."

She picked up the telephone, said, "Give me an outside line, Gertie," and dialed the number.

She sat at her desk, the receiver at her ear, waiting.

"No answer?" Mason asked.

"Apparently no answer," she said. "I can hear the sound of the phone ringing and . . . wait a minute."

She was silent for two or three seconds, then said, "Hello—hello."

She cupped her hand over the mouthpiece, turned to Mason and said, "That's funny. I heard the ringing signal quit right in the middle of the ring. I could have sworn someone picked up the phone, and I thought I heard breathing, but when I said 'Hello,' no one answered."

"Perhaps your connection was broken," Mason said, "and you imagined the sound of the breathing."

"I'd have sworn someone took the receiver off the hook," Della Street said.

"Probably Rose Keeling," Mason said. "She had been warned and thought perhaps you were the belligerent Dolores Caddo, calling to make certain she was in."

"Well, if I were Dolores Caddo I'd be on my way up there right now," Della said, "because I'm satisfied she's in. Someone took the receiver off the hook."

Mason said, "It's twenty minutes to twelve now—too early for lunch—I suppose I've got to go back to this confounded brief."

He picked up the typewritten list of authorities, said, "I guess we're ready to start dictating the brief in final form, Della. What do you suppose a woman like Dolores Caddo sees in a chiseling two-timer like her husband?"

"Probably she sees a certain element of financial security," Della Street said. "Caddo can keep a lot of his business stuff under cover, but she has her rights under the community property law, and sooner or later she'll cash in on them—and perhaps there's a certain element of affection there. She's really fond of him but recognizes his weaknesses and she's trying her best to control them."

Mason nodded, then said, "In addition to all that, Della, the woman really enjoys violence. She loves to invade some boudoir and start smashing things, throwing things and raising hell generally. Being the wife of a heel gives her that privilege. The average woman who has been making a play with a married man doesn't have much chance to resent a violent visit from the 'outraged' wife. I gather Mrs. Caddo wouldn't willingly change her partner—although she may have some romantic side dish her husband might like to know about. However, this speculation isn't getting this brief finished. Gosh, Della, how I hate briefs!"

She laughed and said, "It's like making a boy practice at the piano. You let your mind seize on every possible excuse to break the monotony."

Mason said, "Well, we can copy this statement of the case on the rough draft. Then we'll go on from there. Let's see. . . . All right, Della—take this down: *'At the time of the trial the court permitted the following evidence to be introduced over the objection of the appellant.'* Now, Della, we'll copy the transcript on page 276, the points that I'm underscoring in pencil."

Della Street nodded, and Mason busied himself for several minutes with marking up the reporter's transcript of the trial, then said, "Be sure to copy this evidence and after each excerpt from the evidence, put in the page of the reporter's transcript, Della. Now let me see that case in the hundred and sixty-fifth California Reports. I want a copy from that. But first I'll make an introductory statement to show how we think the doctrine laid down in that case is applicable."

Mason took the book which Della Street handed him, and, having started to read the case, became engrossed in the language of the decision. After some ten minutes he said, "All right, Della, we'll go ahead with the brief. Now take this: *'In California there is a long line of cases setting forth the principle that such evidence is admissible only for the purpose of proving intent, and when admitted, it must be limited by the court to a proof of intent. In the case at bar, there was no such limitation. The jury was left to consider the evidence without restriction, nor was there any real attempt to prove intent by this evidence. Present counsel for the appellant was not his counsel at the time of trial, but trial counsel did protest vigorously to the court, although apparently no motion was made to limit the evidence to a consideration of intent, nor was any instruction submitted. However, as was said in one of the leading California cases . . .'* Now, Della, you can copy the parts of this case in the hundred and sixty-fifth California that I'll indicate with lines along the margin of the page."

Della Street nodded, and Mason put in some ten minutes marking the portions of the decision which he wished incorporated in the brief.

The telephone on Della Street's desk rang and Della Street, picking up the receiver, said, "Gertie, Mr. Mason told you he didn't want to be disturbed. . . . How's that. . . ? All right, just a minute."

Della Street turned to Mason. "Gertie said Marilyn Marlow is on the line and is almost hysterical. She wants to talk with you, says it's terribly important."

Mason said irritably, "Hang it! I just got Dolores Caddo out of my mind. I suppose Marilyn Marlow is covered with ink and filled with contrition and . . . Oh well, it's quarter past twelve and almost time to go out to lunch. Let me talk with her."

Della Street moved the phone on its long extension over to Mason's desk.

Mason said, "Hello. This is Perry Mason talking."

Marilyn Marlow's voice was choked with emotion. "Mr. Mason, something . . . something terrible has happened. It's . . . it's awful!"

"Did you see Dolores Caddo?" Mason asked.

"No, no. I haven't seen her. This is something worse than that. Something awful!"

"What is it?" Mason asked.

"Rose Keeling."

"What about her?"

"She's . . . she's dead!"

"What happened?" Mason asked.

"She's dead in her apartment. She's been killed."

"Where are you?" Mason asked.

"In Rose Keeling's apartment. It's a flat, part of a four-flat house, and . . ."

"Who's with you?"

"No one."

"When did you get there?"

"Just now."

"Are you actually in the house?"

"Yes."

"She's been murdered?"

"Yes."

Mason said, "Don't touch anything. Are you wearing gloves?"

"No, I . . ."

"Any gloves with you?"

"Yes."

"Put them on!" Mason said. "Don't touch a thing. Sit down in a chair and fold your hands on your lap. Stay there until I get there! That address is 2240 Nantucket Drive?"

"That's right."

Mason said, "Sit tight. I'm coming."

He slammed the receiver back on the telephone, rushed to the cloak closet, grabbed his hat and pulled out a topcoat.

"What is it?" Della Street asked.

"Rose Keeling's been murdered. You stay here and run the office—no, come along with me, Della. Bring a notebook. I may want a witness and I'll sure as hell need an alibi."

CHAPTER 9

Perry Mason slid his car to a stop at the curb in front of the Nantucket Drive address.

The building was a four-flat house, and Mason, running up the steps, quickly picked the entrance to Rose Keeling's flat, a second-floor, southern exposure.

Mason tried the door. It was locked. He buzzed on the bell, and a moment later an electric door release opened the door for him.

Della Street and Mason crowded through the door, and the lawyer took the steps two at a time, arriving at the upper corridor several steps in advance of Della Street.

Marilyn Marlow, white and shaken with the shock of what she had found, was waiting in the reception hallway.

"All right," Mason said, "let's have it fast. What happened?"

"I . . . I came to see Rose Keeling. She's . . . she's in there on the floor by the bathroom."

Mason said to Della Street, "You'd better stay here, Della."

He walked rapidly down the corridor, looked in at the open door of the bedroom and looked briefly at the sprawled white body lying motionless against a sinister red background.

For a brief moment the lawyer surveyed the ingredients of the tragedy, the packed suitcases, the nude body, the clothes on the bed, the open bathroom door. Then he turned back down the corridor toward the living room.

"Where's the phone?" he asked.

Marilyn Marlow indicated the telephone.

"You picked up the receiver and dialed my number. Did you call anyone else?"

"No."

Mason said, "That telephone call puts us in a spot."

"What do you mean?"

Mason said, "At twenty minutes to twelve I called this number. Someone was here. Someone evidently who didn't want the phone to keep on ringing and ringing. The receiver was gently lifted off the cradle and . . ."

"Why, that's right," Marilyn Marlow interrupted. "When I came here, the receiver was lying beside the telephone. It had been left off the cradle. I had to put it back and then wait for a minute for the line to come back in service."

Mason nodded, said, "The person who lifted the receiver was probably the murderer. We caught him in the middle of what he was doing, and the continued ringing of the telephone either made him nervous or else he was afraid it would attract attention, so he took the receiver off the hook. His fingerprints will be on the receiver. The hell of it is, yours will be on there too."

"Well, what's wrong with that? I'll tell the police exactly what happened and . . ."

"That's what we're coming to," Mason said. "We may not want to tell the police exactly what happened."

"Why not?"

Mason said, "You probably have never stopped to figure it out, but it was considerably to your advantage to have Rose Keeling out of the way."

"What do you mean by that?"

Mason said, "Rose Keeling was a subscribing witness to that will. She was threatening to change her testimony. As long as she was alive, she could do it. Now that she is dead, she can't do it. You can use the testimony that was given by her at the time she went on the stand when the will was being admitted to probate. Do you understand that?"

"Yes."

"How long have you understood it?"

"Well—Mr. Caddo was the first one to point it out to me clearly."

"Do you mean he suggested that it might be to your advantage to have Rose Keeling put out of the way?"

"Heavens, no! He only said that if Rose Keeling could be made to skip out, it would help."

Mason's eyes were boring steadily into those of Marilyn Marlow. "You knew that Rose Keeling was going to be really difficult to keep in line?"

"Yes, I knew it. I told you that."

"And you also told Caddo?"

"Well, yes."

"In other words, Caddo got under your skin pretty much. You talked quite a bit about your affairs."

She started making nervous patterns on her dress with her left forefinger. "I guess I told Caddo *too* much."

"How did you happen to spill everything to him?"

"I didn't. He has that insinuating way with him. He had found out quite a lot, surmised a lot more, and he had that sort of—well, that sort of take-it-for-granted attitude that's rather hard to deal with. He'd assume things and sometimes it was hard to differentiate between what I told him and what he'd just taken for granted on his own."

"You'd told him quite a bit, however?"

"Well, one way and another, he'd found out quite a bit about the situation."

Mason said, "I telephoned you and told you Mrs. Caddo was on the warpath."

She nodded.

"You were to warn Rose Keeling."

"Yes."

"And you did so?"

"Not right away."

"Why not?"

"Something happened that—well, the situation became complicated."

Mason said, "For the love of Mike, snap out of it! You've told a lot of this stuff to a perfect stranger who came along and handed you a good line, and now you're trying to get reticent with your own lawyer. Get your cards on the table."

She said, "The situation changed immediately."

"What changed it?"

"A letter."

"Who wrote it?"

"Rose."

"Where is it?"

She opened her purse, took out an envelope and handed it to Mason.

Mason looked at the canceled stamp, at the pen-and-ink address, at the postmark which showed an imprint of 7:30 P.M. of the day before.

"When did you get this?"

"This morning. It was in the morning mail."

Mason pulled note paper out of the envelope and read the pen-and-ink letter signed by Rose Keeling.

When he had finished reading it, he read it aloud for the benefit of Della Street:

"Dear Marilyn:

"I don't like to write this letter. Your mother and I were close friends. I would do anything for her, but I can't perjure myself. The plain truth of the matter is that my testimony when I got on the witness stand the first time was false. I tried to fix things so I could help your mother. Actually, I was out of the room at the time that will was signed, if it ever was signed. I've tried to tell you about this in a nice way, so I could break it to you easy, but you thought I had my hand out and wanted some money or something. Nothing could have been farther from my thoughts. I was very friendly with your mother and I let that friendship distort my testimony when I was on the witness stand, and my conscience has been bothering me ever since. I have tried to break it to you easy, but I can't; so now I'm breaking it to you the hard way. Sincerely yours,

"*Rose.*

"You got that letter this morning?" Mason asked Marilyn.

She nodded.

"You had it when I telephoned you?"

"Yes."

"But you didn't tell me about it?"

"No."

"Why?"

She said, "I felt certain it was—well, that Rose had made hints before and that I hadn't done anything about it, and now she was trying to jar me into doing something. I knew that if I told you about it, you'd be very ethical and tell me I couldn't pay her a cent."

"But you intended to make some promise to pay her?"

"I didn't know exactly what I did intend to do. You see, Mr. Mason, that letter is a lie. She *was* in the room when that will was signed. The testimony she gave when she was on the witness stand was the absolute truth. My mother told me so, and Ethel Furlong told me so. Ethel is a square-shooter. She has a good, clear memory, and she recalls everything that happened just as clearly as if it had been yesterday. Mr. Endicott was lying there on the bed and . . ."

"We'll talk about that when we've got more time," Mason interrupted. "What I want to do right now is reconstruct your time schedule for this morning."

"Well, I got this letter and I didn't know *what* to do about it. You see, the thing would have been different if I'd thought there was any possibility the letter told the truth, but I simply knew that it didn't. Then you telephoned me about Mrs. Caddo and I was rather noncommittal. I felt for a minute it would be a mighty good thing if Dolores Caddo did go over to see Rose and make a scene. I thought something like that might give Rose Keeling something else to think about."

"But you had this letter when I telephoned you?"

"Yes."

"And what did you do after I telephoned you?"

"I thought things over for a while. Then I decided to ring Rose up. I got her on the phone and told her I wanted to talk with her. I was planning to tell her over the phone about Mrs. Caddo, but her manner wasn't at all like that letter. She had been crying and she said, 'Marilyn dear, please come over here right away. Please!'"

"What did you do?"

"I jumped in my car and came over here."

"And what happened then?"

"Rose said, 'Marilyn, I want to talk with you but I want to get my nerves quieted first. Will you please drive out to the tennis courts and play a couple of sets of tennis, and *then* we'll talk.' Well, I told her I would, but that I'd have to go back to my apartment and get my tennis things and that I thought I'd bring my playsuit along and change here."

"Then what happened?"

"She gave me a key and told me I should walk right in when I returned. She said she had been giving me a raw deal, but things were going to be different now."

"Well, I went out, drove to my apartment, stopping to do my grocery shopping on the way, got my tennis things and drove back here. When I got here I found the door downstairs was open an inch or two so I didn't need the key. I came up here—and found this. I called you almost at once."

"Did you drive directly here from your apartment?"

"No. I went to my bank first."

"Why did you do that?"

She said, "I didn't know just what was coming, Mr. Mason. I suppose I was foolish, but I thought that if Rose was trying to hold out for a little money, I might—well, I *might* give her some.

"You know, Mr. Endicott gave mother some jewelry before his death. Most of it was stuff that had been in the family for a while, but some of them were more modern pieces. Mother had sold a few of those pieces to get a little money to carry on with, and I'd inherited that money when she died. It was in a joint account, but there isn't much left. I was going to need financial help if I did anything with Rose. I went to the bank and asked them if I could get a little money if I needed it."

"What did the bank tell you?"

"They were very nice."

"You didn't tell them what you wanted the money for?"

"Not in so many words. I told them I had some expenses coming up in connection with this will contest and in trying to protect my inheritance. The bank explained to me that they couldn't underwrite my will contest, that it couldn't gamble on the outcome of that; but that within reasonable limits they would let me have some money, with the understanding that if the will contest didn't come out right, I'd turn the jewelry over to them as a pledge."

"They didn't ask for jewelry in advance?"

"No."

"How much jewelry is there?"

"The bank says it's worth easily seventy-five thousand dollars— the amount that's left."

"How much did your mother sell?"

"Not much. Five or six thousand dollars' worth."

"What time did you talk with Rose Keeling on the phone?"

"About eleven-ten."

"And then you came here?"

"Yes."

"What time?"

"Oh, I'd say eleven-twenty-five or so."

"What time did you get back here?"

"Just about four or five minutes before I telephoned you."

"And what did you find?"

"As I said, the door was partly open. I pushed it the rest of the way open, walked in, closed the door and found things just as they are now."

"Did you look around any?"

"Just as far as the bedroom. I called out, 'Yoo-hoo, Rose,' and walked back to the bedroom and . . . you know what I saw. I was sick at my stomach. I backed out and—well, I got to the telephone and called you."

Mason said, "Wait here. Don't move. Don't touch anything. Keep your gloves on. I'm going to take a look."

"Want me?" Della Street asked.

Mason shook his head and said, "It's pretty sticky, Della. Evidently it was done with a knife. You sit here. Be careful not to touch anything and keep an eye on Marilyn. See that she doesn't go to pieces."

Marilyn said, "I'll be all right now, Mr. Mason."

Mason retraced his steps down the corridor into the bedroom, taking care not to touch anything, and de-touring the pool of crimson which was still welling out from the nude, white body which lay on the floor, partially on its side, the arms flung outward, as though in that last plunge Rose Keeling had tried to break the force of the fall as she hit the floor.

There were two suitcases which had been packed with great care. They were open on the floor near the dresser. Some folded clothes had been placed on top of the dresser. On the bed lingerie and stockings were neatly laid out. On the floor, beneath the bed, rumpled into a ball, was a street dress, the bottom part of the garment now soaked with blood.

Between the figure on the floor and the bathroom was a bath towel which had spots of blood on it. It had been dropped to the floor directly in front of the bathroom door.

Mason skirted the red pool to look into the bathroom.

The air was still steamy and moist. Paths of water-trickles were still evident on the mirror where moisture had condensed and run down the glass.

The bathroom itself contained a medicine chest, clothes hamper, mirror, tooth-brush rack and the conventional bathroom fixtures. There was not so much as a drop of blood in the bathroom.

Mason turned back to inspect the bedroom once more. A pair of tennis shoes, a tennis racket still in a press, and a can containing three tennis balls were near the closet door. The tennis racket was propped against the wall. The can of tennis balls lay crosswise on the tennis shoes.

Flecks of white caught Mason's eye and he leaned over to inspect those flecks more closely.

They seemed to be ashes which had been dropped from a cigar and had spread out in a little cluster of light ash. Just inside the bedroom door was a place where a cigarette, about one-third smoked, had been dropped to the floor and had gradually burnt itself out, leaving a long streak of ash and a charred place on the floor.

Mason tiptoed back from the bedroom, looked out into the kitchen and into a dining room. Through that an open door led into a bedroom and another bathroom. This bedroom evidently had not been occupied. There was a disused air to the place, and the white counterpane on the bed was lightly dust-covered.

Mason returned to the living room.

Della Street glanced up quickly, then swung her eyes significantly toward Marilyn Marlow.

Marilyn Marlow was sitting with her gloved hands folded on her lap. Her white face emphasized the patches of orange rouge which were plainly visible against the pallor of her skin.

Mason said quietly, "Marilyn, are you telling me the truth?"

"Yes."

"The whole truth?"

"Yes."

"Rose Keeling told you she wanted to play tennis?"

"Yes."

"She's quite a tennis player?"

"Yes."

"This is rather a big place for one woman."

"She had a friend staying with her up until about two weeks ago. They shared the expense."

"Even so, it's a pretty big place."

"Rose had a lease on it. She's had it for some time. It's a long-term lease. She got it at a low rental. She can take some woman in with her and charge her almost enough to pay for the whole flat. I know that."

"She rents it furnished?"

"Yes."

"She gave you a key to get in with?"

"Yes."

"You used it?"

"No. I found the door open."

"Where's the key?"

Marilyn said, "Heavens, I don't know. I . . . I guess I laid it on a table here somewhere."

Della Street pointed to a little table which held a few magazines, some volumes of phonograph records, and a radio.

The key glinted near the radio.

Mason carefully picked up the key, then blew on the table in order to eliminate any possible outline in case a thin, hardly visible layer of dust might have been covering the table. He dropped the key in his vest pocket.

Marilyn watched him with fascinated eyes.

Mason said, "Marilyn, if I stick my neck out to help you, can you ride along with me and play, ball?"

"What do you mean?"

"Can you protect Della and me in case we help you?"

"Yes. I'll do anything. Why?"

Mason said in a low, kindly voice, "You have too much at stake here, Marilyn. That letter you received this morning would absolutely crucify you. It's unreasonable to believe that Rose Keeling would have written you a letter like that and then acted the way you said she did."

"I can't help it, Mr. Mason. I'm telling you the truth."

"I think you are. The point is that no one else would believe it. No jury on this earth would ever believe it. To the police, it would look very much as though you had received that letter, as though you had gone up to see Rose Keeling and had found her packing, found her obdurate, refusing to retract the statements she had made. You knew that if Rose could be kept from changing her testimony, you could use the old testimony she had given when the will was first offered for probate. You knew that if she changed her testimony, your entire inheritance would go out the window. You were in a tough spot. You came to see Rose and found her putting the finishing touches on her packing. She was getting ready to go away. You couldn't afford to let her go. You killed her, but as an afterthought you put out the tennis things. You knew where she kept them."

"Mr. Mason, that's utterly, absolutely absurd. I would never have done anything like that!"

"I'm not talking about what you did," Mason said. "I'm telling you what the police will think you did. Furthermore, the minute that letter is made public, your chance of inheriting property under Endicott's will is almost nil."

"I realize that."

"Even if Rose Keeling can't change her testimony, the contents of that letter spread out in the public press will have the effect of antagonizing everyone against you."

"Yes, I know."

"And your fingerprints are on the telephone receiver. Evidently the prints of the murderer are on there too, because the murderer must have been the one who picked up the telephone receiver and moved it so the phone would quit ringing."

She nodded.

Mason said, "There are times when a lawyer throws the rule book away, when he has to go by hunches. There's some evidence that makes me believe some other person came here in the sixty minutes between your talk with Rose Keeling on the telephone and the time when you returned. But that evidence is nothing I can bring into court."

"Can you tell me what it is?"

"It's better that you don't know."

Mason said to Della Street, "Do you think you can take a jolt, Della?"

She nodded.

"I want you to look here a minute."

She followed Mason down the corridor, paused in recoil at the door of the bedroom.

Mason said, "Don't touch anything. Stand here. Take a look. Get it all straight. I think those are cigar ashes in there by the bed. You can see where a cigarette burned a two-inch groove in the hardwood floor there. Notice the clothes that are packed in the suitcase and the folded clothes on the dresser."

Della Street said, "She was packing up to leave."

"And taking a bath," Mason said. "Notice the lingerie laid out on the bed."

Della Street nodded.

"She wouldn't have taken a bath *before* she went to play tennis," Mason said. "She was evidently killed just as she emerged from the bathroom."

Della Street looked around at the bedroom, said, "That's a traveling outfit that was laid out on the bed. She wasn't intending to play tennis. She was going somewhere. Either she lied to Marilyn about the tennis, or Marilyn was lying to us."

Mason said, "I think Marilyn is telling the truth—but I can't see why Rose Keeling would have taken a hot bath just before going out to play tennis."

"Can we look around any? Open drawers?" Della asked.

He shook his head. "We've gone too far as it is. We don't dare touch a thing, not even a drawer handle. Come on, let's go back and see what Marilyn's doing."

Mason held his finger to his lips for silence, tiptoed down the corridor. Della Street, puzzled, followed behind him.

Marilyn Marlow was seated at the little table which held the telephone. Her lips were a thin line of grim determination, and she was busily engaged in polishing the telephone receiver with a pocket handkerchief.

"What are you doing, Marilyn?" Mason asked.

She gave a sudden guilty start, dropped the receiver, then, realizing she was caught, defiantly picked it up again and continued polishing.

"I'm taking my fingerprints off that receiver."

Mason said, "You are probably also removing the fingerprints of the murderer."

"I can't help that!"

"What have you done with the letter?" Mason asked.

"I still have it in my purse."

Mason said, "You shouldn't have taken the fingerprints off the receiver."

"I'm not going to be connected with this, Mr. Mason! I can't afford to be."

Mason said somewhat wearily, "Okay, Marilyn, this is one of the times when I stick my neck out for a client. I suppose I shouldn't do it. I know damn well I'll be sorry for it before the case is finished, but when something like this happens, I can't help it. Circumstances have framed you and put you into an impossible position."

"What are you going to do?"

"We're all going out. We're going to leave the door slightly open. You're going to get in your car and go home. Della Street and I are going to come back as soon as you've driven away. We'll find the door partially open. We'll walk up here and find things just as you see them now. Then we're going to telephone the police."

"Telephone the police!" Marilyn Marlow exclaimed in dismay.

Mason nodded.

"Why, that will bring them here and link you with it and . . ."

Mason said, "I can't help it, Marilyn. I can cut a corner now and then, but I don't dare to fail to notify the police when I've stumbled on something like this. Otherwise I'd be an accessory after the fact. However, when I talk to the police, I'm going to tell them only about my *second* visit to the flat. I'm going to tell them I came up to see Rose Keeling, that I had Della Street with me, that the door must have been pulled shut but hadn't quite caught so far as the spring latch was concerned, that we rang the bell and took it for granted that the buzzer would signal for us to come up. We thought we heard that signal, pushed at the door and the door opened, as though the latch had been released by the electric control at the top of the stairs. We went up and to our surprise found no one in the living room. We looked down the corridor, in the bedroom, saw what had happened and telephoned the police."

"You're not going to say anything about me?"

"Not unless I'm asked specifically," Mason said. "Naturally it's never going to occur to the police to ask me if that was the first time I'd been in the flat this morning. I'll tell them what happened and it will be the literal truth. I simply won't volunteer the information that I'd been here once before."

"And you want me to destroy that letter?"

Mason said, "That letter will crucify you. In a way it's evidence. It's evidence against you. As a lawyer, my only advice to you would be to turn that letter in to the police. If, however, you choose to ignore that advice, and destroy that letter, make a damn good job of destroying it. Burn it up where you can grind the ashes into a powder. And dispose of the ashes somewhere! Do you understand?"

"I . . . I think I understand."

Mason said, "Come on, then. Let's go down the stairs and get out of here. We'll leave the door unlatched, so we can push it open."

"You're going to do all this for me?" Marilyn Marlow asked.

Mason said, "When you look me in the eyes and tell me you had absolutely nothing to do with the death of Rose Keeling."

She came close to him, put her hands on his shoulders; her eyes looked up into his. "Mr. Mason, I tell you by all that I hold sacred I had nothing to do with her death. I'm telling you the truth. I'm telling you exactly what happened."

Mason nodded. "All right," he said, "I'll take your word for it. Let's go."

She glanced dubiously at Della Street.

Mason laughed. "Don't worry about Della. She's been under fire before."

"What will happen," Marilyn Marlow asked, "if they *should* put two and two together? If they should find out what had happened?"

Mason said, "If they're that clever, they'll find out who really killed Rose Keeling."

"Yes, I suppose so," she said in a tone that failed to show any indication of enthusiasm.

"The question is," Mason said, "will you back up my play? I'm risking a lot for you. Will you?"

"Mr. Mason, I'll never, never tell a soul. You can count on my loyalty one hundred per cent. One thousand per cent!"

"One hundred is enough. Let's go."

CHAPTER 10

Lieutenant Tragg came out of the bedroom and said to Mason, "You haven't touched anything?"

"Just the telephone receiver."

"How did you happen to be here?"

"Rose Keeling is a witness on a will."

"Who's the beneficiary under the will?"

"A woman by the name of Marlow. She's dead."

"When did she die?"

"A couple of months ago."

"Whom are you representing?"

"Her daughter."

"What's the name? What's the address?"

Mason gave him Marilyn Marlow's name and the address of her home.

"Know her telephone number?"

"Sure. I called her."

"What do you mean, you called her?"

"I called her at the same time I called you."

"From here?"

"Yes."

"You've got a crust!"

"Notifying my client of a development like this? Don't be silly."

"Telephone anyone else?"

"No."

"Just the two calls?"

"That's all."

"Who came here? How did you get in?"

"The door must have been unlocked. We rang the bell and waited for the buzzer to sound, unlatching the door. I pushed. The door opened. I thought the buzzer had done it. I must have been mistaken. The latch must not have been caught."

"So you walked right up?"

"That's right."

"And started prowling through the woman's flat?"

"Della Street was with me."

"Who found the body?"

"I did."

"Did Miss Street go in the bedroom?"

"No. She stayed here in this room."

"What did you do?"

"Backed right out."

"And then called me immediately?"

Mason said sarcastically, "What did you think we did, sit here and soak up atmosphere for fifteen minutes and *then* call you?"

Tragg chewed meditatively on his cigar. "Any theories about it?"

Mason said, "Sure. She was all packed to go away. She was taking a bath. The clothes she was going to wear were all laid out on the bed."

"That's quite obvious."

"She'd done everything she needed to do to get started, done all the packing and stuff of that sort. Taking the bath was the last thing she'd planned to do before dressing and leaving the flat."

"Even a cop knows that!" Tragg said, grinning.

"Therefore," Mason went on, "she must have intended to be on her way within a reasonable time after she took her bath. If you call the airport, you might find there was a reservation in her name on a plane going somewhere. Unless, of course, there was a railroad ticket in her purse, and if there wasn't, there might be a ticket held in her name at one of the ticket windows."

"You think she was making a long trip?"

"Just taking a glance at those suitcases, I'd say she had been planning to take quite an assortment of clothes."

"No other ideas?"

"No."

"What did this Marilyn Marlow say when you telephoned her and told her Rose Keeling had been murdered?"

"She wanted to ask me a lot of questions. I didn't have time to answer them, so I hung up."

"Why?"

"Because I wanted to call you."

"You mean you called her first?"

"That's right."

"You're supposed to notify the police immediately, at a time like this."

"That's why I only took a second or two to give her the information that Rose Keeling had been murdered, and then hung up."

Tragg said, "It's a damn good thing you've got Della Street with you."

"Isn't it?"

"What did you want with Rose Keeling?"

"I wanted to see her about the will. I wanted to get a statement."

"About what?"

"Her testimony in the will case."

"What about it?"

"I wanted to check with her, that's all."

"Ever met her?"

"No."

"Why the sudden rush to get her statement?"

"No sudden rush. I'd been putting it off."

"Know what her testimony would have been?"

"Sure. She'd already testified when the will was admitted to probate. Now there's going to be a contest after probate. I was just checking up as a matter of routine, to see if there were any new angles that hadn't been covered in her previous testimony. I wanted to get the general background."

Tragg stroked the angle of his jaw with the tips of his fingers. "The more I think of it, Mason, the more I think I'll just keep you and Della Street out of circulation for a while." He turned to one of the plainclothes officers and said, "Take Mason and Della Street downstairs and put them in a police car. Keep them there until I tell you to let them go. Be sure they don't do any telephoning, don't have any communication with anyone else, and don't let them do any whispering. If they want to talk with each other, listen in on what they have to say."

Mason said, "That's a damn outrage, Tragg. I'm busy; I've work to do!"

"I know you have," Tragg said soothingly, "but I want to make certain the work you have to do doesn't interfere with the work *I* have to do."

"And how long do we have to stay in custody?" Mason asked.

"Until we finish our investigation here."

"When will that be?"

"When I feel that I've found out all there is to know."

CHAPTER 11

Mason and Della Street sat in the rear seat of the big police sedan. The chunky, uniformed cop who occupied the front seat had enormous shoulders, a thick neck, heavy forehead, small, deep-set eyes, a huge chin and a battered nose that had apparently been flattened and left largely to its own devices, so far as healing was concerned.

Mason leaned over to Della Street, said in a low voice, "Della, there's one thing . . ."

"No whispering!" the officer growled.

"I was merely giving some instructions to my secretary."

"Keep your voice up when you do! I'm supposed to listen in."

"I don't think anyone has any right to tell me what tone of voice I should talk in, or what instructions I should give to my secretary."

The officer merely held open the door on the left side of the car, got out, opened the door at the back, climbed in and pushed Mason over to one side of the car and said, "Get over, buddy. I'll sit between you. The 'Loot' said you weren't to do any whispering, and when Tragg says you're not to do any whispering, as far as I'm concerned, you're not to whisper."

Mason said, "Tragg has no right to order anything of that sort."

"Okay. Have it your way. I don't aim to stop you from doing anything that's legal, so go right ahead and whisper. You can whisper across me. Whisper all you want."

They sat in silence for several seconds. Then Mason said, "The verbal IQ of our esteemed contemporary of the governmental enforcement staff seems to be limited to the vernacular."

"And so?" Della Street asked.

Mason, watching the officer's expressionless countenance, said, "We might try polysyllabic circumlocution. The elimination of one of the subscribers to a clause of formal attestation enhances the importance of the remaining member of the trio who were present at the time of testamentary execution."

"*Now*, what the hell!" the officer protested.

"Necessitating any remedial measures on our part?" Della Street inquired.

"Not necessarily remedial," Mason said, "but precautionary."

"In what way?"

"In view of the chirography transmitted yesterday, it might be well to ascertain specific details from the survivor of those present at the ceremonies incident to legalizing the cause of the testamentary controversy; and in the event I should be unavoidably detained, you might be able to expedite matters in that direction prior to inter-rogations by . . ."

"Say, bust it up. Bust it up!" the officer said. "What the hell's the idea? Want me to get tough?"

"You certainly can't put gags in our mouths, simply because Tragg wants us held for a while as material witnesses."

"How the hell do I know what he wants you held as?" the offi-cer asked. "I can sure as hell clap the bracelets on you, Mr. Mason, and handcuff you right around the pillar on that porch. And if you're thinking of getting away from here any time soon, it's going to make it a lot easier if I told the 'Loot' you weren't trying to slip anything over. If I tell him you tried to foul me up with dictionary chatter, you'll be here a long time."

"Yes," Della Street said, "I suppose that has its points, and, any-how, on that one matter I see no need for additional clarification."

"Who are you talking to? Me?" the officer asked.

Della Street nodded.

"Well, when you want to sing to me, make it a straight solo. Don't warble, just sing."

Della Street laughed. "Pardon me, I forgot."

"Forgot what?"

"Nothing."

Della Street turned to Mason. "Possibly a matter of emergency might result in a portion of the clerical force incident to the transaction of your business being liberated for the purpose of . . ."

"Oh, nuts!" the officer said. "You folks keep asking for it! Now, shut up. Another word out of either one of you and I'll separate you so you won't have a chance to talk."

He climbed back into the front of the car, pressed the button which brought in the car police radio and said, "Car ninety-one, car ninety-one. Ring Lieutenant Tragg. Tell him the two birds I'm holding at his orders insist on singing funny tunes. What does he want to do about it?"

"Car ninety-one," a voice asked, "relaying a message to Lieutenant Tragg?"

"That's right. You know where he is. There's a phone there. Get him."

Mason said, "After all, our conversation was merely a . . ."

"Shut up!"

Mason shrugged his shoulders and said, "Well, of course, if that's the way you . . ."

"I said shut up, and meant it!"

Mason winked at Della Street, lapsed into silence.

The officer swung around in the seat, his beady, deep-set eyes regarding them in sullen appraisal.

A few moments later the door of the flat where Rose Keeling had been murdered opened and Lieutenant Tragg hurried across the porch and down to the car. "What's the trouble?" he asked.

The officer gestured with his thumb. "These two birds keep on singing," he said. "I broke up the whispering, and then they started a lot of dictionary stuff, back and forth, stuff that was over my head."

"All right, Mason," Tragg said. "I thought you could take a hint. I see you can't. Get out!"

"But, Lieutenant, I was merely . . ."

"Get out!"

The officer opened the door, reached in and grabbed the lapels of Mason's coat and said, "When the 'Loot' says *out*, he means OUT. YOU coming?"

"I'm coming," Mason said.

"Come with me," Tragg ordered.

Mason followed him up to the porch. Tragg turned abruptly, said, "Wait a minute, I have some instructions to give the officer."

Mason sat on the rail of the porch while Tragg moved part way down the cement walk which led to the sidewalk.

Tragg and the officer conversed in low tones for a moment or two, then the officer started back toward the car. Tragg returned to Mason. "What were you two trying to put over, Mason?"

Mason said, "I feel I've been inconvenienced about enough. After all, Lieutenant, I've told you all I know, and *I* have work to do."

Tragg nodded.

"Moreover," Mason said, "there's a lot of stuff at the office that Miss Street has to take care of."

Tragg pursed his lips, started to say something, checked himself.

"One of us has to get back," Mason insisted.

Tragg apparently changed his mind. He called out suddenly to the officer in the police car, "Take Miss Street up to Mr. Mason's office, leave her there and then follow instructions."

"Okay," the big officer said, and almost immediately little puffs of smoke began to come from the exhaust of the big police car.

"You can come back upstairs with me," Tragg said to Mason. "I want to talk with you a little further."

"Only too glad to oblige," Mason said.

The big police car rocketed into motion.

"I'd like her to get there in one piece," Mason said.

"Oh, sure, sure," Tragg assured him casually. "That officer will handle her as though she were a crate of eggs. He's one of the best drivers in the business."

"He seemed unduly suspicious."

"That depends on what you mean by 'unduly,'" Tragg said. "He said you were trying to whisper."

"I wanted to give Della Street some instructions about a business matter."

"You can trust our discretion."

Mason said, "I don't have to trust anyone's discretion. I have a right to run my business, and I certainly don't have to broadcast instructions to my secretary over a police network . . ."

"Okay, okay," Tragg interrupted, "no hard feelings, Mason. I merely wanted to make sure I had a straight story out of you. Now, let's take a few minutes here, and then I see no reason why you can't be on your way. Show me just how this door was standing partially open when you came here."

Mason said, "Now, I'm not certain about that, Tragg. I thought I heard a buzzer somewhere, and—you know how these electric buzzers release a door catch."

Tragg, watching Mason narrowly, nodded his head. "Go on," he said curtly.

"Well," Mason said, "I rang the bell and then I *thought* I heard a buzzer. I can't be absolutely certain of it. I pressed against the door, and the door opened, so I naturally assumed my ring had been answered."

"You don't know whether the door was ajar or not?"

"I acted rather mechanically. I heard what I thought was a buzzer, and pushed the door."

"You don't think it was a buzzer now?"

Mason said, "A dead woman can hardly push a buzzer button."

"That's right," Tragg said, and then added after a moment, "You had Della Street with you?"

"Yes."

"Of course, Mason, you wouldn't want to suppress any evidence."

"What do you mean—evidence?"

"Just what I said."

"I take it," Mason said, "that you are referring to evidence concerning the murder. As far as any other evidence is concerned, I not only have a right to suppress it, but it becomes my duty to do so."

"How do you figure that?"

"I'm supposed to protect the interests of my clients. I'm supposed to keep their confidences."

"Their confidences, yes, but that doesn't mean you can suppress any evidence."

"I can suppress evidence of anything I damn please," Mason said, "just so it isn't evidence that points to a crime."

"There might be a difference of opinion," Tragg said, "as to just what evidence points to a crime and just what doesn't."

"Perhaps."

"I wouldn't want you to think you had the final decision in that matter."

"You think I'm holding something back?"

Tragg said, "I'm interested in how you got in, that's all."

"I told you."

"Obviously, you must have been mistaken when you say you thought you heard the buzzer."

"That, of course, is a logical conclusion."

"Do you know of any motive for the murder?" Tragg asked.

"I had never even met the woman."

"Nurse, wasn't she?"

"So I understand."

Tragg said, "Well, sit down here, Mason. I'll be finished with you in a few minutes. I'll be back as soon as I've checked up on some stuff in here."

Mason sat down in a chair in the living room and Tragg went back to the bedroom. Mason, from time to time, saw brief white flashes of light in the hall as the photographer in the bedroom shot off flash bulbs. The lawyer impatiently looked at his watch, nervously pulled a cigarette case out of his pocket, snapped it open, struck a match and started smoking.

The officer who was standing in the doorway on guard said, "If you don't mind, Mr. Mason, you can put that burnt match in your pocket. It might be confusing if you dropped it in an ashtray."

Mason nodded, and pushed the burnt match down into his pocket.

The door from the south bedroom opened, and Tragg said, "All right, Mason, I don't think there's any need to detain you any longer. You have your car here?"

"Yes," Mason said.

"We've got nothing more to ask you right at the present time. You can't remember anything else?"

"I think I've told you all I can," Mason said.

"*Okay*," Tragg said breezily, "on your way," and to the officer at the door, "Let Mr. Mason *out*."

Mason said good afternoon to Tragg, walked past the officer, down the stairs, walked a half block to where he had parked his car, got in and drove until he saw a sign announcing a telephone pay station.

Mason dropped a coin, dialed his office, and in a matter of seconds had Gertie on the line.

"Quick, Gertie," Mason said, "I want to get the address of Ethel Furlong, the other witness to that will, and . . ."

Gertie's voice was sharp with excitement. "Della Street's already got it. She went tearing out there in a taxi. It's way out on South Montet Avenue—number 6920."

"Thanks," Mason said. "Don't let anyone know where I am. In case the police should telephone, simply tell them I haven't showed up at the office yet but that you're expecting me. You say Della went out in a taxi?"

"Yes."

"How long ago did she leave?"

"About three or four minutes ago. The police brought her to the office. She said they certainly gave her one wild ride. That big cop goes like mad, and, of course, with the siren . . ."

"I understand," Mason said. "I presume I can get there about as soon as she does."

"Mr. Mason, can you tell me what's happened? Della Street was in too much of a hurry . . ."

"I am, too," Mason said. "It'll keep. Just close up the office at five, Gertie, and go on home."

"Aw gee, Mr. Mason, I'd like to stay if there's anything I can do."

"I don't think there is. I'll phone you if I need you. Good-by."

Mason jumped in his car and made time out to the cross-town boulevard. It was a twenty-minute drive to where South Montet Avenue crossed the boulevard in the fifty-two-hundred block.

Mason turned right, and had only gone two blocks when he overtook the taxicab in which Della Street was riding.

Mason drew alongside and pressed the button of his horn.

Della looked up, first with apprehension, then with glad surprise. She tapped on the glass, signaling the driver to stop.

When the driver had brought his cab to a stop, Della Street paid him off and climbed in with Mason.

"How did you do?" Mason asked her.

"Swell, but my gosh, I had a wild ride up to the office!"

"The cop try to pump you?"

"No."

"Not a word?"

"No."

"Try to date you?"

"No."

Mason said, "There's something funny about that chap, but I don't know what it is. Now let's go to see what Ethel Furlong has to say."

They found the number to be an apartment house on the west side of the street. Della Street ran her hand down the list of cards and said, "Here she is—apartment 926."

She pressed the bell repeatedly.

There was no answer.

Mason frowned. "Just our luck not to have her home, Della.

Press one of the other buttons. We'll see if we can't get someone to let us in."

Della Street pressed two or three buttons at random, and, after a moment, someone buzzed the catch on the outer door.

Della Street and Mason entered the building and took the elevator to the ninth floor.

As they approached the door of 926, Della Street said, "There's an envelope pinned to the door."

"Probably a note saying when she'll be back," Mason said.

They walked rapidly down the corridor. Della Street, in the lead, said, "It's an envelope addressed to you, Chief."

Mason said incredulously, "It has *my* name on it?"

"That's right."

Della Street handed him the envelope, which had on the outside the words, "Mr. Perry Mason," written in the even, regular strokes of a literate hand.

Mason pulled back the flap on the envelope. "Still damp," he said. "It was sealed only a minute or two ago."

He unfolded the note, read the message and then suddenly broke into laughter.

"What is it?" Della Street asked.

Mason said, "I'll read it to you:

"'Dear Mr. Mason:

"'Thanks very much for the tip which enabled us to get Ethel Furlong's story before you had a chance to foul it up for us. Tragg had called the office of the Probate Clerk and had her name and address. Thanks to your erudite conversation with the estimable Miss Street, I was able to anticipate your plans. You may be interested to know that I had high marks in forensic debate and was on the college debating team which won the 1929 conference championship. My physiognomy became badly marred because of a mistaken impression that I was possessed of the necessary pugilistic ability to carve a career for myself in that profession. Don't worry about Ethel Furlong. She's in nice safe hands, and by the time we get done with her, we'll have her story all down in black and white, with her signature at the end of it. After that, it won't do much good to have you try to change it. Best wishes.

"'Driver of Car 91.'"

Della Street said indignantly, "Why, the dirty. . . !"

Mason, grinning broadly, said, "It shows the danger of judging people by the way they look. He sat there and played dumb and let us tell him all of our plans."

"Just where does that leave us?" Della Street asked.

"Temporarily," Mason said, "it leaves us behind the eightball."

"And what do we do now?"

"Return to the office," Mason said, "and start Paul Drake doing a lot of leg work. And the next time we meet a 'dumb' cop, Della, we'll forget the broken nose and cauliflower ear, and look him over to see if he has a Phi Beta Kappa key hanging from his watch chain. Let's go."

CHAPTER 12

The two Endicott brothers and the one sister had moved into the big mansion home which had been left them under the terms of George Endicott's will.

Years ago the house had been one of the show places of the city. Now it was an anachronism, a big wooden-gabled structure with side porches, spacious grounds, shade trees, lawns, summer houses, terraces, winding walks and sunken pools. It seemed more a museum than a dwelling.

Mason turned his car in at the driveway, which, together with the big garage, had been constructed as a modern improvement. The hard-surfaced driveway cut through in a businesslike straight line past the winding walks which followed the contours of the terraced grounds.

The lawyer stopped his car under the protecting portico of what had once been a shelter over a carriage entrance. He climbed three stairs and rang a bell which jangled sharply in the dark bowels of the ancient house.

Mason rang a second time before he heard slow steps, and then the door was opened by a man whose bald head, fringed with white hair, whose sharp, piercing eyes, beaklike nose and thin lips gave him the appearance of a reincarnated predator.

"I would like to see any one of the Endicott family," Mason said.

"I'm Ralph Endicott."

Mason handed the man his card. "I'm Perry Mason, a lawyer."

"I've heard of you. Won't you come in?"

"Thank you."

Mason followed Endicott in through a gloomy, paneled passage-way redolent with the splendor of a bygone age.

His guide opened the door and said, "Won't you step in here, please, Mr. Mason?"

This room was thoroughly in keeping with the rest of the house, a large, spacious library, in the center of which was a massive mahogany table on which were three huge table lamps. The shades, some four feet in diameter at the bottom, were composed of heavy leather, and the clustered lamps on the interior poured forth illumination upon the huge table and sprayed light out through the openings in the tops of the shades.

Three chairs had been drawn up at this table. Two of them were occupied, and the third, which evidently was where Ralph Endicott had been sitting before he went to answer the bell, was pulled slightly back from between the other two.

The two people who looked up at Mason's entrance had a certain family resemblance.

Reflected light from the big reading lamps on the table splashed illumination on their faces and etched them into white brilliance against the somber background of booklined shelves.

"Mr. Mason," Ralph Endicott said, "permit me to introduce you to my brother and sister. Mrs. Parsons, may I present Mr. Perry Mason, a lawyer. And this, Mr. Mason, is my brother, Palmer Endicott."

"Good evening," Mason said, giving his most cordial smile. "I'm very pleased to meet you."

The others bowed coldly.

"Won't you be seated, Mr. Mason?"

"Thank you," Mason said.

Ralph Endicott drew up a chair for Mason directly across the table from where the others were sitting, then walked around to take his place once more in the third chair between the other two.

Mason had a chance to size up the brother and sister while Ralph was seating himself.

Palmer was a thin-faced, bushy-haired individual, somewhere in the seventies. He had about him a look of perpetual skepticism. Lorraine Endicott Parsons quite evidently lavished care upon herself, such care as could be given in home treatments. She sat haughtily erect in stiff-backed, uncompromising truculence. Her face had begun to sag, but her chin was up; her hair was frosty white, and there was the cold ruthlessness of self-righteous respectability in her posture. There was about all three of them an appearance of shabby gentility which added to the over-all family resemblance. Clothes were dark in color, old-fashioned in cut, and well worn.

"Just what do you want, Mr. Mason?" Ralph Endicott asked.

"I'm a lawyer," Mason said. "I'm representing interests adverse to you. You have a lawyer, Paddington C. Niles. I tried to call him. His secretary said he was on his way here. I don't want to talk with you until he arrives."

"What do you want to talk about?" Ralph Endicott asked.

"Rose Keeling is dead. I want to ask you about circumstances which may have led to her death or . . ."

"Rose Keeling dead!" Mrs. Parsons interrupted with cold disbelief. "She can't be dead. That would greatly embarrass us. Are you *certain* of your facts, Mr. Mason?"

She regarded him as though she expected him to wither and crawl under the table under the impact of her disapproving stare.

Mason said, "She's quite thoroughly dead. Someone stabbed her as she stepped out of the bathtub. I'm investigating that murder, and time is precious. I'd like to know whether any of you have been in touch with her recently. All I want to know is whether you saw her today, whether she phoned you and, if so, when."

Ralph Endicott said slowly, "This, of course, was the thing we had to fear."

Mrs. Parsons said, "A creature who had stooped to taking advantage of a man's incompetencies and depriving his relatives of what is justly theirs, would stop at nothing."

"Meaning?" Mason asked.

"I am making no specific accusations."

"That sounded like an accusation."

"You are free to interpret my remarks any way you wish."

"My I ask whom you're representing?" Palmer Endicott inquired.

Mason shook his head. "My client is not willing to have an announcement made at the present time."

"I take it you're not representing the authorities. There's nothing official about your investigation."

"Not in the least," Mason said. "I want you to have your lawyer, and I want to know if any of you had been in touch with Miss Keeler earlier in the day. That's all I want to know."

"Why?"

"Because a murder has been committed. I'm trying to get the time element straightened out. I want to know when she was killed. And I'm anxious to find out the latest hour at which she was alive. I think she may have called one of you today. I don't give a hang about the nature of the conversation. I only want to know the time of the conversation. Your lawyer's supposed to be here. I want him present. Where is he?"

"He's coming," Ralph Endicott said. "When we heard your ring we felt certain that it was Mr. Niles. He's due here now for a conference. That's why we're sitting in the library."

Mason said, "I want to see him. I . . ." He broke off as the electric bell boomed a summons through the house.

"That will be Niles now," Mrs. Parsons said with calm conviction.

Ralph Endicott pushed back his chair, said, "Excuse me," went to the door and returned in a few moments with a florid-faced man in the fifties who beamed optimism and geniality.

"Mr. Niles," Ralph Endicott said as though presenting two fighters in the ring. "Mr. Mason."

"How are you, Mr. Niles," Mason said, shaking hands. "I'm glad to meet you."

"I've heard of you," Niles said. "Seen you in court several times, but never have had the pleasure of meeting you. How do you do? And may I ask what you're doing *here*?"

Mason said, "I am trying to get some information about a matter which is outside the issues of the will contest. I told these people I wanted their lawyer present. I understood you were here."

"What is the nature of the information you want?" Niles asked, instantly suspicious.

Mason said, "I'm investigating the death of Rose Keeling."

"The *death* of Rose Keeling!" Niles echoed in astonishment.

"That's right."

"But she's not dead. She . . ."

"She *is* dead," Mason said. "She was murdered some time around noon today."

"Good heavens!" Niles said. "This complicates the situation."

Mason said, "I'm trying to account for her time during the early part of the day. I had reason to believe she might have been in conversation with one of the Endicotts."

"What caused you to believe that?"

"My detectives tell me there is evidence that Rose Keeling gave one of your clients a check today. I want to know when and what for."

Niles pursed his lips thoughtfully. "Did you come here to see me?"

"I wanted to ask some questions of your clients. I rang your office. Your secretary said you were here. Naturally I wanted your permission, although I could have secured the information through more orthodox and more disagreeable channels."

"How?"

"I could have told my friend, Lieutenant Tragg on Homicide, that I thought it would be a good plan to check on the Endicotts. That would have dragged their names into the newspapers and ultimately had a far more disastrous effect on the will contest than an informal chat of this sort."

"Well, let's sit down and get this thing straightened out," Niles said.

Ralph Endicott said, "As far as I'm concerned, I can shout what I have to say from the housetops. I think it would be a good plan to let the newspapers know exactly what happened."

"Not the newspapers!" Lorraine Parsons said coldly. "The newspapers are vulgar. They are sensational. They cater to the lowest section of humanity and present news with the vulgar sensationalism which appeals to readers of that type."

Niles said, "I think we'll excuse you for a few minutes, Mr. Mason. I want to talk with my clients about this. And then if we have any statement to make, we'll make it formally."

"Time is short," Mason reminded him.

"Why are you in such a hurry to get that information?"

"I have reasons."

"What are they?"

Mason smiled, and shook his head.

"You want *us* to put *our* cards on the table while you hold all the aces up your sleeve," Niles said.

Mason said, with some anger, "Have it your own way. I'll put in a call for Lieutenant Tragg and then I'll read the answers in tomorrow morning's paper."

"I think, Mr. Mason," Mrs. Parsons said acidly, "that Mr. Niles' request is quite in order. You may wait in the . . ."

"Reception hallway," Palmer Endicott cut in firmly.

Mason grinned and said, "I'll wait in my car. I'll wait five minutes. You can make up your minds within that time to talk with me or with the police, whichever you see fit."

"I don't see what the police have to do with . . ."

"Please!" Niles protested to his clients, then turned to Mason. "Go out and wait in your car, Mason."

Mason bowed. "Five minutes," he said, and left the room.

Five minutes to the second after the lawyer had settled himself in his car, he started the motor, inched his way past Paddington Niles' car, got to the garage, turned around and started to drive past the house and out the driveway.

He had gone perhaps fifteen feet when the side door was flung open and Ralph Endicott, running out, waved frantically at him.

Mason braked his car to a stop.

"Come in, Mr. Mason! Come right in," Endicott called, his voice tremulous with excitement. "We're waiting for you. We *want* to talk with you."

Mason stopped his car, leaving it so that it blocked the driveway. He got out and said, "I thought you'd decided to let me go to the police."

"No, no, no. Not yet. Come right in. We perhaps ran a few seconds over the time, but only a few seconds—just a few seconds, Mr. Mason."

Mason followed Ralph Endicott back into the library.

They looked up as he entered.

Paddington C. Niles was frowning. His face had an expression of perplexity. Palmer Endicott, with an attempt at cordiality that was foreign to his nature and made his words utterly incongruous, said, "Sit right down, Mr. Mason. Sit right down and be comfortable."

Lorraine Endicott Parsons actually managed a frosty smile. "*Do* sit down, Mr. Mason."

Mason seated himself at the far end of the table.

There was a moment of silence, while Ralph Endicott resumed his chair and cleared his throat.

"Go ahead," Mason said.

"Would you like to tell him, Niles?" Ralph Endicott asked.

Niles shook his head. "This is all a bit sudden, as far as I'm concerned. You tell the facts to Mason and I'll listen while you go over them again. But be *sure* of your facts."

"Oh, certainly," Ralph Endicott said testily.

Mason lit a cigarette. "Let's go," he said.

Ralph Endicott said, "In the beginning, Mr. Mason, I came to the conclusion that the purported will my brother was supposed to have executed was the result of fraud, undue influence and various other illegalities. The nurse who attended him saw to it that his mind was never entirely clear, and at a propitious moment she suggested the signing of this will."

Palmer Endicott, having made his attempt at cordiality, had now slumped down in his chair, listening to his brother's statement with cold cynicism. Lorraine Parsons nodded her head slowly, signifying her acquiescence.

"I don't want to talk about the will contest," Mason said impatiently.

"Well, we do."

"All I want to know is the time you talked with Rose Keeling. I want the exact hour as nearly as you can recall."

"I'm coming to that," Ralph Endicott said, "but I'm coming to it in my own way. Since you're here, we may as well talk about the whole case. We *might* reach some understanding."

Mason said, "I'm only prepared to talk about the murder."

"Well, listen to what *I* have to say, then," Endicott said.

The others nodded approval.

"I assumed," Ralph went on, "that the witnesses to the will were equally culpable with the so-called beneficiary. I assumed that there must have been some financial benefit to them in the transaction, and I felt certain that no matter how my brother might have been drugged, no matter how much disease and undue influence had clouded his mind, he would never voluntarily have made such a will. That will was written by the beneficiary. It was then shoved under his nose and he was told to sign."

"That doesn't coincide with the testimony given by the two subscribing witnesses," Mason said.

"Just a moment, just a moment," Endicott said rapidly. "I'm coming to that."

"All right. Go ahead."

"So, I approached Rose Keeling. I explained to her exactly how I felt about it, and at first Miss Keeling refused to co-operate with me in any way or give me any information other than the parrotlike statement she had been paid to make."

Mason puffed silently at his cigarette.

"Then," Ralph Endicott went on, "her conscience began to bother her. She finally told me a most remarkable story."

"What's the story?" Mason asked. "Let's get down to brass tacks."

"It was an extraordinary story. She stated that Mrs. Marlow had taken up the matter of the will with her on the day that it was executed, that she had told her that her patient, who was really wealthy, desired to make a will in her favor and that he had dictated to her the terms of the will; that his right hand was paralyzed so that he could not sign with his right hand, but that he would sign with his left hand."

"At that time the will was already drawn?"

"The will was already drawn in the handwriting of Mrs. Marlow. She said that my brother had dictated the terms of the will. She also told Rose Keeling that if Rose would sign as a witness and the will stood up, Rose Keeling would receive a substantial amount of money. Rose Keeling had no way of knowing what Mrs. Marlow promised the other witness, Ethel Furlong, but it is assumed that substantially the same promises were made.

"The three nurses entered the room where my brother was lying. Mrs. Marlow said to him, 'Now, Mr. Endicott, I have drawn up the will the way you wanted it. You sign here.' My brother said, 'I can't sign with my right hand,' and Mrs. Marlow had said, 'All right. Go ahead and sign with your left hand.'

"Thereupon my brother suggested that she read the will to him in the presence of the witnesses, and she said, 'No, no, that isn't necessary. These two nurses are on duty here on the floor and they may be called out at any time. They can't take enough time from their other patients to sit around and listen to this. It's drawn up just the way you wanted it drawn up. You sign here.'

"My brother George seemed a little bit uncertain about whether he would sign or not without having it read to him. But at just that moment the floor superintendent looked into the room and said, 'What's the matter in here? The call lights are on all over the floor.' Mrs. Marlow had thereupon hastily hidden the will and Rose Keeling had said, 'I'll take care of the lights.' She had dashed out of the room and found three lights. Two of them were patients who required only minor attention and one from a patient who took longer, about five minutes. When she had finished with those duties, Rose Keeling returned to the room, and Mrs. Marlow was then holding in her hands the document supposed to have been signed by my brother, and she said, 'It's all right, Rose, he's signed the will and everything's all right. Just go ahead and sign here as a witness. You want her to, don't you, Mr. Endicott?'

"And," Ralph Endicott went on triumphantly, "my brother, George, said nothing. He was lying there with his eyes closed and was breathing regularly. Rose Keeling thinks that he was either asleep or that while she was out of the room, he had been given a heavy hypodermic of morphine. However, Mrs. Marlow was popular and Rose Keeling was thoroughly in sympathy with having her get something for the nursing and attention she had given my brother. So she signed as a witness.

"Later on, after my brother had died, Mrs. Marlow came to Rose Keeling and told her there were certain formalities that the lawyers would ask about, and told Rose substantially what to say. She told Rose that there had been an outright gift of certain jewelry and that she was going to keep some of this jewelry, but was going to sell some of it to raise some immediate money.

"She did this, selling some diamonds, which I understand brought in the neighborhood of ten thousand dollars. My brother's collection of jewelry, many of the pieces heirlooms, was worth at least a hundred thousand dollars. The story that I now get is that some two weeks before his death, in the presence of Ethel Furlong, he had given the jewelry to Mrs. Marlow and told her that he wanted her to have that jewelry, that he had no use for it; that there would be no descendants of his to wear the jewelry and that she was to take it and do what she wanted to with it. Mrs. Marlow had some cash. She gave Rose Keeling a thousand dollars in cash and told her that when the estate was finally distributed, if everything went all right, Rose Keeling would get another nine thousand dollars."

Mason said, "Quite easy to make up a fairy story like this, now that Rose Keeling is out of the way. I thought you'd probably do something like that, which was the reason I told you I would only give you five minutes. However, you've collaborated on a pretty good scenario. It's as fast a job as I've ever seen. You should be in Hollywood."

Niles said hastily, "That's the story they told me as soon as you left the room, Mason."

Mason merely smiled.

"However," Niles went on somewhat testily, "there's proof of this."

"Proof?" Mason asked.

"Exactly," Ralph Endicott said. "Rose Keeling's conscience began to bother her. I received a telephone call from her, stating that she wanted to see me at once upon a matter of the greatest importance. That call came in about seven-thirty this morning. I finished my breakfast and went to her apartment. I arrived there approximately at eight o'clock. I found Rose Keeling in an extremely nervous state. She said she had agreed to do something which preyed on her conscience and that she just simply couldn't go through with it. She told me that she had received one thousand dollars from Mrs. Marlow, that she was satisfied that one thousand dollars came from the sale of jewelry which had virtually been stolen from the estate; that, inasmuch as I was one of the heirs and represented the others, she had decided to surrender that money and ease her conscience. Whereupon, she handed me her check for one thousand dollars, drawn on the Central Security Bank, and gave me a carbon copy of a letter she had sent to Marilyn Marlow."

Mason's eyes narrowed. "A carbon copy?" he asked.

"Yes."

"How had the letter been written? On a typewriter?"

"No. In pen and ink, but she had a clear carbon copy."

"May I see the carbon copy of the letter?" Mason asked.

Ralph Endicott said to Niles, "How about it, Niles? Shall we show him the carbon copy of the letter?"

"I see no reason for not showing it to him," Niles said. "Since you've gone this far and told him this much, I'd tell him the whole thing. Put all the cards on the table."

Endicott opened a billfold which he had taken from his pocket while Niles was speaking, and handed Mason a sheet of note paper. "There it is," he said.

Mason glanced through the letter. It was a carbon copy of the letter which Marilyn Marlow had received and which she probably had by this time destroyed.

"Very interesting," Mason said, his voice and face expressionless as he handed back the carbon copy. "When did all this take place?"

"At approximately eight o'clock this morning."

"That was at Rose Keeling's flat?"

"Yes."

"How long were you there?"

"Perhaps half an hour in all."

"What did you do when you left there?"

"I see no reason to go into that. It involves purely private affairs. I assume you are only interested in Rose Keeling's . . ."

"Go ahead and tell him," Niles grunted. "You've admitted having seen Rose Keeling, and if she's been killed, you'd better go on with your story."

"It's a lot of purely personal trivia," Endicott protested.

"Go on with it, Ralph," Mrs. Parsons ordered, "otherwise you seem evasive. Tell Mr. Mason where you went."

Ralph Endicott frowned, said, "Very well. It is a lot of utter trivia. I left Miss Keeling's place at approximately eight-forty in the morning. I went from there to the office of an automobile agency where I have had a new car on order for some time. I felt certain that they were cheating on me and letting cars out the back door. I had been twenty-fourth on the list several months ago and was advised that I was fifteenth on the list as of this date. I made something of a scene. I left there at approximately nine o'clock. I had an appointment with my dentist at nine-fifteen. I was with him until nine-fifty-five. I remember the time because I had been thinking about that check while I was in the dentist's chair. I knew it was an important piece of evidence. If I cashed it, then it would be returned to Rose Keeling by the bank when it sent her her canceled checks. If I held it as evidence, she might change her mind and stop payment on it.

"Just before I left the dentist's, I conceived the idea of holding the check but having it certified. I consulted my watch. It was a few minutes before ten. I hurried to the bank and reached the cashier's window at about ten-five. When he certified the check, I asked him to be certain to note the time of certification. You can see he wrote it on the check, 10:10 A.M.

"From the bank I went to a chess and checker club. I arrived there at about ten-twenty and started playing in a tournament in which I was a contestant. I played continuously until about three-thirty. Then I had a sandwich and a malted milk and drove home in my car—a model A Ford. I have been here ever since.

"Here is the certified check, in case you wish to examine it."

"I presume you can verify all these times," Mason asked, taking the check Ralph Endicott handed him.

"As a matter of fact, I can very easily. As it happens, I was playing chess on a time limit, and inasmuch as I am considered one of the champions there, there was a record kept of the games and of the time consumed in the games. However, I consider all of this as absolutely beside the point and quite irrelevant."

Mason, who had been examining the check, said, "You saw her sign this check?"

"Yes."

"I notice there's a somewhat smeared but still fairly legible fingerprint on the back of this check."

"Let's see it."

Mason pointed out the smudged fingerprint.

"Probably my fingerprint," Ralph Endicott said casually.

"Made in ink?"

"That's right. I remember now I started to endorse the check, and the cashier told me that I shouldn't endorse it. If I wanted to have it certified, the certification would show the check was good as gold. He said I wasn't to endorse it until I was ready to cash it."

Mason said, "Well, let's just check on this ink-smeared print. If it's your fingerprint, let's find out."

Endicott burst out, "I consider this damned impertinent!"

"So do I," Niles said.

"I don't," Palmer Endicott said calmly. "If we're going to put our cards on the table, let's put them all on the table. Rose Keeling was murdered today. Ralph was with her. He received a check from her, and he went to the bank and presented that check to have it certified. Under the circumstances, he's going to have to account for every minute of his time, and if he can't do it right now, I, for one, want to know it."

Ralph Endicott turned to him irritably. "What are you trying to do?" he said. "Casting insinuations?"

"I'm not casting any insinuations," Palmer said calmly, his eyes still fixed on his folded hands, his outward demeanor one of extreme placidity, "I'm merely checking. I want to know, myself, just as much as Mason does."

"My own brother!" Ralph snorted.

"And doing you a great favor," Palmer said.

"Yes," Ralph said sarcastically, "I know just how much of a favor you want to do me." He drew his index finger in a circular cutting motion across the front of his throat.

Niles said hastily, "Come, come, gentlemen, remember that Mr. Mason is here, and that Mr. Mason is representing adverse interests. Frankly, I see no reason for letting him question your word or indulge in any cross-examination."

Palmer Endicott pushed back his chair, said, "You folks can do whatever you want to, but as far as *I'm* concerned, I'm going to find out about that fingerprint, and I'm going to find out about it right now."

"Ralph isn't trying to keep anything from you, Palmer," Lorraine Parsons said acidly. "It's merely that we object to discussing family affairs in front of this . . . this lawyer."

Palmer Endicott said, "The trouble with Ralph is he thinks he's too smart. He's always gilding the lily and painting the rose. If he'd only learn to confine himself to the evidence and tell the simple truth, we'd all be better off. If it hadn't been for that time he tried to dress things up and make the evidence look better ten years ago, we wouldn't have been dependent upon inheriting under our brother's will. We could have been independently rich and . . ."

"Palmer!" Lorraine snapped. "We *won't* go into that."

"I was merely mentioning . . ."

"Well, don't."

Palmer walked into the next room, said, "Well, there's an ink pad in the writing desk. Can you make fingerprints from an ordinary rubber stamp ink pad, Mr. Mason?"

"I think so," Mason said.

Ralph Endicott said, "This is all foolishness."

Niles shifted his position uneasily in his chair. "I don't approve of . . ."

Palmer Endicott returned to the room, carrying an ink pad and a sheet of paper. "Here you are," he said to Ralph Endicott, holding the paper out in front of him.

"A blank sheet of paper and an ink pad. Let's see your fingerprints."

Ralph Endicott said angrily, "You're crazy, Palmer."

"Crazy like a fox," Palmer said. "Come on over here and take your fingerprints."

He moved over to a small table at the far corner of the room, put down the sheet of paper and inked pad, said, "I'll be getting a drink while you're doing it."

"Do I have to?" Ralph Endicott asked the lawyer.

"I would say not," Niles said.

Palmer Endicott, standing in the door of the butler's pantry, said quietly and forcefully, "Go over to that table and put your prints on that paper. Do you all want Scotch and soda?"

Mrs. Parsons said, "I think Scotch and soda would suit us all, Palmer, but I don't think Mr. Mason would be comfortable drinking with us."

Ralph Endicott walked over to the small table, inked his fingers and sullenly pressed them down on the sheet of paper.

Palmer Endicott, standing in the doorway, said, "Never let it be said that the Endicotts were remiss in hospitality. Scotch and soda, Mr. Mason?"

"Please," the lawyer said.

Palmer Endicott left the room.

Ralph Endicott, having finished with the prints of his right hand, placed his left hand on the pad and transferred a set of finger-prints to the paper. He waved the paper in the air so that the prints would dry, then brought it over to the table and placed it in front of Mason. His face was sullen.

Mrs. Parsons said, "I, for one, bitterly resent the aspersions which are being cast upon the family. The Endicotts have at times been impecunious. They have *never* been dishonorable."

There was an uncomfortable silence while Mason studied the fingerprints.

Palmer Endicott returned from the butler's pantry with a half bottle of Scotch and glasses containing ice cubes. "How's it coming?" he asked Mason.

Mason, comparing the fingerprints, said, "It looks to me like a thumbprint—I think—that's right. It's the right thumbprint. They check absolutely."

"I'll take a look for myself," Niles said, and, crossing over to Mason, peered over the lawyer's shoulder. At length he nodded. "That's right," he said, "they do seem to check."

Palmer Endicott poured Scotch into the glasses. He used no jig-ger for measurement, and it was noticeable that he tried to conserve the Scotch as much as possible. When he splashed soda into the glasses, the resulting mixture was a very faint amber color.

"I hope you're satisfied now," Ralph said.

Palmer Endicott moved the tray over to offer his sister a drink. "I'm not satisfied. I'm merely convinced. Of course, Ralph," he went on musingly, "you had no incentive to kill her. You had no motive, as far as I can see. But you sure as hell did have an opportunity."

"I did not!" Ralph said indignantly. "She was alive and well when I left her, and I'm willing to bet the autopsy will show she was killed a long time after that."

"Do you know the time of death, Mason?" Niles asked.

Mason said, "I *think* it was around eleven-forty."

"Well, we'll find out from the police," Niles said.

Palmer Endicott, sipping his drink, slowly nodded.

Mason said, "I notice on this check that when Rose Keeling signs her name, she uses a very soft pen. She writes with a vertical hand and there is a good deal of shading on the strokes."

Niles nodded. "I'd noticed that."

"But on this carbon copy of the letter, there is none of that."

"Naturally not," Lorraine Parsons said. "That was written with an entirely different pen. Kindly don't try to confuse the issues, Mr. Mason."

Mason smiled affably. "That's the very point I was getting at, Mrs. Parsons. This note must have been written with a ball-point fountain pen. Otherwise so clear a carbon copy would have been impossible."

Mrs. Parsons said acidly, "That is the same handwriting, absolutely the same vertical penmanship as the signature on the check which the bank has certified."

Mason grinned. "Don't misunderstand me. I was merely raising a point."

Ralph Endicott turned to Niles. "Well, what do you think of it?" he asked the lawyer.

Niles said, "I think you have been more than frank with Mr. Mason. I think you have gone out of your way to tell him things that you certainly did not need to tell him."

"I want him to get the whole picture," Ralph said.

"He certainly should have it now."

Mason pushed back his chair. "I think I have it. Thank you."

Niles shook hands. Palmer Endicott came around the table to shake hands. Lorraine Parsons bowed a cold good night, and Ralph Endicott merely bowed without offering to shake hands.

Mason left the place, got in his automobile, drove to the first pay station he could find and called police headquarters.

Lieutenant Tragg was out.

"I want to leave a message for him," Mason said.

"Okay, we'll take it."

"Can you get him on the phone?"

"I think so. We can put out a radio call for him. What's on your mind?"

Mason said, "Tell him that Ralph Endicott presented a check to be certified at the Central Security Bank shortly after ten o'clock today. The check was dated today, was payable to him, and had been signed by Rose Keeling. Is that important?"

"If that's true," the voice at the other end of the line said, "it's important as hell."

"Okay," Mason said, "it's true."

He hung up and dialed the number of Marilyn Marlow.

After a moment or two she came to the phone.

"Are you alone?" Mason asked.

"No."

"Boy friend?"

"No."

"Girl friend?"

"No."

"Police?"

"Yes."

Mason said, "The wind's going to blow! Within the next hour they'll have a carbon copy of the letter you destroyed. Don't deny you received it; say it made you so mad you . . ."

Mason heard a peculiar sound at the other end of the line, then a suppressed exclamation.

The lawyer hesitated a moment, then went on talking casually. "I think the murder case is as good as solved. I find that Ralph Endicott presented a check for certification shortly after ten o'clock. The check was dated today and was signed by Rose Keeling. That should put him in the position of being the last one to see Rose

Keeling alive. My advice to you is to co-operate in every way you can with the police, and tell them everything, because I think the murder will be cleared up in a few hours."

There was silence at the other end of the line.

"Are you there?" Mason asked.

Lieutenant Tragg's voice, coming over the wire, said, "Well, thank you very much, Counselor, for your advice. I thought perhaps I'd better see what was going on when Miss Marlow had such an attack of monosyllables. I just thought it might be you asking questions."

"What the devil are *you* doing there?" Mason asked.

"Following my profession," Tragg said.

"Well," Mason told him, "that's what I'm doing."

"So it would seem."

"You sound disappointed," Mason said.

"Not disappointed. Only startled. It's such a strange sensation to listen in on a conversation you're having with a client and hear you suggest that the client should co-operate with the police."

"Oh, I always do that," Mason said breezily. "It's not often that you hear me, that's all. Have you been in touch with Headquarters lately?"

"Why?"

"I rang up and left a tip for you."

"The hell you did!"

"That's right. About this check."

"Is that on the square?"

"Sure it is. Hang up and Headquarters will be calling you."

Tragg said, "And just in case this is a grandstand, Mason, and you intend to call Headquarters as soon as I've hung up, I'll dial Headquarters right from here and get them on the line and find out if the information is already in there."

"It will be," Mason said. "But what are you doing with Miss Marlow?"

"Questioning her."

"Well, she'll give you the answers," Mason said.

"Yes," Tragg commented dryly, "I had just about come to the conclusion that she knew *all* the answers. Remember now, don't try to call Headquarters, because I'm going to beat you to it."

And Tragg hung up.

Mason dialed his office. Gertie answered the phone.

"What are you doing?" he asked. "Running a night shift?"

"Miss Street said things might be moving rather fast tonight, so we thought we'd wait around. She brought in some hot dogs and coffee and we're just sitting here talking."

"Della's there?"

"Right here."

"Put her on."

Della Street came on the phone, said, "Yes, Chief."

"Thank heavens you're there!" Mason told her. "We've got to work fast. Get out your form book. Make an application for a writ of *habeas corpus* for Marilyn Marlow, state that she is being detained by the police without any charge whatever having been placed against her, that her detention is, therefore, unlawful and illegal. Then make out a writ of *habeas corpus* for a judge to sign and be sure that the writ provides that she can be admitted to bail, pending the hearing on the writ. Have you got that?"

"Okay, Chief. Gertie and I will hammer it out right away."

"That's fine," Mason said. "We haven't a second to waste."

"The police have taken Marilyn Marlow?"

"They are going to," Mason said.

"And then what?"

"Then," he said, "we run up against a very ticklish, very delicate and personal problem. Ralph Endicott has a carbon copy of a letter which he claims Rose Keeling sent Marilyn Marlow yesterday."

"Oh, oh!" Della exclaimed in dismay.

"Exactly," Mason told her, and hung up.

CHAPTER 13

Marilyn Marlow sat under the glare of a pitiless light which threw every fleeting expression on her face into sharp visibility.

The detectives and officers who sat in a circle around her were vague, indistinct, shadowy objects back of the glare of this light.

"Can't you get that light out of my eyes?" she asked.

"What's the matter?" Sergeant Holcomb's sneering voice asked. "Are you afraid to let us see into your eyes?"

"I'm not *afraid* to let you see into my very mind," she said indignantly, "but that thing gives me a headache. It's wearing me out. The glare is like driving at night when you're tired and meeting an endless string of headlights."

"Come, come," Sergeant Holcomb said, "let's not talk about the light. Let's talk about the case. The quicker you tell us about that, the quicker the light will go off."

"Those diamonds you've got on," another voice said, "where did they come from?"

"I've told you where they came from. My mother was a nurse. She nursed George P. Endicott for months before he died. He knew he was going, along toward the last, and he gave her the family jewelry. He said there was no one to take over after he was gone."

"Except two brothers and a sister."

"He cared nothing about them. They never came to see him while he was in the sanitarium. It was only after he died that they became affectionate. Then they moved into his house and took charge of everything they could get their hands on."

"Rather vindictive, aren't you?" Sergeant Holcomb said.

"I'm simply trying to tell you the truth."

"Okay," a voice from the shadows said, "what about the diamonds?"

"These were some of the jewels. He gave them to my mother and I inherited them from my mother when she . . . when she passed away."

A voice that was rasping and taunting, a voice which seemed only to make sneering, sarcastic, nasty remarks, came from far back in the shadows, hurtling another accusation at Marilyn Marlow. "Your mother was a nurse. She was nursing Endicott. She had a lot of dough when he kicked the bucket. How do you know she didn't help ease him out of the picture?"

Marilyn Marlow started to get up out of the chair. "Are you accusing my mother of murder?" she blazed. "Why, you . . ."

A big hand clapped down on her shoulder and pushed her down. "Sit down, sister. Just answer questions. Never mind pouring on the abuse. Now, when did you see Rose Keeling last?"

"I . . . I can't remember just when it was."

"Saw her today, didn't you?"

"I . . . I can't remember just when . . . I saw her. . . ."

"Oh, quit stalling. Bring that other dame in, Joe."

A door opened. A woman came in who stood as a vague, indistinct object back in the very dim shadows beyond the brilliant light.

"Take a look at her," a voice said. "Ever seen her before?"

Marilyn Marlow said, "I can't see who it is."

The sneering voice said, "*You* ain't the one we're talking to. We're talking to the witness. Ever seen this dame in the chair before? The one under the light?"

"Why, yes," a woman's well-modulated voice said.

"Okay, okay. Where did you see her?"

"She's the woman I was telling you about, the one I described to you, the one I saw coming out of Rose Keeling's flat, the one . . ."

"Hold it, hold it!" the voice cautioned. "Never mind spilling everything in front of the suspect here. But this is the jane you saw, the one you were telling us about previously?"

"Why, yes. That's right."

"Okay. That's all. Take her out, Joe."

The feminine figure was whisked out of the door.

"Okay, baby," the voice said, "come on, let's come clean. Let's have it and get it over with."

Marilyn Marlow, confused, said, "I *tried* to see Rose Keeling."

"Sure you did. You went to her flat today. Okay, now, tell us what happened. And if you try to lie, that'll put your pretty neck right in the middle of a hemp loop."

"I . . . I just went there."

"Don't kid us like that. You went inside. This witness saw you coming down the stairs and leaving the place. She's described the whole business. She just had an idea something might be wrong, and she was keeping an eye on everybody that came and went. We've got the whole timetable. Now, *you* try holding out on us and *you'll* be inside looking out. You come clean and explain things satisfactorily and *we'll* give *you* a break. We have to know that you're on the up-and-up. Now, why didn't you tell us you went to Rose Keeling's flat?"

"I . . . well, I really didn't see her."

"What do you mean, you didn't see her?"

"She . . ."

"Yes, go on."

Sergeant Holcomb said irritably, "I tell you, we're not going to get anywhere with the dame! She's giving us the runaround. We've got everything we need on her, everything that happened. We know everybody who came and went, and the time they came and went, thanks to this witness."

Marilyn Marlow said desperately, "I tell you, she was dead when I got there!"

The room suddenly became tense with a sudden silence. No one moved. No one spoke. It was for the moment as though no one breathed.

Marilyn Marlow plunged on desperately. "I went there to see her. I went up, and—well, she was dead."

"How did you get in the door?"

"I had a key, but I didn't have to use it. The door was open when I got back."

"Who gave the key to you?"

"Rose. She wanted me to come up and go play tennis with her. She gave me a key so I could walk right in and go up the stairs."

"What did you do with the key?"

"I left it on the table."

"Then what happened to it?"

"I don't know. I guess . . . someone could have taken it—*anyone*."

"Sure, sure!"

"I tell you, *anyone* could!"

"Okay. Let's forget the key for the moment. What happened after you got in?"

"She was dead."

"Why didn't you tell us this before?"

"I . . . I didn't want to get mixed up in it."

"Well, you're mixed up in it now. You'd better come clean. What happened?"

"She was lying there on the floor just as . . . just as you found her."

"Come on, come on," the sneering voice said. "Don't forget that we've got a tab on everyone that came and went. We want to know the truth with no more runaround. You'd better explain while the explaining is good!"

She said desperately, "Well, Mr. Mason came there at my suggestion."

Once more there was one of those sudden tense silences.

"Go on," the sneering voice said.

That silence had been too abrupt, too exultant. It suddenly occurred to Marilyn Marlow that she had given them information they had not had before, that in some way this thing was a plant. She said, "I don't think I care to tell you anything else."

"Now, ain't *that* something!" the sneering voice said. "She traps herself. She admits she's in the room with the murdered person. She admits she was there when the crime was committed and now she goes hotsy-totsy and says she doesn't care to discuss it with us. Wouldn't that jar you?"

"I *wasn't* there when the crime was committed!"

"Oh, yes, you were, sister. Don't try to lie out of it now. It's too late."

"I tell you I wasn't!"

"Yeah, you claim you came in there afterwards. What did you do with the knife?"

"I tell you I didn't have any knife. I didn't have anything to do with it. I . . ."

"So you go call up Perry Mason," Sergeant Holcomb interrupted. "And what did Mason do?"

"I tell you I'm not going to talk about things any more. If you want to get any statements out of me, I insist that I see my lawyer before I say anything."

"No use locking the stable door after the horse's been stolen," Holcomb said. "You've admitted you were there. You've admitted you called Perry Mason and got him to come. Now then, what did you two hatch up? How did it happen that Mason slipped you out of there?"

"I'm not saying anything."

"You said you called Mason up. How does it happen your fingerprints weren't on the telephone receiver?"

She clamped her lips shut in a tight line.

Questions were coming at her now, thick and fast. Her eyes were weary from the pitiless glare of the brilliant light. Her ears ached with the words that were being bounced off her eardrums. Her nervous system was raw and quivering from the beating it had taken, and these incessant sneering questions pounding in on her consciousness made her cringe as though from a series of actual blows.

"How about that letter you got from Rose Keeling? What'd you do with it? Why did you destroy it? Who told you to destroy it?"

She tried to assume an external appearance of calm disdain.

"Come on," Sergeant Holcomb said, "let's hear the rest of it. You knew that if she changed her testimony you were licked on the whole will case. Your only hope was to murder her so that she couldn't change her testimony."

"Yes," the sneering voice said. "Then you could use the testimony she'd given at the probate of the will and get by on that."

Marilyn Marlow sat silent.

"Notice that she isn't denying it," the voice taunted.

"We've accused her of murder, and she hasn't denied it. Remember that!"

"I do deny it!" she stormed.

"Oh, you do? We thought you'd quit talking."

"I'm denying that I murdered her."

"But you do admit you were in the apartment after she was dead, and you didn't notify the police."

"I . . ."

She realized suddenly she was being trapped into further conversation, and clamped her lips shut.

"Come on," Sergeant Holcomb said, "let's have the rest of it."

She sat silent, quivering inwardly, but trying to preserve a calm exterior.

"Okay," Sergeant Holcomb said, "let's let the newspaper reporters take a crack at her."

Someone opened the door. Men came pouring into the room. Someone said, "Look up a little, Marilyn."

A flashlight blazed into brilliance, but her eyes were so accustomed to the glare of the big light that she hardly noticed the flash bulb.

Other flashlights shot off in succession. Photographers moved about, pointing cameras. Then a newspaper man said, "Okay, Miss Marlow. How about a little statement. It isn't going to hurt you any, you know; give you an opportunity to get your side of the case presented to the readers."

"No comment," she said.

"Come, come, Marilyn, don't be like that. That's being dumb. That's not going to do you any good. A lot depends on public sentiment and public sentiment goes a lot according to first impressions. Get your story before the readers right at the start of the case. Look at all these gals who kill 'em and get off. Every one of them took the newspaper readers into their confidence right at the start."

"No comment," she said desperately.

They hounded her for some five minutes more, trying every expedient to get her to talk.

Then they took more photographs and left.

The police started on her once more, and Marilyn Marlow, by this time so thoroughly weary that her very soul felt numb, could hear her own voice mouthing words which sounded as if the words were emanating from her mouth through the medium of some ventriloquist saying from time to time, "No comment. . . . No comment. . . . I will not discuss the matter until my attorney is here. . . . I demand that you call my attorney."

They were at her like a pack of yapping dogs, worrying the heels of some high-strung, nervous horse. She felt that she wanted to run, if only some avenue of escape would open up. . . .

A door opened. She sensed a tall figure standing in the doorway. A man's quiet voice said, "What's going on here?"

Sergeant Holcomb said, "We're getting a statement from Miss Marlow."

"How are you getting it?"

"We just asked her questions. We . . ."

"Shut off that light!" Lieutenant Tragg ordered. "Shut it off instantly!"

A light switch clicked and suddenly her tired, aching eyes were able to relax as the bright light ceased to beat into her brain through her weary eyes.

"I sent Miss Marlow up here for questioning," Lieutenant Tragg said angrily. "I didn't mean that she was to be browbeaten. She's just a witness."

"Witness, hell!" Sergeant Holcomb said. "I don't want to seem disrespectful, Lieutenant, but she's admitted to being in the house just about the time the crime was committed. She claims that Rose Keeling was dead at the time, but there's no evidence to back her up. And then she called Perry Mason. She got Mason to go up there, and Mason evidently fixed things up so she could take a powder. She admits that she used the telephone in there to call Mason. Remember, her fingerprints weren't on the receiver, just Mason's prints, not another print there. The thing had been wiped and polished clean as a whistle."

"Nevertheless," Tragg said angrily, "I do not care to have Miss Marlow submitted to the indignity of an inquisition. You men get back to your posts. I've left assignments for you. Get out and get busy. Try and get some evidence by using your head and your feet instead of mouths."

With the glaring overhead light out, Marilyn Marlow could see Lieutenant Tragg clearly now, a tall, somewhat slender, well-knit individual whose clean-cut features were a welcome relief from the heavy faces of the officers who had been leering at her.

There was a general scraping of chairs, a shuffling of feet. Men sullenly left the room, until finally only Lieutenant Tragg was there with her.

"I'm sorry about this, Miss Marlow. Was it really quite terrible?"

"It was ghastly," she said with a note of hysteria creeping into her voice. "That light got to beating down on me until—I just couldn't get away from it anywhere. I . . ."

"I know," Tragg said sympathetically.

"It gave me a beastly headache and . . . I hardly knew what I was saying."

"I understand. Won't you come into my office?"

He escorted her through a door into an inner office, gave her a comfortable chair, carefully turned the desk light so that the blessed shadow enveloped her, left the light shining on the desk blotter and on Tragg's features.

Tragg took a cigar from his pocket, then paused with the match halfway to the cigar. "Do you mind?"

"Not at all."

He lit the cigar, settled back in the chair, said casually, in a well-modulated voice, "The life of an officer is not a happy one."

"No, I suppose it isn't."

"I have been going all day," Tragg said, "hitting a pretty hard pace. This whole case is, of course, a tragedy to you. To me it's just another case, one that has to be investigated and cleaned up."

He took the cigar from his mouth, stretched, yawned, regarded the tip of the cigar for a moment, then puffed out more blue smoke. "I guess Rose Keeling was a rather peculiar girl," he said.

"I think she was."

"Any idea how she happened to write you that letter?"

"What letter?"

Tragg said, "The one that she sent you. I believe yesterday. The Endicotts have a carbon copy of it."

"No, I don't know what caused her to write it."

"Think there was any truth in it?"

"Definitely not. I don't think there was anything irregular about the execution of that will. I talked with her before Mother died and I've heard her tell what happened several times, and I just can't account for that letter."

"By the way," Tragg said quite casually, "the carbon copy of that letter isn't the best evidence. Of course, we can use it if we have to, because it's a *bona fide* carbon copy and there's no question but it's in the handwriting of Rose Keeling. But I'd like to have the original. Do you happen to have it with you?"

He extended his hand as casually as though he had asked her for a match.

"Why, I . . . no, not with me."

"Oh, it's at your apartment?"

"I . . . I don't know where it is."

Tragg raised his eyebrows. "You received it yesterday—or was it this morning?"

"This morning."

"Oh, yes, I see. That is the reason you went to see Rose Keeling."

"No, Lieutenant. Frankly, it isn't."

"No?"

Lieutenant Tragg raised his eyebrows with just the right expression of polite incredulity.

There was an apologetic knock at the door. Tragg frowned, said, "I don't want to be disturbed."

The door opened a crack.

"Skip it," Tragg said over his shoulder. "I'm busy. I don't want to be disturbed."

A man's voice said, "I'm sorry, Lieutenant. I'm a deputy sheriff and these papers have to be served right now."

"I don't want to have any . . . oh, all right, I'll take them."

The deputy sheriff walked into the room, holding papers in his hand. He said, "I'm sorry, Lieutenant. You understand it's all in the nature of a duty. We have to do it and this lawyer is burning my tail."

"What are you talking about?"

"Writ of *habeas corpus* for Marilyn Marlow," the deputy sheriff said, "ordering that she be brought into court day after tomorrow at two o'clock and in the meantime that unless there is some charge filed against her, she be released on bail in the sum of twenty-five hundred dollars. Perry Mason is downstairs depositing twenty-five hundred dollars in cash with the bail clerk. He'll be up here with a receipt in a matter of seconds."

"Thanks for telling me," Tragg said. "Get out."

The deputy sheriff left the room, pulled the door shut behind him.

"This isn't going to get you anywhere," Tragg said irritably. "These are the tactics lawyers use when they have guilty clients."

Marilyn Marlow said nothing.

"Now then," Tragg said, "suppose you tell me a little more about why you really went to see Rose Keeling, and . . ."

Knuckles sounded on the door and then the door opened and Perry Mason said, "I'm sorry, Tragg. That's all."

"You get the hell out of here," Tragg said. "This is my private office. I . . ."

"Stay here till you rot!" Mason said. "Come on, Miss Marlow, *you're* leaving."

"The hell she is," Tragg said.

"The hell she isn't," Mason told him. "She's released on bail on *habeas corpus*. Here's the bail receipt and you have a writ of *habeas corpus* served on you, stating that she is to be released on bail."

"Unless she's charged with something," Tragg said.

"Go ahead and charge her," Mason said. "Put any charge against her and I'll have bail."

"Suppose I charge her with murder?"

"Then I won't have bail," Mason said, "because I can't get it."

"All right, you crowd my hand and I'll charge her with murder."

"Phooey!" Mason said. "If you charge her with murder, then you've laid an egg that you can't hatch."

Tragg said, "You push me and I will."

"Go ahead. I'm pushing you. I'm representing Miss Marlow. She's been released on *habeas corpus*. She's going with me. There's an officer here to see that the court order is carried out. The order specifically states that she is to be released from custody, pending a hearing on the *habeas corpus*, upon giving bail in the sum of twenty-five hundred dollars. That bail has been put up in cash and I have here a receipt from the bail clerk. Come on, Miss Marlow."

Marilyn arose from the chair. She thought for a moment that her knees would buckle and she would pitch forward on her face. But she took a deep breath and started walking, expecting every moment to hear a blast from Lieutenant Tragg.

Tragg, however, sat there, stiff in hostile silence, while. Mason held out his hand to take her arm. The deputy sheriff took the other arm.

"You're going to regret this, Mason!" Tragg said.

"I don't think so."

"Incidentally, I have some questions to ask *you*."

"Come to my office any time," Mason said.

"I might have you come here."

"Not without a warrant, Tragg."

"I might get a warrant."

"That's your privilege."

The door closed. The deputy sheriff said, "Well, I guess that's all, Mr. Mason."

"Just see us out of the building, if you will," Mason said.

He helped Marilyn Marlow down the stairs.

"You're trembling," he said.

"I'm a wreck," she admitted. "I just want to get somewhere where I can cry. I think I'm going to have hysterics."

"Was it bad?" Mason asked.

"It was terrible."

Mason shook hands with the deputy sheriff. "Thanks a lot."

"Okay, Mr. Mason. I was just doing my duty. You had the papers. I was ordered to serve them, and I served them."

"Thanks again," Mason said.

She heard the rustle of paper, caught a glimpse of green currency, then Mason was helping her into his automobile and the car was purring away through the city streets.

"What happened?" Mason asked.

"It was terrible, terrible, terrible, terrible. . . ."

She felt her voice rising higher and higher. The word "terrible" was wedged in her mind. Her tongue kept repeating it without any conscious volition on her part.

Mason suddenly slammed the car to a stop. "Forget it!" he said. "Seconds are precious. They may charge you with murder at that. Go ahead and tell me what happened. Start crying after you've told me what happened. And save the hysterics until we're out in the clear."

There was something in the granite-hard eyes of the lawyer that brought back a measure of her self-control.

She said, "Lieutenant Tragg asked me to come to his office. He asked me to show him some of the jewelry that my mother had been given by George Endicott. Then Lieutenant Tragg suggested very tactfully that I'd better wear as much of it as possible, because if I left the place alone, it just might be that some sneak thief might get in and . . ."

"Did they photograph you?" Mason asked.

"The police? No."

"Anyone take pictures?"

"Yes. The newspaper men came in."

Mason swore under his breath.

"What's the matter?"

Mason said angrily, "It's the way the police play ball with the newspapers."

"What do you mean?"

"A nice bit of publicity for the police," Mason said. "They got you all dolled up in the jewelry that your mother had received from Endicott. Then the newspapermen are permitted to photograph you. They'll have pictures all over the morning papers with the caption, 'HEIRESS BEING QUIZZED AT OFFICE OF LIEUTENANT TRAGG OF HOMICIDE SQUAD, WEARS FORTUNE IN JEW-ELRY MOTHER RECEIVED FROM DEAD BENEFACTOR.'"

"Oh!" Marilyn said, and the word was an exclamation of dismay.

"Go ahead," Mason said. "What happened after that?"

"Lieutenant Tragg, it seems, was delayed, and I was sent up to meet Sergeant Holcomb and three or four other officers."

Mason said, "And then, I suppose Sergeant Holcomb started questioning you."

"Yes."

"And," Mason went on, "they put you in a chair with a bright light beating on your face. They formed a circle around you and a lot of other people came in, and they started yelling at you and throwing questions at you before you had a chance to answer, making all kinds of nasty insinuations and accusations and . . ."

"Yes," she said.

"And then Lieutenant Tragg suddenly showed up and was very fatherly and gentlemanly and apologetic and took you into his office, and the relief was so great that you felt he was the most wonderful gentleman."

"Why, yes! How did you know what happened?"

Mason said, "It's police routine, just part of the psychological third-degree. One man pounds a witness until she's almost crazy, gets everything he can out of her, and then when she gets to the point where she won't talk, a signal is flashed and another man comes in and takes the part of a perfect gentleman and . . ."

"You mean that was all an act?"

"All an act."

"Why, I don't believe that Lieutenant Tragg is that sort."

"Lieutenant Tragg," Mason said, "has a job to do. He's given instructions as to the methods he has to employ. He doesn't have a thing to say about what he does and what he doesn't do. He's a cog in a machine. The police have to get results. They have to make people talk. They use all sorts of methods. Some of them are damned ingenious. Don't make the mistake of thinking the police are dumb."

"Well, those first people certainly were dumb. They . . ."

"I'll bet they got a lot out of you, at that."

"They didn't until that witness identified me."

"What witness?"

"The woman who saw us all going in and going out of Rose Keeling's flat."

Mason said wearily, "Nine chances out of ten that was another police frameup. The witness was just a stooge. You didn't see her clearly?"

"No."

"Did she definitely state what time you came in? And what time you went out?"

Marilyn Marlow thought for a moment, then said, "No, she didn't. She just said that I was the woman she had seen leaving at the time she had previously told the police."

Mason sighed. "That's an old gag. She hasn't seen anyone. She was probably a stenographer in one of the police departments, working nights, or else she was a deputy clerk from the bail-bond office. She didn't even know where Rose lived. She'd never seen you before in her life."

Marilyn Marlow sucked in her breath.

"And what did you tell them?" Mason asked.

She said, "I guess—I guess that did it! I thought she had seen us all going in and coming out, and I—I was trying to save you and I told them that *I* had been the one who had telephoned you to come and . . ."

"And admitted you were there and left the place?"

"Yes."

"That clinches things," Mason said. "They'll charge you with murder."

"And when that happens, what will it do to you?"

Mason said grimly, "Plenty!"

CHAPTER 14

Della Street was waiting up when Mason unlocked the door to the private office.

She jumped up out of the chair and ran to him.

"Della, what are *you* doing here?" Mason said. "It's midnight."

"I know, but I couldn't have slept if I'd gone home. What happened?"

"They made her talk."

"How bad was it?"

Mason hung his hat on a hook in the coat closet and said, "It's a mess."

"Was the *habeas corpus* in time to do any good?"

"Just in time to salvage some of it. But a lot of it had gone by the board."

"How much?"

Mason said, "They worked the old gag on her. First, Sergeant Holcomb batted her around and then Tragg came in and was the perfect gentlemen. He's good at that. People feel his heart's in the right place and sob out their souls to him."

"What did she tell him?"

"Told him about the letter, about telephoning me, and, by implication, told them that I had either wiped fingerprints off the receiver of the telephone or had given her a chance to do so. That's the part that's going to hurt. Tragg will really go to town on that."

"But she didn't tell them specifically that she had wiped the prints off the receiver or that you had intimated she should?"

Mason shook his head. "Not specifically. It's a plain inference from what she did tell them."

"Where is she now?"

Mason grinned, and said, "Right now she's out on *habeas corpus*. She's not a fugitive from justice and she's where the police are going to have one hell of a time finding her. Darned if I know why I do it, Della! But I always do."

"Do what?"

"Stick my neck out for my clients. I should have taken the case just the way any other lawyer would have; taken the facts as they were and let the chips fall wherever they might. But no, I'm not built that way. I'm always a pushover for a client who is having the breaks go against her."

"After all," Della Street said, "we're not too certain that Marilyn Marlow is as innocent as she sounds."

"I can't picture her as being guilty," Mason said.

"Not of murder, perhaps, but I do think she's holding out on us somewhere along the line. I'm not satisfied with any explanation that has been made so far of why that ad was put in the lonely-hearts magazine. I still don't think we know what she wanted with Kenneth Barstow."

Mason sat down at the desk, lit a cigarette, sighed wearily, then said to Della Street, "I told Paul Drake to be waiting for me. I gave him a few chores to do. Get hold of him on the telephone, will you, Della? We'll get him in and then let him go to bed."

"Are *you* going to get some sleep?"

"Darned if I know. I'm in what is sometimes referred to as 'an unenviable position.' I should have known Marilyn Marlow would have cracked the minute they started putting the pressure on her. She isn't built right to withstand a lot of rough stuff."

Della Street said, "We have her word for what happened prior to the time we arrived there at Rose Keeling's flat—her word and that's all!"

Mason nodded and said, "Get Drake on the line."

Della Street put through the call, and a moment later had the detective on the line.

"This is Della, Paul. The Chief's here now. Want to come down. . . ? Okay, I'll have the door open for you."

Della Street hung up the telephone, crossed over and opened the door. A moment later they heard the sound of Drake's steps in the corridor and then the tall detective droop-shouldered his way through the door and flopped in limp fatigue into the big easy chair.

Della Street closed the door.

Drake spun around so that he adopted his favorite position of sitting crossways in the chair.

"What do you know, Paul?"

"A lot of stuff," Drake said. "I've checked Ralph Endicott's alibi. You wanted me to. Police were checking it right along at the same time, so it was a cinch. It's absolutely okay, completely watertight."

"No question?"

"None whatever. Aside from ten or fifteen minutes between the time he left the dentist's office and the time he got to the bank, every second of his time's accounted for. And he didn't leave the chess games until three hours after the murder had been committed."

Perry Mason started pacing the floor of the office, his coat unbuttoned, his thumbs pushed in the armholes of his vest, his head thrust forward in thought.

Abruptly he said, "I telephoned you about this other witness, Ethel Furlong. Did you get in touch with her?"

Drake nodded.

"What about her?"

The detective thumbed through the pages of a notebook, said, "The police had her, giving her a shakedown. They let her go. My man interviewed her. The police were interested in finding out about the will and about what had happened. She tells a straightforward story. No one had ever offered her any money, either one way or the other. She was a witness to the will. Eleanore Marlow, Marilyn's mother, called two nurses from the floor, Ethel Furlong and Rose Keeling. She told them that Mr. Endicott wanted to execute a will and wanted them to be witnesses. She says that Rose Keeling was called out on an emergency call at about the time the will was being read to Mr. Endicott, but that she returned before the will was signed and that when Endicott signed it, both of the nurses as well as Eleanore Marlow were in the room with him; and that he had to sign with his left hand, but that he seemed to be perfectly aware of what was going on; and he specifically stated to them that this was his will and he had signed it and that he wanted them to sign as witnesses."

"Ethel Furlong is positive about that?"

"Positive."

"Had Rose Keeling approached her with any proposition?"

"Nothing."

Mason resumed pacing the floor.

"Of course," he said after a few moments, "Marilyn Marlow called a turn when she said that *she* had to hold two witnesses in line in order to get anywhere. But the other side only needed to have *one* of the witnesses lined up to win their case.

"When you come right down to it, it makes you a little hot under the collar to think of these brothers and sisters, who never gave a damn for George Endicott in his lifetime, sitting out there in his house and plotting and planning to beat Marilyn Marlow out of her inheritance. Apparently someone had made a payoff to Rose Keeling, and I don't think it was Marilyn Marlow. But Endicott says it was and the police are going to be pretty apt to take his word for it."

Drake said, "It could be, of course, that *both* Ethel Furlong and Rose Keeling received a thousand bucks to make their testimony come out right, and Ethel Furlong is staying put. Rose Keeling was having an attack of jitters."

Mason said, "It's possible, but I don't warm up to the idea. What about Caddo, Paul? What did you find out about him?"

"He and his wife had a battle and she threw an inkwell, I guess. He sent a suit out to the cleaners that was all spotted with ink. You knew, didn't you, that the police found a playsuit with the blouse ripped open and ink spattered over it?"

"No. Where?"

"In the soiled clothes hamper of Rose Keeling's flat."

Mason was excited now. "Was it Rose Keeling's sunsuit?"

"Apparently it was."

"Any police theories on that?"

"None. They think she had been filling a fountain pen, and . . ."

Mason gestured Paul Drake to silence, resumed pacing the floor, then abruptly he turned to face the detective.

"Rose Keeling must have been murdered when she was leaving the bathroom."

"Yes. Apparently she was hit over the head with some blunt instrument, probably a blackjack," Drake said. "She wasn't stabbed until after she'd hit the floor."

Mason stopped his pacing abruptly. "How's that?"

"Someone sapped her before she was stabbed."

"That's interesting!"

"Why would they do that, Chief?" Della Street asked.

Mason said, "Probably someone hiding behind the door, waiting for her to come out of the bathroom. The minute she did, this person hit her on the head. He did that because he had to be certain she wouldn't make any noise and he wasn't certain he could make a clean-cut stab that would kill her instantly. What about the time of death, Paul?"

"Right around twelve o'clock."

Mason said, "The way I figure it, Della Street telephoned at just about the time the murder was being committed. The murderer was lying in wait for Rose Keeling to come out of the bathroom. The phone started ringing. That didn't suit the murderer at all. He was afraid Rose might wrap a towel around her and rush out to answer the telephone. He knew that if that happened, she'd be on the run and he wouldn't stand any chance to sneak up behind her and club her."

"So you think the murderer was the one who picked up the receiver to make the telephone quit ringing?" Drake asked.

"I can't figure any other explanation right at the present time. Do you know whether the police noticed any cigar ashes on the floor of Rose Keeling's bedroom, Paul?"

Drake shook his head. "If they noticed them, they're keeping quiet about it. They haven't told the newspaper men—I don't think they found any."

"Have your men looked around, Paul?"

"Naturally we couldn't get into the flat. There's a vacant lot on the south. The police looked around it a bit, thinking perhaps the murderer had tossed the knife out of a window in Rose Keeling's flat after the crime had been committed. They didn't find anything. My men looked around in the lot after the police left. I was with them. We searched every inch of it."

"No dice?" Mason asked.

"No dice."

Mason paced the floor for a few moments, then asked, "You didn't happen to notice any half-smoked cigar out there in the vacant lot while you were searching for the knife, did you?"

Drake shook his head, then said, "Wait a minute. I remember Kenneth Barstow poking a half-smoked stogie with his foot. Barstow is quite a cigar smoker and claims to be a connoisseur of good cigars. He poked a half-smoked cigar with his foot and said, 'That just goes to show, even the cops can't finish the nickel cigars they sell nowadays.'"

Mason's eyes narrowed. "It was half smoked, Paul?"

"Just about half smoked."

"A stogie?"

"A regular rope," Drake said. "One of those black stogies the cops chew on. It takes a man with a strong stomach to smoke more than half of one."

"And Barstow likes *good* cigars?"

"That's right, the best," Drake said.

Mason again started pacing the floor.

"Of course," Drake pointed out, "insofar as that inheritance is concerned, there'll be a lot of public sympathy on behalf of the brothers and sister."

"Why?" Mason asked, snapping the question over his shoulder. "After all, they're—well, the *rightful* heirs."

"What do you mean by that, Paul?"

"They're the blood relatives."

"And they didn't give a damn about George Endicott until after he died. There's altogether too much sloppy thinking about the *'natural'* relatives being entitled to inherit. The only real protection an elderly man or a sick man has in this world is the power to dispose of his property the way he wants to. That enables him to reward special service and special attention if he gets it, and it enables him to hold his relatives in line. If a man couldn't make a will leaving his property to whomever he wanted, relatives would simply crowd him into the grave as fast as they could—that is, lots of them would."

Drake said, "Of course, if your theory is correct, Perry—about the murderer being the one who lifted the receiver off the telephone—well, in that case the fingerprints on the receiver would have been the most important bit of evidence in the whole case."

Mason said nothing.

"Just how *did* Marilyn Marlow get into the apartment?" Drake asked.

"She says Rose Keeling gave her a key."

"How come?"

Mason said, "Marilyn went to see Rose. Rose wanted to play tennis. Marilyn went back to her apartment to get her things. Rose gave Marilyn a key so Marilyn could get in when she came back. Marilyn went home, came back and found Rose murdered. However, Marilyn says that she didn't get in with the key. She says the door to the street at the foot of the stairs was actually open an inch or two when she returned, so she just pushed it open and walked in."

"That's Marilyn's story?"

"That's her story."

"When did she leave Rose?"

"Right around eleven-thirty-five. Perhaps a few minutes earlier."

"When did she get back?"

"She wasn't in any particular hurry. She had some things to do. She bought some groceries and stopped by her bank. She got back about twelve-five."

"And in that time the murder had been committed?"

"That's right. Marilyn phoned me right around twelve-fifteen."

"You figure right around eleven-forty was the time of the murder?"

Mason nodded.

"When did Marilyn get to the bank?"

"Not in time to give her an alibi. No one remembers seeing her in the grocery store."

"And Rose gave Marilyn a key?"

"Right."

Drake said, "You aren't going to like this, Perry, but after we gave Marilyn Marlow a green light to go ahead with Kenneth Barstow she told him she'd fix up a tennis game with Rose Keeling and she wanted him to get her a key to Rose's flat, either by hook or crook. She said Rose had sold out and Marilyn said if she could get in and search the place at a time when she knew Rose would be playing tennis or something that would keep her occupied so Marilyn could have the time to search the way only a woman could. . . . She quit there. She didn't tell Kenneth exactly what she expected to find."

Mason said, "Keep Kenneth out of circulation for a while, Paul."

"He'll be discreet, Perry."

"Unless they ask him too much. Caddo knows about him."

"That's right."

"Of course you can't blame Marilyn."

"You mean *you* can't," Drake said, grinning.

"Well, what the hell, Paul, Rose Keeling *had* sold her out. She simply *had* to get evidence one way or another."

There was silence for a few moments. Then Mason said, "That ink-stained, torn playsuit is a clue."

"What about it?"

"I have a theory on it."

"Mrs. Caddo?"

"Could be."

"Want us to do anything there, Perry?"

"No, not yet, anyway. I'm going to have a talk with Dolores Caddo, just for the fun of the thing."

"If you can get any fun out of that," Drake said, "go to it."

"You have Caddo's home address, Della?" Mason asked abruptly. She nodded.

"You've made a *complete* check on Ralph Endicott?" Mason asked.

"His story checks absolutely," Drake said.

Mason said, "I hate to dismiss him from the list of suspects, but I guess we'll have to. My own hunch is that the murder was committed right on the dot of eleven-forty. That's the time we telephoned and someone lifted the receiver off the hook."

Drake said, "Well, so far they can't *prove* that anyone has wiped fingerprints off the telephone receiver, Perry."

"That's so far," Mason said grimly. "Only my prints were on that receiver. That makes it look as if I'd tried to save my client by wiping her prints off the receiver and when I did that, I wiped the murderer's prints off."

"Some people would think it looked that way," Drake said tonelessly.

"I didn't do it, Paul."

Drake raised his eyebrows.

"Marilyn did it," Della said.

Drake's face showed relief. "That'll let *you* out, then, Perry. Gosh, I was worried. The minute Tragg can show the murderer must have picked up the receiver at eleven-forty, that Marilyn telephoned you around twelve-ten and that you phoned the police, but that *only* your prints were on the receiver—well, that gives him quite a case against you, Perry. It's pretty strong circumstantial evidence that you sent Marilyn home and tried to save her by wiping her prints off the telephone receiver. But if you and Della can both swear Marilyn did that, it'll put you off the spot."

"We can't swear that, Paul."

"I thought you said you could."

"We can't. It wouldn't be fair to our client."

"If you don't, it won't be fair to you."

"If we do, it'll just about clinch the case against her. We have to protect our client."

"Not to the extent of taking blame yourself, Perry! Surely you don't have to go *that* far."

"Hell," Mason said, "I go all the way for a client, Paul, and now I'm going to try to start a family fight in the Caddo family. This *should* be good."

CHAPTER 15

Some five minutes after Mason had rung the doorbell for the first time, Robert Caddo came shuffling down the corridor and opened the door.

A heavy woolen bathrobe was thrown around his shoulders. Beneath the robe, his legs showed in striped pajamas. His feet were encased in soft leather slippers. His hair, left long and trained to cover as much of the baldness of his head as possible, now hung down over one ear and gave him a ludicrous, lopsided appearance. There were sleep puffs under his eyes and a slightly dazed expression on his face.

"Hello," Mason said. "I want to come in."

Caddo said, "You . . . why, what's happened?"

"Plenty," Mason said, and pushed his way past Caddo.

The house was cold, with the chill of midnight. The windows had been opened for ventilation.

Caddo switched on lights, went around lowering windows and pulling shades. Mason found the button which controlled the gas furnace and turned it on.

"It's cold in here," Caddo said. "I'm shivering."

"Perhaps you need a drink," Mason told him.

Mrs. Caddo's voice, from an upstairs bedroom, called, "Who is it, Bob?"

"Mr. Mason, the lawyer," Caddo said. "You were at his office earlier today."

Bare feet thudded on the upstairs floor. Then, after a moment, there was the sound of light, quick steps in house slippers, and Dolores Caddo, a robe wrapped rather tightly around her, glided into the room.

"Hello," she said to Mason, and smiled, then embellished the smile with a quick wink. "I'm sorry for what I did today."

Mason said, "Just what *did* you do today?"

"You know what I mean, calling at your office and making a scene." And again she winked at him, then added hastily, "Bob says he saw you right afterwards and that he's going to make things right with you. I told him not to squander his money—*our* money— because the hurt was mainly to your dignity. I hope you'll be a good sport about it."

"What other places did you go today?"

Caddo said, "After all, Mr. Mason, this is a very disagreeable subject. Can't we. . . ?"

"No," Mason said. "I want to know where she went."

She said gleefully, "I went to see Marilyn Marlow. I couldn't find her. I had to put her on my list for tomorrow, but I saw Rose Keeling."

"What time?"

"Right around eleven-thirty."

"Throw any ink?"

She said grimly, "Believe me, that little tart will keep grub hooks off a married man in the future. I went places with her."

"At what time?" Mason asked.

"Around eleven-thirty. It took me a little time to find her. I wasted some time trying to get Marilyn Marlow located, but Bob's dear friend, Miss Marlow, was hiding out."

"I tell you, my love, that it was only a business matter. Purely a business matter!" Caddo said desperately. "And if you had given Mr. Mason a chance to explain, he would have told you that. As a matter of fact, I never even saw Rose Keeling in my life."

"Well, I saw her," his wife said, "and, believe me, I put the fear of God into her."

"What was she doing when you got there?" Mason asked.

"Dolling herself up for a tennis game. She had on one of those leg-showing suits, a nice, flimsy little thing. Well, I fixed that! I ripped it down the back and said, 'Why not show 'em all of you, dearie? Why just tease them?' And then I took my fountain pen and snapped ink all over her."

"My love, you didn't!" Caddo said, his voice filled with dismay.

"I certainly did!" his wife said. "And any time you think you're going to cut corners, just remember one thing. I'll find out about it sooner or later, and when I do, I'm going to make a scene that will teach people a married man isn't fair game."

"But, my love! This was a business matter. I could have made a lot of money out of it."

"How?" Mason asked.

Caddo said, "Well, I . . ." He stopped abruptly, his sentence unfinished.

Dolores said, "Don't think you can get your lawyer to front for you. Have I got to start getting rough all over again?"

Mason said, "I'm interested in what happened with Rose Keeling."

"Well, suppose you go ask Rose Keeling. She *should* have a very vivid recollection of what happened."

"Unfortunately, I can't."

"You mean she's skipped out?"

"Rose Keeling," Mason said, "is no longer with us. She was murdered at approximately eleven-forty this morning."

In the silence that followed, the little noises made by the gas furnace as the metal of the heating system expanded in the growing heat sounded as clear as pistol shots.

Robert Caddo said sharply, "Damn it, Dolores, I told you that one of these days your temper would get the best of you! Now you've really done it."

"Shut up," she said.

Mason said, "Perhaps if you'd tell me more about your visit with Rose Keeling . . ."

"Phooey," she said. "What are you trying to do, pin a murder charge on me?"

Mason said, "I have reason to believe that the murderer must have entered the place very shortly after you left."

She said, "Wait a minute. Where do *you* fit into this picture?"

Mason said, "I'm trying to investigate . . ."

"You're interested in finding out about the murder?"

"Yes."

"Why?"

Mason said, "I'm an attorney. I'm trying to clear it up."

She said, "You're an attorney and you're representing someone. When you started in on this case, you were representing my husband. Bob, you haven't asked Mason to do anything about the murder, have you?"

Caddo shook his head, but said, "Really, my love, this is serious. Mr. Mason is one of the best lawyers and . . ."

"And Mason is representing someone right now," Dolores said. "He's trying to pin something on me so he can protect someone else."

"But, my love, you admitted you were there," Caddo said.

"Well, he's juggling things around so that it makes it appear that the murder was committed right at the time I was there. . . . What kind of monkey business is this, anyway?"

Mason said, "I'm simply trying to get the facts, that's all. You didn't kill her, did you?"

"Phooey," she said. "I threw ink on her and tore off a few of her clothes and then I tried to give her a good spanking, but she got away from me and ran into the bathroom and locked herself in. . . . I think, Bob, we won't do any more talking."

Mason said, "It would be of considerable assistance if you would tell me . . ."

"Well, I won't!" Dolores Caddo said.

"If I could apprehend the real murderer, it would keep some innocent person from being falsely accused."

"Yes, I know," Dolores said. "But suppose you get bighearted about this other person and try to pin things on *me?*"

"You've already said you were there, my love," Caddo said in a panic. "You'd better go ahead and explain now. Otherwise Mason will go to the police."

"Let him go to the police," Dolores said.

"I can, you know," Mason told her.

"Phooey!"

"I mean it."

"There's a phone. Go to it."

Mason walked over to the telephone, said, "It suits me just as well this way as the other."

He picked up the receiver, dialed police headquarters, asked for the Homicide Department and wanted to know who was in charge.

"Who is talking?" a voice asked.

"Perry Mason."

"Wait a minute. Lieutenant Tragg just dropped in. I'll put him on."

Mason heard Tragg's voice saying, "Yes, Mason, what is it?"

"You must be working overtime."

"I am—thanks to you."

Mason said, "Perhaps I can give you a real break this time."

"Your breaks aren't the kind we're looking for."

"This one is," Mason said. "I'm talking from the home of Robert Caddo, who runs the Lonely Lovers Publications, Inc., and puts out a magazine entitled 'Lonely Hearts Are Calling.' He . . ."

"I know all about him," Tragg said. "The rackets department had him up once or twice."

Mason said, "Robert Caddo had been interested in Rose Keeling. Dolores Caddo found out about it. She went to Rose Keeling's flat at eleven-thirty and, according to her own statement, beat up one Rose Keeling and threw some ink around. Rose Keeling shut herself in the bathroom. Dolores says she isn't doing any more talking. Are you interested?"

Tragg's voice showed eagerness. "Where are you?"

"At Caddo's residence."

"This isn't some frame-up, trying to spring your client?"

"I'm telling you the truth."

"I'm coming right down," Tragg said. "Hold everything."

He slammed down the phone. Mason dropped the receiver into place.

"Well?" Dolores Caddo said.

Mason said, "Lieutenant Tragg was somewhat skeptical."

"Probably thinks you're trying to get some of your clients out of trouble."

"Perhaps."

"What's he going to do?" Caddo asked.

"We'll have to let subsequent events determine that."

Mrs. Caddo said, "Well, mix a drink, Bob. We don't have to neglect the social amenities just because this lawyer is trying to pin a murder on me."

"I wish you'd talk frankly to us, my love," Caddo said, his voice sharp with anxiety. "You know, love, you have this ungovernable temper and . . ."

"Why, if you aren't joining the procession!" Dolores said. "Don't think you can get rid of me and have that Marlow woman by pinning a murder on me. You two-timing buzzard! I want a Scotch and soda. And get some of that *good* Scotch. Don't use any more of that prune-juice combination."

"But, my love, if you were there and . . ."

"Get that drink!"

"My love, won't you please . . ."

"All right," she said, "I'll get it myself," and started for the kitchen.

Caddo said in a low voice to Mason, "Look here, Mr. Mason, can't we square this somehow?"

"I'd like to have your wife tell exactly what happened," Mason said, "I think it's the best way to . . ."

"Bob!" Dolores called angrily. "What have you done with that Scotch?"

"Just a moment, my love. Just a moment, just a moment," Caddo said, and with ludicrous haste ran toward the kitchen, the bathrobe trailing out behind him.

A few moments later he was back. "Just why did you come here, Mr. Mason?"

"I wanted to get the facts."

"But you must have had some way of knowing that Dolores was there. There must have been something . . ."

"Well, there was."

"What was it?"

Mason shrugged his shoulders and said, "What difference does it make? She says she was there. I found the evidence. The police will find the evidence."

Caddo walked over to stand on the register, which was now spewing out heat from the gas furnace. The hot air billowed the bathrobe into flapping motion.

"Well," Mason said at length, "what do you plan to do?"

"I don't know," Caddo said.

Mrs. Caddo brought in a tray with glasses, put the tray in front of Mason and said, "Take your pick, just so you'll know that you're not being poisoned."

Mason picked the middle glass.

Dolores took the tray over to her husband, then took the remaining drink, placed the tray on the table, and sat down.

They sipped their drinks for a few moments in silence.

Caddo started to say something. His wife frowned him into silence.

The sound of a siren cut through the night. The scream descended into a low-throated growl and a car slid to a stop in front of the house.

"Let the police in, darling," Dolores said to her husband.

"Yes, my love," he said meekly, and went down the corridor and opened the front door.

Lieutenant Tragg and a plainclothes man came pushing into the room.

"Hello, Mason," Tragg said. "What's this all about?"

Mason said, "This is Dolores Caddo, Lieutenant Tragg, and her husband, Robert Caddo."

Tragg pushed his hat over on the back of his head, said, "What's this about Dolores Caddo going to see Rose Keeling?"

Dolores sipped her drink and said, "Damned if I know. It's an idea Mason had. He thought he could make it stick."

Mason said, "Dolores Caddo is inclined to have fits of temper whenever her husband has been philandering. She thought he had been seeing Rose Keeling. Mrs. Caddo called at my office earlier in the day and said she was on her way out to see Marilyn Marlow and Rose Keeling and that she intended to make something of a scene. Naturally, I called to ask her what had happened."

"Go on," Tragg said.

Mason said, "She has just admitted to both of us that she had been in Rose Keeling's flat about eleven-thirty, that she had distributed a little ink around, torn Rose Keeling's clothes, and tried to administer a spanking. Miss Keeling broke away from her, got into the bathroom and locked herself in. So Mrs. Caddo went out."

"And the time?" Tragg asked, eyes glinting.

"Eleven-thirty," Mason said.

Tragg turned to Mrs. Caddo. "What about it?"

Dolores Caddo looked at her husband with wide-eyed astonishment. "I'll be a dirty name," she said.

"What about it?" Tragg repeated.

"That's the wildest fairy tale I ever heard," Dolores Caddo said.

"Didn't you see Rose Keeling?"

She shook her head. "I've never seen her in my life."

Tragg looked at Mason.

Dolores Caddo turned to her husband. "What about Rose Keeling, honey? Do you know her?"

"I have never seen her," Caddo said, running his tongue along the line of his lips.

"Mrs. Caddo," Mason said dryly, "is given to throwing ink in her fits of temper. Is that right, Mrs. Caddo?"

She said to Lieutenant Tragg, "I don't know what's going on here, but you're the law. You'd ought to see that we get a square deal."

"Tell me exactly what happened," Tragg said. "Then I'll see what can be done."

She said, "I went to call on Mr. Mason this morning. I had a talk with him. Shortly after I left, my husband went there. He said at that time Mason told him I'd thrown ink all over his office. Mason had smeared some ink on his face to make it look natural and apparently had put some scratches on his face with lipstick. I'd never touched him; I was a perfect lady.

"Then tonight Mason came down here and accused me of having gone to see Rose Keeling. I told him I'd never seen her in my life. He walked over to the telephone and called police headquarters and told you that fairy story. I can't figure it out."

"You hadn't told him you had seen Rose Keeling?"

She shook her head.

"You're certain?"

She nodded.

Robert Caddo cleared his throat. "I was here all the time, Lieutenant. She certainly never said anything like that!"

"You were both together here?"

"That's right. Mason rang the bell and got us up out of bed. He said he wanted to talk with us. We mixed a drink and Mason accused my wife of having gone to see Rose Keeling. She said she didn't even know Rose Keeling. Then Mason went over and called you up."

Tragg looked over to Mason.

The lawyer put down his drink, said, "I'm sorry, Lieutenant."

"You got anything more to say than that?"

Mason shook his head.

"By God!" Tragg said. "One of these days, Mason, you're going to step all over your tonsils. What the hell's the idea rushing me down here on a bum steer like this? You're mixed up in this thing up to your necktie, and you're trying every way you can to get out. What's this about her calling at your office and you smearing ink on your face?"

Mason said, "I've been guilty of underestimating Mrs. Caddo's intelligence, Tragg."

"And, by God, you're underestimating mine!" Tragg said. "And for your personal information, we've now found some evidence that really connects your client with the murder. By ten o'clock in the morning I'll have a warrant for her. If you hide her after that I'll nail you as an accessory."

"Who's his client?" Mrs. Caddo asked.

"Marilyn Marlow," Tragg said.

"That woman!" Mrs. Caddo exclaimed, and then added, "Did she kill this girl—what's her name?"

"Rose Keeling. Yes, she killed her."

"How do you know?" Mrs. Caddo asked.

Tragg grinned. "Among other things, we've found the murder weapon in her possession."

"Well," Dolores Caddo said, "you certainly shouldn't want anything more than that!"

Mason said, "Before you go overboard on this thing, Lieutenant, I want to tell you what happened. Caddo wanted to get a lead on Marilyn Marlow, who was advertising in his magazine as a lonely heiress. At that time I think he was telling me the truth. He wanted to protect himself against a charge of false advertising. But once he found out who she was and had a look at her, he had an idea he might trade his wife in on a new model."

"That's a lie!" Caddo said.

"Naturally," Mason went on, "he didn't map out a plan of campaign all at once. He became convinced Marilyn was playing a game of some sort. He thought that he might be able to edge into the picture so that he could get a little money—and if he had to do it by some form of blackmail, he wasn't going to be *too* squeamish. However, in the back of his mind was an idea that Dolores had given him about everything she had to offer, and it might be a good plan to shine up to Marilyn Marlow, feeling that he just *might* be able to hit the jackpot."

"What was the jackpot?" Tragg asked.

"Reno," Mason said. "Trading Dolores in on a more streamlined model with more money."

"That's a lie, my love," Caddo said. "Don't listen to him. He's simply trying to make trouble."

Dolores threw back her head and laughed. "How well I know it! He thinks I'm jealous. Well, Robert, darling, I know you wouldn't do anything like that. You love me, and I know you love me."

"Thank you, darling."

"In the first place," Dolores went on, "you couldn't have got to first base with this heiress, and in the second place if you had, I'd have beaten your damn brains out before you could have stolen second base."

"Yes, my love."

"You know better than to try to two-time me. You might let your foot slip once in a while, but you wouldn't really try to walk out on me."

"No, my love."

"You know what would happen if you did."

"Yes, my love."

Dolores smiled at Lieutenant Tragg and said, "Can't you do something to keep this lawyer from trying to break up a perfectly happy marriage?"

Mason picked up his hat. "My congratulations, Mrs. Caddo. I hope you haven't played *all* your trumps."

"I haven't," she said sweetly. "Do stick around and have a drink with us, Lieutenant. My husband has some excellent Scotch in the kitchen. This prune juice is just some imitation stuff we dug out for this lawyer."

"I'll let you out," Caddo said to Mason.

"Don't bother," Mason told him. "I've found my way out of worse places than this, Caddo. Good night!"

CHAPTER 16

Mason stopped at an all-night restaurant, dialed Della Street's apartment.

"Hello, Della. Gone to bed yet?"

"No. I've only been here a few minutes. What's happened?"

Mason said, "I ran into something."

"At Caddo's?"

"Yes."

"Want to tell me about it?"

"I think I do. How tired are you?"

"Not at all. I'll wait."

"I'll be right out," Mason promised.

He jumped into his car, made time through the night streets to Della's apartment.

She had left the door slightly ajar so he could enter without knocking.

"Hello," she said. "What do you want, Scotch and soda or coffee? I have them both."

"Coffee," Mason said. "I just had a drink."

She poured him a big cup of coffee, added cream and sugar, brought out crackers and a plate of assorted tea biscuits.

Mason seated himself at the table, sipped the coffee gratefully, munched on tea biscuits, and said nothing.

She sat quietly across the table from him, refilling his coffee cup when it was half empty, waiting for him to think his way through the situation which confronted him.

At length Mason pushed the plate of tea biscuits away from him and took out his cigarette case. He held a pocket lighter for their cigarettes, then settled back in the chair and said, "I went to Caddo's place. Caddo was a very much subdued individual. His wife admitted she'd been out to take Rose Keeling apart. She arrived about eleven-thirty, she says. That's apparently approximate. She made a scene, tore Rose Keeling's sunsuit, threw some fountain pen ink just as Rose Keeling made a dash for the bathroom to keep from being spanked. Rose slammed the bathroom door and locked it. Mrs. Caddo went out."

"Chief!" Della Street exclaimed, her eyes big. "That accounts for it. That takes Marilyn Marlow off the spot."

"Wait a minute," Mason said. "Get the rest of it. I called Lieutenant Tragg. He came out there in a rush. I told him my story. Mrs. Caddo was just as sweet as honey on hot cakes. She told Tragg she'd never said any such thing. Caddo blinked, and backed her play. He said he'd been present during every minute of the conversation. He said nothing like that had been said; he thought perhaps I was trying to work some clumsy, amateurish third-degree on his wife."

"What did Tragg do?"

"When I left they were buying Tragg a drink. Everybody was chummy and hotsy-totsy."

"Can Tragg be that dumb?"

"It's not that he's so dumb. He's completely hypnotized with the idea that Marilyn Marlow is the one he's after. He can't see any angle that doesn't make Marilyn it. He's found some new evidence. He *says* he's found the murder weapon in Marilyn's possession."

Della Street's face showed startled dismay.

"So," Mason went on, "I guess our *habeas corpus* didn't do much good. They'll charge her now."

"Chief!" Della exclaimed, "how could they have found—oh, Lord!"

Mason nodded glumly.

After a minute or two, Della Street said, "But why did Mrs. Caddo tell you that she'd been out there if she was going to lie later?"

"She may be smart. It may have been because she didn't know Rose was dead until I told her. I spilled it because I thought she must know it. In other words, I'd pick her as the one who did it. She *may* have decided that a play like that was the best way to convince me that even if she had been out there, she had nothing to do with the killing. She may be really smart, that Caddo woman."

"What's going to happen now?" Della Street asked.

Mason said, "If we let events take their natural course, about ten or eleven o'clock in the morning Tragg will call at my office. He'll say in effect, 'Mr. Mason, you have Marilyn Marlow concealed somewhere. You know where she is. She's charged with first-degree murder. I have here a warrant for her arrest. I want her. I'm calling on you to produce her. If you continue to conceal her, so help me, I'll name you as an accessory and drag you in too.'"

"What can we do to stop that?"

"Nothing—once it happens. A murder warrant will have me on a spot."

"Then between now and morning you have to think of some way of heading off Lieutenant Tragg?"

He nodded.

She smiled, reached across the table, put her hand over his and gave it a reassuring squeeze. "I take it," she said, "you're about to hatch up some skulduggery."

"We've got to find a red herring somewhere."

"Where?" Della Street asked.

Mason grinned and said, "That, my dear young lady, is the object of the meeting."

She quietly got up from the chair, went to the kitchen, brought back the coffee pot and refilled Mason's cup. Then she filled her own.

She returned the coffee to the stove, raised the rim of her cup as though proposing a toast to the lawyer, and said, "Here's a good-by to sleep."

"Good-by to sleep," Mason said, and touched coffee cups, and then again they sipped their coffee and smoked cigarettes.

An alarm clock that was somewhere in the kitchen, ticking away the seconds, began to sound increasingly audible in the night silence which wrapped the apartment house.

Mason said thoughtfully, "We have to get some new evidence which will incriminate someone else."

"How about putting a different interpretation on some of the evidence that Tragg already has?" Della Street asked.

"I'm turning that one over in my mind," Mason told her. "It would be a slick stunt if we could figure some way of doing it. Nice business if you could only get it!"

Mason's thumb and forefinger slid down into his right-hand vest pocket, brought out a key, started tapping on the table with the key.

"What's that?" Della Street asked.

"That," Mason said, "is the key that Rose Keeling gave Marilyn Marlow, the key that enabled her to open the door and get into Rose Keeling's apartment, the key she left on the table and the key I picked up and put in my pocket."

"Oh, oh," Della Street said.

"Are you reading my mind?" Mason asked.

She said, "I'm two paragraphs ahead of you."

Mason said, "The big trouble with the case, as far as we are concerned, is that no one has a motive for killing Rose Keeling except Marilyn Marlow. The Endicotts are pure as the driven snow. Quite apparently it was to their interest to have Rose Keeling live. The very thing that gives Marilyn a motive gives Ralph Endicott a clean bill of health."

"Plus an alibi, of course," Della Street said dryly.

Mason nodded thoughtfully.

"And with Mrs. Caddo," Mason said, "we have a peculiar situation: A jealous wife going out to raise the devil with a woman who she thought had been philandering with her husband. Her husband probably went tearing after her, trying to explain that, after all, it was merely a business proposition, that he was trying to cut himself a piece of cake by horning in on a will contest. Probably of all the alibis Robert Caddo ever had, this was the only one that he stood any chance of putting over. As soon as he could find his wife, he could convince her that she had better lay off. Now, according to the way events developed, he must have found her *after* she saw Rose Keeling and *before* she called on Marilyn Marlow. Otherwise, Marilyn Marlow would have had some ink stains and perhaps a few facial blemishes to add to her other troubles."

"Stay with it," Della Street said, smiling. "You're doing fine."

"And then," Mason went on, "we run up against the fact there's no motive for anyone to have committed the murder, other than Marilyn Marlow."

"And," Della Street said, "by a rare coincidence, *we* have the key to Rose Keeling's flat. Is that the sequence of ideas you're seeking to impress upon my mind?"

Mason said, "It's a temptation, Della."

"Well, why not?" she asked.

"Several reasons," Mason said. "One of them is that the police have undoubtedly photographed everything in the apartment. The other one is that they may have a guard on the job."

"If they've completed their photographing and map-making, wouldn't they simply lock the flat up and leave?"

Mason said, "They're a little short-handed on the police force. There's a very good chance that such is the case."

"Well?" Della Street asked, smiling.

Mason grinned. "Get thee behind me, Satan."

He continued to tap the key on the table.

Della Street refilled the coffee cups.

Mason said, almost wistfully, "It's a lot of fun to yield to temptation, Della."

"Isn't it!"

"Once this damned idea has got in my mind, I can't seem to think of anything else."

"Just what could we do?"

"*We* couldn't," Mason said. "It's something I'd have to do by myself, a chance I'd have to take . . ."

Della Street firmly shook her head.

"No need of both of us getting in a mess," Mason said hastily. "In case something should go wrong, I'd need you to run the office."

She said, "If we did get caught, we could say that we were just looking for evidence."

"Yes, we could *say* that."

"And we might get away with it."

"We *might*."

"What's the worst thing against Marilyn Marlow, Chief?"

"Its hard to tell which is the *worst*," Mason said. "If Tragg has a knife found in Marilyn's possession, he'll claim that's the murder weapon and that, of course, will be the worst thing that could happen. I think he's found a knife that *could* be it, but I don't think he can prove it's the murder weapon. However, Marilyn's whole story is so utterly implausible. Here was Rose Keeling packing her suitcases, ready to leave town. She had written Marilyn Marlow, telling her that the will was no good. She had given Ralph Endicott a check for conscience money—the first installment of bribe money she had received. Of course, I'd take that with a grain of salt, Della. I think that it wasn't entirely a matter of conscience. I think Ralph Endicott made some promises, but I don't know how we're going to bring that out. The fact remains the girl was packing her suitcases, ready to leave town. Yet Marilyn wants people to believe Rose told her that she wanted to go play tennis. And Dolores Caddo could substantiate that story if she only would tell the truth. But she won't and that leaves Marilyn stuck with her story."

Mason was thoughtfully silent over his coffee.

Suddenly Della Street said, "Gosh, Chief, I've got an idea. If— it's so simple that it would be a cinch, and so daring it scares me."

Mason cocked an eyebrow in her direction.

"Look," Della Street said, the excitement making her voice run the words together, "how do *we* know she was packing? Everyone takes it for granted she was packing because the clothes were neatly folded and were in the suitcase and on the top of the bureau. But suppose that when it comes to a showdown, we can show that she was unpacking?"

Mason frowned thoughtfully, then his face broke into a smile. "Darling!"

"Just a few little things here and there," Della Street went on. "Clues that would naturally have escaped the untutored, male eyes of the blundering cops, but things that you could bring out in front of a jury, things that would really mean something, particularly if we have some women members on the jury."

"We'll get the women on the jury," Mason said. "But how are we going to find these little things that will make it appear she was unpacking instead of packing?"

Della Street said, "You leave that to me," and made a run for her bedroom, emerging presently with a fur coat, and a jaunty hat perched on one side of her head.

"What's holding us back?" she asked.

Mason said, "My damn conservative disposition."

"I was afraid of that," she told him.

Mason got to his feet, took Della Street into his arms and kissed her. She laughed up at him, and he said, "Why is it your feminine charms are never so alluring as when you've thought of some piece of skullduggery?"

"It's a subject we can discuss later," she said. "Right now we have work to do. Suppose Tragg's having the place watched?"

"That's what we'll have to find out."

"And if we get caught?"

"We're just looking for evidence—and if Tragg doesn't believe that, your feminine charms will have to go to work again," Mason replied.

"On Tragg? Let's not get caught," Della Street said.

CHAPTER 17

Mason drove his car slowly past the four-flat house.

"Take a good look, Della."

"I'm looking."

"All dark?"

"Dark as the inside of a pocket."

"We'll drive around the block," Mason said, "and look for a police car. There's a chance a guard might be sleeping inside the flat. If so, he'll have a car parked around here somewhere."

They cruised slowly around the block, watching the license numbers of the parked cars.

"See anything official?" Della Street asked.

Mason said, "I think we're in the clear, Della. We'll circle around a couple more blocks, just to make sure."

"How strong are we going to go after we get in?" she asked.

Mason said, "Just strong enough to rattle these birds on cross-examination and drive home a point to the jury. When you come right down to it, Della, no one knows whether Rose Keeling was packing to leave town or whether she had been planning on leaving town and was unpacking the suitcases when she was murdered.

"When the trial starts, the D. A. will put Lieutenant Tragg on the stand and ask him what he found when he discovered the body. Tragg will state that he found the body nude, sprawled on the floor in front of the bathroom door with the feet toward the bathroom, the air in the bathroom still steamy, the temperature of the tub warmer than that of the surrounding air, indicating that she had been taking a bath; that he'd found clothes on the bed and all that, and then he'll go on to state that there were two suitcases open and that she had been packing those suitcases.

"You can leave it to Tragg to slip that in very skillfully before anyone can make an objection. Then I'll move to strike out the statement that she was packing, on the ground that that was a conclusion of the witness, and the D. A. will say wearily, 'Oh, yes, that can go out if you insist that it's a conclusion, Mr. Mason.' And then he'll turn to Tragg with a superior smile and say, 'Just what *did* you find, Lieutenant? Since Mr. Mason objects to having you say that the girl was packing, just what did you find?'

"And then Tragg will say, 'I found two suitcases in front of the dresser. There were some folded clothes on the dresser. The fold on the clothes was of exactly the right dimension to enable them to fit into the suitcase when they were placed on top of the clothes already in there. The suitcases contained articles of feminine clothing which we had identified as having belonged to Rose Keeling in her lifetime.'"

"Then what?" Della Street asked.

"Then," Mason said, "the District Attorney will turn to the jury with something of a smirk, as much as to say, 'You see what a technical chap this Mason is and how he's trying to resort to all kinds of technicalities in order to keep his client from being convicted.' Those are little tricks of courtroom technique but they can be used to put a defense attorney at a disadvantage."

"And after we get in the flat? Then what?"

"Then," Mason said, "after we get in the flat, we'll know a lot more than we do now. We'll let Tragg slip in the statement that she had been packing her suitcases at the time of her death, and make no objection to it. But when we start our cross-examination, we'll say, 'Lieutenant, your assumption was that this woman had been packing. How do you *know* she was packing? How do you know she wasn't *un*packing?' And Tragg will sarcastically say, 'She hadn't been any place, had she? Or do you claim she kept her clothes in her suitcases and then once a week or so she put them in the bureau drawers just to give them a treat?' And then the judge will frown, the jury smile, and the people in the courtroom laugh.

"And then I'll start asking him specifically about the articles that were in the suitcase and will bring out the evidence that shows she was unpacking instead of packing. And that will make it appear that I knew what I was talking about all along, that the District Attorney has missed a bet, and, more important than all, it will keep from crucifying Marilyn Marlow with that story she's telling. In other words, if Rose Keeling had been packing, she never would have invited Marilyn Marlow to come back and play tennis. If she had been unpacking, she could very well have done so. It's just a little thing, but it may mean the difference between conviction and acquittal in a murder case. In one way Marilyn Marlow's story *has* to be a lie, and in the other way it *may* be the truth. How about this block, Della? Have you seen anything that looks like a police car?"

"Not a thing so far."

Mason said, "Well, we can't comb the whole city. We've got the key. Let's take a chance."

"Okay by me," Della said. "Where are you going to leave the car?"

"Right in front of the flat," Mason told her.

"Isn't that dangerous?"

"Sure it's dangerous. The whole thing is dangerous. The minute we walk in there, we're playing into Tragg's hands. If he should spot us, he'll arrest us for burglary."

"But we aren't *taking* anything."

"Burglary," Mason said, "is a matter of intent."

"What do you mean?"

"A person who enters a building with intent to commit larceny or any felony is guilty of burglary."

"You mean if we were caught inside the building, we wouldn't have any defense?"

"We'd have to convince a jury that our intent in entering the building wasn't to take anything. That might be quite a job. The police would claim we intended to take something out with us."

"What, for instance?"

"They wouldn't need to specify. They'd claim it was some bit of evidence we didn't want to have found by the police. Oh, what's the use, Della. We just can't afford to get caught."

She laughed. "I was just getting posted on the law."

"Do you want to wait in the car and . . ."

"Don't be silly."

"I can go in and take a preliminary look around . . ."

"What would you know about fixing evidence so it would look as though a girl had been unpacking instead of packing? You'd botch it all up. Any man would. Don't be silly, let's go."

Mason slid the car to a stop in front of the flat.

"Do we do any more reconnoitering?" Della asked.

"Definitely not. Anyone who might happen to be looking out from one of the adjoining houses would immediately think we were guilty of something. We walk right up to the place, just like we were police detectives getting evidence. Just like this."

Mason led the way across the sidewalk, fitted the key to the door of the flat.

"And go right up?" Della Street asked.

"Right up," Mason said. "After all, the housing shortage being what it is, the neighbors might think some friend of the chief of police had made a new lease on the flat before they had the body moved out. Just don't turn on the lights, Della. We'll use flashlights and keep the beams shaded."

Mason produced two small flashlights which he had taken from the glove compartment of his car, and they moved cautiously up the stair treads.

"Keep a little to one side," Mason warned. "The sides of the treads don't creak as much. I don't want the people in the flat below to hear steps moving around up here."

"The building's constructed rather substantially," Della Street said.

"I know, but just take it easy."

Keeping to the side of the stair treads, they moved cautiously up to the second floor. Mason, keeping the beam of his flashlight shielded, moved quietly through the living room, down the short stretch of corridor and into the bedroom.

The body had been moved, and where the red pool had been there was now only a sinister stain. Chalk marks on the floor outlined the general position of the body when it had been found.

"They've dusted everything for fingerprints," Mason said, "but aside from that, they've left stuff just as it was."

"Then they haven't made an inventory of the things that were in the suitcases?"

"I don't think so. They probably just lifted the edges of the various garments. They may intend to do some more photographing or bring in some more witnesses. Perhaps later on they'll close these suitcases and take them up to the District Attorney's office. All right, here you are, Della. Get busy."

Della Street bent over the suitcases. Mason held his flashlight so it gave her a circle of illumination.

Della Street's deft fingers ran through the garments.

"What do you make of it?" Mason asked.

Della Street said, "She was either going to get married or she was going on a trip of some importance. She certainly put her finery in here and lots of it. Looks to me as though she's raided her hope chest. She went heavy on lingerie and nighties . . . expensive stuff."

"How can you make it appear she'd been unpacking instead of packing?"

"Give me time, Chief, I'll have to figure that one out."

Her skillful fingers raised the folds of each one of the garments without disturbing the manner in which it had been packed.

"I'll tell you one thing," Della Street said in a low whisper. "The girl was a darn good packer and I don't think there was anything hasty about the way she did this packing, either. It's been done very carefully."

"Stay with it," Mason said. "See what else you can find."

Della Street ran through the other suitcase, then said, "She evidently hadn't packed one side of it. What are the clothes on the dresser?"

Mason raised the beam of his flashlight so Della Street could inspect them. Suddenly she whistled.

"What's the matter?" Mason asked.

Della Street said, "Chief, the theory of the police is that these garments were folded and placed on top of the bureau so they could be put into the suitcase?"

"That's right."

Della Street shook her head. "She couldn't have folded them that accurately. You see, the edges are all uniform, just absolutely the dimensions of the suitcase."

Della Street picked the garments up and eased them down into the suitcase. "See, they fit exactly!"

"Well?" Mason asked.

"Don't you get it?" Della Street said, her voice excited.

"Get what?"

"Chief, we're *right!* We had it all the time."

"You mean she *was* unpacking?"

"She was! She had to be. See what happened? She folded these garments into the suitcase, one by one. That's the reason they *exactly* fit the dimensions of the suitcase. As she folded them, they were inside the suitcase. Then when she started to unpack, she lifted out the garments that were on this side of the suitcase and put them on the top of the bureau. . . . Probably something she wanted out from underneath. Then she left them there on top of the bureau. There aren't enough here to fill . . . Let's take a look, Chief."

Excitedly, Della Street opened the bureau drawers.

"Look," she said breathlessly, "look at *these* garments! They're folded exactly in the same way the others are. Let's see."

Della Street carefully picked up a blouse and super imposed it on top of the pile of garments on top of the bureau.

"You see what I mean? She *had* started to unpack! She really had, Chief! She'd taken these garments out of the suitcase, placed them on top of the bureau; and then she was proceeding to put them back in the bureau drawers, and because the dimensions of the suitcases were somewhere near those of the drawer, she hadn't bothered to fold them again, but had left them folded just as they had been to go into the suitcase."

Mason said dubiously, "You don't think it could be just a coincidence? It . . ."

Della Street said, "If you think it's a coincidence, just try it. Try to take a garment and fold it so that it is exact in the dimensions of its fold. You can't do it, unless you have something to hold it, something that keeps it in size. You need a box or a suitcase, or . . ."

"Let's get out of here," Mason said abruptly. "We'll get a court order demanding that the property be undisturbed. We'll get photographers. The thing now is to get official access to these premises before the police have mixed everything up."

Della Street said, "But even if they do, we could testify. I could say that . . ."

Mason's laugh was harsh. "A fat chance!" he said. "You'd get on the stand and testify to what you had seen and the District Attorney would take you on cross-examination and say sarcastically, 'What sort of visibility did you have, Miss Street? What kind of light were you using?' And you'd say, 'A flashlight,' and then the District Attorney would ask you what time of night it was, and you would say, 'About one-thirty in the morning,' and . . ."

"Well, what difference does it make what time it was?" Della Street demanded. "Facts are facts."

"Sure they're facts," Mason said, "but the District Attorney would make it appear that you and I had entered the building so that we could refold those garments so they would just fit into the suitcase and . . ."

"But we didn't do it."

"You'd say we didn't do it, Della, but when you come right down to it, what *did* we come in here for? Suppose we'd had to do it?"

Della Street thought that over for a moment, then said, "All right, let's get out of here."

"The irony of it is," Mason went on, "that the evidence was actually here all the time. If I'd only used my eyes when I was in here. If I'd pointed it out to Tragg then . . . Oh, what's the use? Let's go."

They tiptoed down the passageway, through the living room to the head of the stairs, then cautiously descended, once more keeping over to the side of the treads so as to avoid creaking boards.

They reached the lower landing.

"All ready?" Mason asked.

"All ready," Della Street said.

Mason opened the door.

After the stuffy interior of the flat where the windows had been closed, the freshness of the cool night air fanned them with a sudden chill.

At that moment a light swinging around the corner of the building flooded the porch with blood-red brilliance.

Della Street said, "Good heavens, it's . . ."

"A police car," Mason said.

"Do we run back or . . ."

"Out!" Mason said, and pushed her out to the porch. He followed her and pulled the door shut behind him. He took the handkerchief from his pocket, held it in front of him and made rapid motions.

"What are you doing?" she asked.

"Polishing fingerprints off that key. Raise the front door mat with your foot. Hurry."

She moved the front door mat with her foot. Mason dropped the key to the cement porch where it gave forth a metallic tinkle.

"All right," Mason said. "Hold the rug up."

Della Street's foot held the rug and Mason kicked the key under the rug.

Mason, standing at the door, started ringing the bell. The blood-red spotlight on the police car now held them pinned in its pitiless red beam. The police car slid to a stop. A door opened and closed.

Mason turned and said casually, "We want to get in here. What's wrong with the police guard? Is he drunk? We've been ringing for ten minutes."

A radio officer, followed by a man who hung back in the shadows, came up the walk.

"What the hell's coming off here?"

Mason said, "We want to get into this place."

"You've *been* in it."

"Been in it?" Mason said. "Of course I've been in it. That's why I want to get back in."

"How did you get in?"

"I was here with Lieutenant Tragg," Mason said.

"I don't mean then. I mean you were in just now."

Mason said, "I want to get in. I'm ringing the bell. There must be some officer sleeping upstairs."

"You've been in. You opened that door and went in."

"What are you talking about?"

"Here's a witness who saw you," the officer said.

Robert Caddo stepped forward, said apologetically, "Hello, Mason."

"Why, hello, Caddo," Mason said. "What are *you* doing here?"

Caddo was awkwardly silent.

Mason said to the prowl car officer, "I certainly hope you're not paying any attention to the word of this man."

"What's wrong with his word?"

"As far as I'm concerned, he's a suspect in this murder case. He's already told one bunch of lies to the police."

Caddo said, "You can't talk like that, Mason."

"The hell I can't!" Mason told him belligerently, stepping toward Caddo. "You heard your wife tell me she'd been to see Rose Keeling, and you tried to . . ."

"She didn't tell you any such thing! She . . ."

The radio officer put a big hand on Mason's chest, pushed him back from Caddo. "Keep your shirt on, buddy," he said. "We'll save all this stuff. What I want to know is what you were doing in that house."

Mason said, "I want to get the evidence perpetuated. This man with you is trying his damnedest to get into this flat by some hook or crook, so he can remove some evidence which will implicate his wife."

"That's not true," Caddo said.

Mason laughed sneeringly. "You'd give your right hand to get in there. You've worked up some cock-and-bull story to spring on this officer so he'll let you in."

"I tell you that's not true!" Caddo said. "I was watching this place because I felt certain someone would try to *plant* some evidence that would incriminate Dolores."

"So," Mason said sneeringly, "you came out here, parked a car and stayed all night so you could . . ."

"So I could watch the place," Caddo interrupted. "I saw you driving around and around the block and then I saw you park your car, and you and your secretary went in that flat."

"So you dashed out to find a cop. Is that right?"

"I went to the nearest telephone and put in a call to police headquarters. They contacted the radio car," Caddo said.

"I see," Mason said sarcastically. "And how long after you think we went in did you wait before you went for the radio car? Why did you sit there waiting. . . ?"

"I didn't wait. The minute I saw you at the door, I knew it was going to happen, and I made a dash to the telephone."

"I thought so," Mason said.

"What's wrong with that?" Caddo asked.

"The minute you saw us coming up here to this door," Mason said, his foot touching Della Street's toe, "you went dashing off to the nearest telephone."

"I've already told you that," Caddo said.

"You certainly have," Mason said. "I want you to get the significance of that, officer. The minute he saw us come up here on the porch, he dashed to the telephone."

"Because I knew what you were trying to do. I knew you were going to get in here and plant some evidence on my wife. I'd had a suspicion all along that you'd do something like that. You . . . Hey, officer, that woman is taking this stuff down in shorthand."

"Sure she is," Mason said.

The officer turned. Della Street, standing back in the corner, had taken a shorthand notebook and fountain pen from her pocket and her hand was flying over the page, making dashes and pothooks.

"What's the idea?" the officer asked.

Mason said, "This man who is with you is a congenital liar. He'll change his story just as soon as the full significance of it dawns on him."

Caddo said, "You keep calling me a liar and I'll push your teeth . . ."

"Shut up," the radio officer said to him and then turned back to Mason. "What are you getting at?"

"Do you know me?" Mason asked.

"No."

"I'm Perry Mason, the lawyer."

"Let's take a look at you," the officer said. He pushed Mason over so that the beam of the flashlight shone fully on the lawyer's face. "Damned if you ain't," he said.

"And this is Miss Street, my secretary."

"All right, Mr. Mason. What are you doing here?"

"Trying to get in," Mason said. "Apparently your watchman upstairs is sound asleep. I've been ringing the bell for it must have been as much as ten minutes."

"There isn't any watchman upstairs."

"What?"

"That's right. This place is in my territory. We haven't enough men to leave a watchman up there. I'm supposed to keep my eye on the place."

"No wonder we couldn't get any answer to our ring," Mason said.

"He wasn't ringing," Caddo said angrily. "He's been up there. He and his secretary opened the door and went up."

"*Opened* the door!" Mason said.

"You heard me. That's what I said."

Mason laughed. "What makes you think we opened the door?"

"I saw you. I saw you go in!"

"You saw us go *in*?"

"That's right. You heard me."

Mason laughed. "You saw us come up on the porch and ring the bell. You saw us in the same position that we're in now."

"No, I didn't. I saw you get the door open and actually go inside."

"Oh, no, you didn't," Mason said, and then, turning to the officer, observed, "See I told you he'd try to change his story as soon as he realized what the situation was."

"I'm not changing my story. That's what I said all along."

"That's what he told me," the officer said, "that you two had gone in. He told me that the minute I picked him up at the restaurant where he'd been telephoning. He said that two people had gone in. . . ."

"He *surmised* they'd gone in," Mason interrupted.

"I *saw* you go in," Caddo said.

Mason said condescendingly to the officer, "You see what happened. He saw us come up on the porch and assumed we were going in, so he tore off immediately to get to a telephone. Now that he realizes we didn't go in and that he actually didn't see us go in, he's trying to make up a case."

"I'm not doing any such thing."

"I don't think he is," the officer said. "His story to me was that you'd gone in."

"Don't you get it?" Mason said. "He admitted here three times that *just as soon as he saw us come up on the porch*, he dashed off to a telephone."

"He did, at that," the officer said dubiously.

"That isn't what I meant," Caddo said, raising his voice, "I meant that as soon as you came up on the porch I knew what you were going to do, and I got all ready to make a dash. You opened the door and the minute you did that, I . . ."

"See," Mason said, laughing. "He's trying to lie out of it. I told you he would."

Caddo said, "I never said any such thing."

"I think you did," Mason said.

"I'll leave it to the officer. I . . ."

Mason said, "Della, read just what Caddo *did* say."

Della Street tilted her shorthand notebook so the light struck on the page and then read slowly:

"(Mr. Caddo): 'I didn't wait. The minute I saw you at the door, I knew it was going to happen, and I made a dash to the telephone.'

"(Mr. Mason): 'I thought so.'

"(Mr. Caddo): 'What's wrong with that?'

"(Mr. Mason): 'The minute you saw us come up here to this door, you went dashing off to the nearest telephone.'

"(Mr. Caddo): 'I've already told you that.'

"(Mr. Mason): 'You certainly have. I want you to get the significance of that, officer. The minute he saw us come up here on the porch, he dashed to the telephone.'

"(Mr. Caddo): 'Because I knew what you were trying to do. I knew you were going to get in here and plant some evidence on my wife. I'd had a suspicion all along that you'd do something like that. You . . . Hey, officer, that woman is taking this stuff down in shorthand.'"

"There you are, officer," Mason said. "She took it down in shorthand, in black and white. That's word for word what the man said."

"I think it is!" the officer said. "I think she's got it right."

"Well, that wasn't what I meant," Caddo said. "I know they went in here. I saw them open the door."

Mason laughed. "How did we get the door open?"

"I don't know. Perhaps it was unlatched, or perhaps you had a key."

"Want to search me?" Mason asked, holding his arms out.

"Since you've given me the invitation, I'll take a look," the radio officer said.

He patted Mason's figure first, looking for weapons, then felt of each pocket. "You don't seem to have anything except small stuff," he said.

Mason started emptying his pockets on the porch, turning each one of his pockets wrong-side-out as it was emptied, putting the belongings in a small pile in the center of the light cast by the police car.

Suddenly a porch light clicked on. A woman's voice, coming from a lower flat, shrill with fright, said, "I've telephoned for the police. I don't know what you think you're doing, but . . ."

"We *are* the police," the officer said, showing his badge.

"Well, I telephoned the police station and . . ."

"That's all right. The police station knows I'm here," the radio officer said, his eyes on the growing assortment of stuff that Mason was taking from his pockets.

"There you are," Mason said, showing that each pocket had been turned wrong-side-out. "You don't see any burglary tools there, do you?"

"Perhaps it was a key," Caddo suggested.

"You don't see any key."

"His secretary has it!"

Mason said, "If there's any doubt about that, you can take my secretary to Headquarters and we'll have a police woman search her, officer. But . . ."

"Let me look in your purse," the officer said to Della Street.

He opened Della Street's purse, looked through the miscellaneous contents, pulled out a key ring, said, "What's this key to?"

"My apartment."

"And this key?"

"Perry Mason's office."

"And this one?"

"My garage key."

"Don't let her fool you," Caddo warned. "How do *you* know that's what they are? That key she says is to Mason's office can well be something else. You . . ."

"I don't care what it is," the radio officer said, "unless it's a key to this door. We'll find out about that right now."

One by one, he tried to fit the keys to the lock. None of the keys would slide in.

"Not even the same grooves," the officer said. He returned the keys to Della's purse, closed the purse and handed it to Della Street.

"She's got it down her stocking top," Caddo said. "How do you know . . ."

"Oh, shut up!" the officer told him. "You've been wrong on everything so far. What the hell are you trying to do anyway?"

"I'm trying to see that . . ."

"You've been laying out here watching this apartment?"

"Yes."

"All night?"

"All night."

"That looks fishy to me, on the face of it," the officer said.

Mason merely smiled.

Caddo said impatiently, "I tell you, the guy's clever. I had an idea he'd . . ."

Mason said, "Anyhow, Caddo, you took it on yourself to be a self-appointed watchman for this place. Is that your story?"

"That's right."

"Why didn't you have some police officer accompany you or wait with you?"

"You know why. I didn't have anything to go on except suspicion. I . . ."

"You had a talk with Lieutenant Tragg tonight, didn't you?"

"Yes."

"And at the time of that talk I told Tragg that you had heard your wife admit she'd been out here and had an argument with Rose Keeling."

"I never heard any such statement. My wife never said that, or anything like it."

"But, despite the fact that your wife never said any such thing, you, instead of going back to bed, jumped in your car and came out here to watch this flat, didn't you?"

"Yes."

Mason smiled. "If you'd never known Rose Keeling, how did you know where the flat was?"

"I . . . I had the address."

Mason laughed at the radio officer and said, "If you want to do yourself a good turn, lock this guy up."

The officer's head nodded almost imperceptibly.

Caddo, in a sudden panic, said, "You can't get away with that stuff! Officer, I telephone you when I see people breaking into a house, and you come up and let them talk you out of it."

"Nobody's talking me out of anything," the officer said, "but I don't get the sketch. I don't see what you were sticking around here for instead of being in bed and, personally, I don't think you saw them go in that door. I don't think they got in the door. I think they were standing here ringing the bell. Come on, now, break it up. On your way, all of you. I know who this man is and I can reach him whenever I want him. I'll make a report as to exactly what happened."

"And *I'll* make a report," Caddo said. "When Lieutenant Tragg . . . Damn it, I'll call Lieutenant Tragg myself!"

"Okay," the radio officer said, "go ahead and call him. But I don't see anything here that won't keep until morning. I'll make a report so Lieutenant Tragg can do whatever he wants to."

Mason said, "I demand, for the protection of my client, as well as myself, that a police guard be placed in charge here. I want to see that this evidence is preserved without being disturbed."

"We're short of officers," the man said apologetically. "There's been a lot of crime and . . ."

"I'm making that request," Mason interrupted. "I'm making a formal demand on the police. In view of the fact that it now appears that Caddo is trying to enter that flat, I demand a guard."

The officer said, "I'm going to dump this whole thing in the lap of Headquarters."

Mason said, "You have a two-way radio phone there in your car. Go call them."

"You getting this, Jack?" the officer called out to his partner who had been sitting in the car.

"Some of it."

"Put through a call to Headquarters and tell them Mason is demanding a guard for this place."

"On the ground that one of the interested parties was apprehended prowling around the place," Mason said.

"You mean me?" Caddo asked.

"I mean you."

"I haven't been apprehended and I wasn't prowling."

"All right," Mason said, laughing sarcastically. "Tell Headquarters that one of the chief suspects in the case has constituted himself a self-appointed guard to keep the flat under surveillance. When Homicide hears about that, they'll want a guard."

The officer said, "Okay, just a minute."

He rolled up the window of the car so they could not hear him talking while he put through his call to Headquarters.

A few moments later he rolled down the window of the car. "Okay," he said, "Headquarters is sending out a guard."

CHAPTER 18

Judge Osborn looked up from the papers he had been reading and said, "People versus Marilyn Marlow."

"Ready for the Prosecution," James Hanover said.

Mason arose. "Your Honor, the defendant is in court, represented by counsel. She has been advised of her rights and is ready to proceed with the preliminary hearing. The charge is first-degree murder and I am appearing upon behalf of the defendant."

Deputy District Attorney Hanover said, "In view of Counsel's statement, I will proceed with the evidence at this time. Call Dr. Thomas C. Hiller."

Dr. Hiller was sworn in, droned through a list of his qualifications as an expert medical witness, testified that he had been called to the apartment of Rose Keeling, that he had tentatively fixed the time of death at about noon of the day on which he was called, perhaps a half hour earlier. He had subsequently performed a postmortem. There had been a blow on the head of sufficient force to render the decedent unconscious. Apparently while unconscious, she had been stabbed in the back with a knife having a blade approximately an inch and two-tenths in width and a thickness of perhaps two-tenths of an inch at the heaviest part of the knife. The length of the blade was, of course, something that he couldn't swear to, but it had penetrated the body of the deceased to approximately seven inches.

Dr. Hiller gave it as his opinion that death had been practically instantaneous from the stab wound, but pointed out that also, in his opinion, the stab wound had been inflicted after the decedent had fallen to the floor and was stretched motionless and in approximately the same position as that in which her body had been found.

There had been considerable hemorrhage. The knife had been thrust in from the back or slightly to one side of the back. Microscopic tests he had made of the nails and other tests had indicated to him that the decedent has been bathing but a short time before the fatal injuries were inflicted.

"Cross-examine!" Hanover snapped truculently.

"No cross-examination," Mason said.

Lieutenant Tragg was called to the stand.

He testified to his official position, testified to having been called to Rose Keeling's flat on the day of the murder.

Asked to comment on the condition of the flat when he arrived, Tragg stated that Perry Mason and his secretary, Della Street, were, when he arrived, alone in the place with the body of the murdered woman.

He then went on to describe further the condition of the room, from time to time identifying photographs which were offered and received in evidence as being photographs taken under the supervision of the police force.

Then Hanover brought Tragg around to the effort he had made to find the murder weapon.

"Just tell the Court what search you made."

"I looked through the flat, searching for the murder weapon. I couldn't find it anywhere."

"Now," Hanover said, "I will ask you whether or not you located an automobile belonging to the defendant in this case."

"I did."

"Where was it?"

"In a public rental garage."

"And do you know who had left it there?"

"I only know what was told me."

"You cannot, of course, testify as to that. Is the proprietor of that garage in court, the one who gave you the information?"

"Yes, sir."

Hanover smirked triumphantly.

Mason said, "There's no need to call him. I will stipulate that I drove my client's car into a public storage garage and left it there while my client went to a private sanitarium after she had been released on a writ of *habeas corpus.*"

"Very well," Hanover said. "That will save time. Thank you."

He opened a small handbag, removed a box and approached the witness stand. From the box he removed a knife, stained and encrusted with dried blood.

"Lieutenant Tragg, I'll ask you if you ever saw this knife before."

"Yes, I have seen that knife before. I can identify it because it has my initials scratched on the handle. I found that knife under the floor mat in the trunk compartment of the defendant's automobile. At the time I found it, it was in exactly the same condition as it now appears, except that some of the encrusted blood stains on the blade have been subjected to chemical tests in the police laboratory. This has somewhat altered their appearance. There is also a slight change in the appearance of the knife, in that the handle and portions of the blade have been dusted with powder for the purpose of developing latent fingerprints."

"Were any developed?"

"No, sir, none were developed. The handle had been very carefully wiped, so as to remove all traces of fingerprints."

"That's a conclusion of the witness," Mason protested.

Lieutenant Tragg smiled, and said, "Well, I will put it this way: The handle was absolutely devoid of all latent fingerprints, *all* prints of any sort. Not even the faintest smudge." He added triumphantly, "And, as a man who has had considerable experience with homicide cases and the development of latent fingerprints, I know that such a condition couldn't possibly have existed unless the handle had been very carefully wiped."

"Are you," Mason asked Hanover, "preparing to introduce this knife in evidence?"

"Exactly," the deputy district attorney said.

"Under the circumstances," Mason announced, "there will be no objection. Go right ahead and put it in evidence."

Judge Osborn seemed frankly puzzled. "Of course," he pointed out, "there has been as yet no attempt to show that this is the so-called murder weapon. While it is true that the decedent apparently died from a stab wound, and I gather that the dimensions of the knife are approximately similar to the width of the stab wound, there is as yet no other evidence."

"Exactly," Hanover said. "I have other evidence, Your Honor, which I would wish to introduce."

"But," Mason interpolated, "the deputy district attorney wishes to introduce this knife in evidence. It has been identified as the knife which was found in the defendant's automobile, and I have no objection to it being received in evidence."

"As the murder weapon?" Hanover asked.

Mason's smile was frosty. "I have no objection to it being received in evidence as *a* knife which was found in the back of the defendant's automobile."

"Very well," Hanover snapped, "introduce it on that basis and we'll connect it up later."

Judge Osborn pursed his lips, as though debating whether to make some comment, finally decided against it and said, "Very well, the knife will be received in evidence and marked with the appropriate exhibit number by the clerk. Proceed, gentlemen."

"Now then, Your Honor," Hanover said, "I'd like to excuse Lieutenant Tragg for a moment, put another witness on the stand and then recall Lieutenant Tragg in a few minutes."

"No objection," Mason said.

Tragg left the stand.

"Call Sergeant Holcomb," Hanover said.

Sergeant Holcomb was sworn, testified as to his name, age,

address and occupation, then settled back comfortably in the witness chair.

"You're acquainted with the defendant, Marilyn Marlow?" Hanover asked.

"Yes, sir."

"And did you have any conversation with her concerning her relations with Rose Keeling? Now that's a preliminary question, Sergeant. Just answer it 'yes' or 'no.'"

"Yes."

"When was that?"

"On the seventeenth of this month."

"That was the date the body of Rose Keeling was discovered in her flat?"

"That's right."

"Where did this conversation take place?"

"In the office of the Homicide Squad at police headquarters."

"At that time did the defendant, Marilyn Marlow, make any statements to you as to whether she had been in the flat of Rose Keeling at any time during the day?"

"She did."

"What did she say?"

"Just a moment," Mason said. "The proper foundation has not been laid. There has been no statement on the part of this witness as to whether or not this statement was a free and voluntary statement or whether it was obtained by duress."

"It's not necessary to lay that foundation, Your Honor," Hanover said. "We're not asking for a confession. We're asking only for an admission. It is a well-settled rule that an admission against interest does not necessarily require that it was made voluntarily."

"Nevertheless," Mason said, "I think that what Counsel is claiming as an admission affects the rights of the defendant so that I am entitled to find out first if it was a free and voluntary statement. Your Honor, may I ask a few questions of Sergeant Holcomb on this point?"

"Very well, go ahead," Judge Osborn said.

"There were several officers present when this statement was made?" Mason asked Sergeant Holcomb.

"That's right."

"These officers were grouped in a circle around the defendant?"

"They were around where they could hear."

"How was the room illuminated?"

"With electric lights," Sergeant Holcomb said. "We quit using kerosene before I came on the job."

A ripple of merriment sounded from the spectators.

"Was there one big light in the room?"

"Yes."

"And that was directed full on the face of the defendant?"

Sergeant Holcomb said, "You can't illuminate a room and not have it so that *some* light doesn't shine on the face of the defendant. We try to give 'em service but we can't give 'em *that* much service."

People in the courtroom tittered.

"Wasn't that light so arranged that it concentrated its rays upon the face of the defendant?"

"The defendant was just sitting there," Sergeant Holcomb said.

"Facing the light?"

"That's right."

"Who was questioning the defendant?"

"I was."

"And didn't some of the others question her?"

"*Some* of them, yes."

"Didn't all of them question her?"

"Well, they may have."

"During the time that the defendant was in that room, did some other person enter the room?"

"How do I know? I didn't keep track of everybody that came and went. Perhaps they did. Perhaps they didn't."

"Did anyone enter that room at your suggestion?"

"Perhaps."

"Didn't you ask a young woman to come to that room?"

"I think maybe I did."

"And did you ask that woman to identify the defendant?"

Sergeant Holcomb shifted his position. "Well, yes."

"Had that woman actually ever seen the defendant before?"

"I don't know. I can't tell what people that woman had seen and what people she hadn't seen."

"You instructed that woman before she entered the room to come in the door, to point at the defendant and say, 'That's the woman,' or words to that effect?"

"I told her to come in and identify the woman."

"Who was this person whom you told to enter the room and identify the defendant?"

"A night stenographer in the traffic department."

"And sometime later you signaled Lieutenant Tragg to come in?"

"I may have."

"And resort to a prearranged act by which he dispersed all the officers and took the defendant into his office?"

"Well, what if he did?"

Mason said, "There you are, Your Honor, a typical case of a police third degree."

"I don't think I'll entertain evidence of a confession," Judge Osborn said, "but I will receive evidence as to an admission. Go ahead, Mr. Hanover."

"Now then," Hanover said, "did the defendant make any statement at that time as to what she had done on that day with reference to being in the apartment of Rose Keeling?"

"She certainly did. She said she went to see Rose Keeling, that Rose Keeling was dead, that the defendant went to the telephone and called Perry Mason and that she was responsible for Perry Mason being there. She admitted that she was there in Rose Keeling's apartment right about the time the murder was committed and that she had got in there with a key Rose Keeling had given her."

"Cross-examine!" Hanover said triumphantly.

"The defendant admitted to you that she was in the apartment at about the time the murder was committed?"

"Well, she said she was there and it was about the time the murder was committed, because the police got there very shortly after Rose Keeling had been killed."

"But she didn't tell you that she was there at the time the murder was committed?"

"Well, not in so many words."

"Or at *about* the time the murder was committed?"

"Not in so many words."

"Or that she knew anything about the murder?"

"Not in so many words."

"And did she tell you she entered the apartment with a key?"

"She said she had a key to the flat."

"But did she tell you that she used it?"

"Not in so many words."

"Didn't she say she found the door open or slightly ajar?"

"Well, she may have put across some idea like that, but she had the key and . . ."

"What did she *tell* you?"

"I think she said she found the door open, but she had the key."

"Thank you," Mason said with sarcastic exaggeration of politeness. "That's all, Sergeant Holcomb. Thank you for being such a fair and impartial witness."

Sergeant Holcomb heaved himself to his feet, sneered at Mason and lumbered down off the witness stand.

"Now we'll recall Lieutenant Tragg," Hanover said. "Just take the stand again, Lieutenant."

Tragg returned to the witness stand.

Hanover's voice had an edge of triumphant power. "Now, Lieutenant, when you arrived at the apartment of Rose Keeling, what did you find specifically?"

"I found a house of the type known as a four-flat house," Lieutenant Tragg said. "The flat which had been occupied by Rose Keeling was that on the second story on the south side."

"I'll show you a map and some photographs and ask you if you can identify these."

"That's right," Tragg said. "This is a photograph of the four-flat house. This diagram is a map showing the layout of the apartment where the body was found. The location of the various rooms is shown on this map and the places marked here showing the approximate position of the body. Now this photograph is one that shows the bedroom and the body. This one shows the interior of the bathroom. This one shows the interior of the living room. This one shows the bedroom from another view. This is a close-up of the body. I can identify all of these maps and photographs as showing the things which I have mentioned. In other words, they're true representations."

"I ask these be marked with appropriate numbers and be received in evidence," Hanover said.

"No objection," Mason said. "Let's just get the records straight."

The court clerk stamped the various exhibits, giving them appropriate numbers.

Hanover said, "Now, Lieutenant Tragg, calling your attention to the photograph, People's Exhibit Number Four, I indicate two suitcases."

"Yes, sir."

"Did you notice those two suitcases when you first entered the flat?"

"I did, yes, sir."

"What was in those suitcases, if anything?"

"Clothes," Tragg said, and added quite casually, "she'd been packing up at the time she was killed."

"Oh, indeed!" Hanover said, and added parenthetically, "Taking a trip?"

"She was packing up for a long trip, all right," Lieutenant Tragg said. "She hadn't finished packing when she was killed."

"I see. And over here in the photograph of the living room there's a telephone shown in the picture."

"That's right."

"Now what did you do with that telephone, if anything?"

"Well, we dusted it pretty carefully for fingerprints."

"And did you find any?"

"Fingerprints of only one person," Tragg said. "Those of Mr. Perry Mason, attorney for the defendant."

Judge Osborn leaned forward. "What's that?" he said.

"Just the fingerprints of one person. Perry Mason's fingerprints are on it."

"No other fingerprints at all?"

"No."

"Have you asked any explanation of the. . . ? Well, go ahead, Mr. Hanover."

Hanover said smilingly, "I was coming to that, Your Honor. Now, Lieutenant Tragg, just what happened when you arrived at the apartment?"

"Well, when we first got there to the flat," Tragg said, "we were answering a call which had been put in by Mr. Perry Mason. We found Mr. Perry Mason and his secretary, Miss Street."

"Did you have any conversation with them?"

"With Mr. Mason, yes. He told me that he'd found the door open and had walked in, and that he'd found the body and had telephoned police headquarters. He said he'd also telephoned Marilyn Marlow, his client."

"Did he say anything to you about Miss Marlow having been at the flat?"

"No. Definitely not."

Judge Osborn frowned ominously.

"Now, did the defendant subsequently make any statements to you as to how she happened to be at this flat?"

"Yes, she said she had an appointment to play tennis with Rose Keeling."

"I notice in this photograph of the bedroom, there are tennis shoes, a tennis racket, and a container holding tennis balls."

"That's right. I noticed those particularly."

"Did you have any conversation with the defendant concerning them?"

"Yes."

"What was it?"

"I keep accusing the defendant of putting those things out after she had murdered Rose Keeling, putting them out so as to give a prop to her story about the tennis game."

"And what did she say?"

"She would never admit that she'd done it."

"Did the defendant ever offer you any explanation as to how it happened that Rose Keeling would extend an invitation to play tennis at a time when Miss Keeling was quite evidently hurried packing to get out of town as fast as she could?"

"No explanation," Tragg said, and grinned.

"Now, did you have any conversation about a letter she had received from Rose Keeling?"

"That's right."

"What about it?"

"She said she'd destroyed it."

"I now hand you what purports to be a carbon copy of a letter written in longhand addressed to Marilyn Marlow and bearing the signature of Rose Keeling and ask you if you've ever seen that carbon copy before."

Mason said, "I submit, Your Honor, this certainly falls far short of an identification."

"Marilyn Marlow destroyed the letter. We're entitled to use the carbon copy," Hanover said.

"Certainly you are," Mason said, "provided you establish two things. One of them is that the original has been destroyed or is not available, and, secondly, that this is a carbon copy of that original."

Hanover said, "In view of this technical objection, Your Honor, it will be necessary for me to call other witnesses whom I have not planned to put on the stand. I think there can be no question but what this is a true carbon copy. It would expedite matters if I did not have to call these other witnesses."

Mason said, "You have what purports to be a carbon copy of a letter. If you want to introduce it, you'll have to show that it is a carbon copy. You'll have to show that it is in the handwriting of the person who purported to sign that letter, and you have to go further and prove that the letter of which this purports to be a carbon copy was received by the defendant."

"Very well, if you want to get technical," Hanover said angrily, "I'll do it the hard way. Your Honor, I notice that it is approaching the noon luncheon hour, and if we may have a recess until two o'clock, I believe I can have witnesses here who will go through the long, tedious process of identifying something which the defendant knows very well is perfectly authentic."

"It's your case," Mason said. "Put on the evidence if you want to."

"I most certainly will," Hanover snapped.

"Very well," the Court said, "we'll adjourn until two o'clock. The defendant is in custody and will be remanded. Two o'clock, gentlemen."

CHAPTER 19

Perry Mason and Della Street sat in a secluded booth in their favorite restaurant near the Hall of Justice.

Mason, sipping a glass of tomato juice, said, "Hanover's trying to breeze through the case, making it appear that I'm being unduly technical."

She nodded. "He's making quite an impression on Judge Osborn."

"Osborn," Mason said, "is a fine, honest, direct, upright judge, but he never had much actual courtroom experience. His calendar is crowded and he's in a hurry to get things cleaned up. He falls for tricks like that, whereas a judge who had been more accustomed to rough and tumble courtroom stuff would see what Hanover was trying to put over. Only, then Hanover wouldn't try it. He's pretty shrewd and he knows all of the various judges and how they react."

The waiter served them salad and crackers.

Mason said, "Well, Della, we've seen their atomic bomb now. That knife is the piece of evidence we have to explain or else have our client found guilty."

"What possible explanation *can* there be? It was found concealed in her automobile," Della said. "Gosh, Chief, it looks like curtains for Marilyn. That knife *really* clinches the case against her!"

Mason said, "Not necessarily, Della. There are two possibilities. Either Marilyn Marlow killed Rose Keeling with that knife, or someone is deliberately framing a crime on her."

"Robert Caddo?" Della Street asked, hopefully.

Mason played with his fork. "Darned if I know, Della. There's another significant clue in the fact that Dolores Caddo never did call on Marilyn Marlow and try to make a scene. She admitted to me she called on Rose Keeling. I don't think there's any question but what she's telling the truth. I don't think there's any question but what a visit from Dolores accounts for the torn sunsuit and the ink stains.

"But somehow something intervened before Mrs. Caddo went to call on Marilyn Marlow.

"Now let's suppose that Mrs. Caddo called on Rose Keeling at eleven-thirty. Her time was more or less approximate, but we can assume that it was very shortly after Marilyn left. Mrs. Caddo rang the bell and Rose Keeling probably pressed the electric button which released the catch on the outer door."

Della nodded, said, "Go on, Chief."

Mason said, "Dolores went up and staged a scene. She threw some ink. Rose ran for the bathroom. Dolores made a grab at her, caught the neck of her sunsuit, tore it off, and Rose locked herself in the bathroom.

"Now, if that's what actually happened, Marilyn Marlow has quite a bit of corroboration for her story that Rose wanted to play tennis. And if that part of her story is true, the rest of it *can* be true.

"Rose was not packing. She was unpacking. She suggested to Marilyn that they play tennis, and as soon as Marilyn left the apartment, she jumped out of her clothes and into a sunsuit. She got the tennis things out of the closet and about that time the bell rang. She went to the head of the stairs and sounded the buzzer which opened the door. Dolores Caddo entered and climbed the stairs, probably smiling affably until she got to the head of the stairs, and then, without any preliminary, said, 'So you're the woman who has been making passes at my husband!' and splashed her with ink from a fountain pen she was holding in her hand in readiness for just such a move.

"Rose tried to tell her she hadn't been making passes at anyone's husband, and Dolores grabbed her and tried to spank her. Rose wrenched herself free and that's when the inkstained sunsuit was torn. Rose made a dash for the bathroom and locked herself in. Dolores felt she had done enough to embarrass her husband. I don't think Dolores loses her temper the way she pretends to. She simply puts on an act to impress her husband and make him think twice before he goes out with any woman.

"Moreover, Dolores was frank enough in talking to me about having gone to see Rose Keeling. But when I told her Rose had been murdered, she thought that over and then decided she wanted no part of the entire affair. That's when she started lying to Lieutenant Tragg.

"If she changed her statement to me because of the knowledge that Rose Keeling had been murdered, the statement that I made to her was the first intimation she had that Rose was dead. Naturally, then, she couldn't have been the one who did the killing."

"How about her husband?"

"Now there," Mason said, "we have an entirely different situation. There was some cigar ash in the bedroom. Hang it, I wish I knew whether that burn on the wood floor where the cigarette had burnt down had been made by a cigarette Rose dropped when she was struggling with Dolores Caddo or whether it was dropped there by the murderer.

"It could hardly have been dropped there by Rose Keeling *after* she had taken the bath, and aside from Dolores Caddo's visit, there was no reason for her to have dropped it before she went into the bathroom."

"But the murderer could have dropped it," Della suggested.

Mason said, "Rose Keeling wasn't smoking a cigar. The cigar ashes indicate the presence of a man. If you have both a cigar and a cigarette present at the time the crime was committed, you've complicated the problem a lot. I feel certain that the cigarette must have been dropped by Rose Keeling when Dolores grabbed her, but I don't know how we're going to prove it."

Della Street said, "Somehow I have the feeling that if we could know a little more about what Robert Caddo was doing about noon on the seventeenth we wouldn't have any trouble getting the thing cleared up."

Mason said, "He's not very much of a smoker. He may smoke cigars. I've never actually seen him do so and I've never seen any cigars in his pocket."

"That's right," Della Street admitted grudgingly.

Mason said, "Oh, well, let's eat our lunch and well go back and see what happens this afternoon."

He went ahead with his salad and when he and Della had finished, paid the check and walked back toward the Hall of Justice.

Suddenly Della Street gripped his arm.

"Look, Chief. Do you see what I see?"

Mason stopped, followed the direction of Della Street's gaze.

Robert Caddo, accompanied by Palmer and Ralph Endicott and Lorraine Endicott Parsons, was walking toward the courthouse, and at the moment Della Street spoke, Palmer Endicott was extending his cigar case. Robert Caddo took a cigar and with the practiced skill of a habitual cigar smoker bit off the end, scraped a match into flame, rotated the cigar as he lit it, to get it burning evenly, and then walked on toward the Hall of Justice, the cigar tilted up a jaunty angle. Caddo's facial expression was that of a man who has dined well, is prepared to enjoy a good cigar, and finds himself at peace with the world.

CHAPTER 20

As court reconvened, Judge Osborn said, "Are you ready to proceed with the case of People versus Marlow, gentlemen?"

"Ready for the Defense," Mason said.

"Ready for the Prosecution," Hanover announced. "It gives me pleasure to inform the Court that the additional witnesses whom I wanted to secure are now in court, so that I can authenticate the copy of that letter.

"I believe that Lieutenant Tragg was on the stand, but if it is agreeable to the Court, I would like now to withdraw Lieutenant Tragg once more so that I can call Ralph Endicott."

"No objection," Mason said. "I want it understood, however, that Lieutenant Tragg will be returned to the stand because I wish to cross-examine him on some of the matters concerning which he has already testified."

"You will have ample opportunity to cross-examine the witness," Judge Osborn said.

"I will now call Ralph Endicott to the stand," Hanover announced.

Ralph Endicott nodded somewhat acidly to Mason, took the witness stand and answered preliminary questions, stating that he was the brother of George P. Endicott, deceased, that he had been acquainted with Rose Keeling during her lifetime.

"Now, on the seventeenth of this month," Hanover said suavely, "did you receive from Rose Keeling a carbon copy of a letter she had sent in the mail to this defendant?"

"I did, yes."

"What was that?"

"I received from Miss Keeling a carbon copy of a letter which was in her handwriting."

"To whom was that letter addressed?"

"To Marilyn Marlow."

"The defendant in this case?"

"Yes, sir."

"I'll show you what purports to be a carbon copy of that letter addressed to Marilyn Marlow and ask you whether you have ever seen that letter before."

"I have. Yes, sir. That was delivered to me by Rose Keeling."

"And that letter is in the handwriting of the decedent, Rose Keeling?"

"Yes, sir, it is. I have seen her handwriting. I've studied her signature very carefully. Her signature is appended to the purported will of my dead brother, as a witness."

"And is that the only way you know that letter is in the handwriting of Rose Keeling?"

"No, sir. I discussed the matter with Rose Keeling. She told me that letter was in her handwriting."

"Cross-examine," Hanover said to Perry Mason.

"When did she tell you that the letter was written by her?" Mason asked.

"That was on the seventeenth."

"The day she was killed?"

"Yes, sir."

"And where did this conversation take place?"

"In her flat, in the living room."

"And what time was it?"

"Around eight o'clock in the morning."

"And how did you happen to be there at that hour?"

"She telephoned me and asked me to come there."

"You had a conversation with her at that time?"

"I did. Yes, sir."

"And what did she tell you during that conversation?"

"Oh, Your Honor," Hanover said, "if the Court please, this is going far afield. The only questions I have asked this witness pertain to the letter. Now then, If Counsel goes on a fishing expedition, inquiring about everything they talked about . . . well, Your Honor, I object on the ground that it's not proper cross-examination."

Mason said, "I believe, Your Honor, it is an elemental rule of evidence that when Counsel inquires concerning a conversation on direct examination, on cross-examination opposing counsel has the right to bring out the entire conversation."

"I didn't inquire about this conversation," Hanover said.

Mason smiled and said, "You asked him how he knew it was her handwriting and he said he was familiar with her handwriting, and, moreover, she had acknowledged that it was her handwriting. I then asked him about the conversation, and it appears that the acknowledgment took place in her flat. I am now asking for the entire conversation."

"The objection is overruled," Judge Osborn said.

"Well," Endicott said, "she called me up and asked me to come up there. She told me that she wanted me to have a carbon copy of the letter she'd sent Marilyn Marlow."

"That was over the telephone?"

"Yes."

"So you went to her apartment, or flat, and had a conversation with her?"

"Yes, sir."

"And what did she say?"

"She said that Eleanore Marlow had promised her money to witness a false and fraudulent will, that she had been given one thousand dollars on account, that she knew the will was improperly obtained, that my brother had not known the terms of the will, and she doubted very much whether he had actually signed it; that she had not been in the room when the instrument was executed. Under those circumstances, she felt the thousand dollars which had been received by her from Eleanore Marlow, and which she knew was money raised from the sale of jewelry that also had been fraudulently obtained, should be refunded to me. Therefore, she gave me a check for a thousand dollars to ease her conscience."

"That was the conversation you had in her flat?"

"That's right. Yes, sir."

"On the morning of the seventeenth?"

"Yes, sir."

"And at that time she-gave you a check, which also carries the signature of Rose Keeling, does it not?"

"Yes, sir."

"And when you said that in passing upon the genuineness of the signature of Rose Keeling to this letter you knew that it was her handwriting, I presume you're being guided in part by a comparison of the signature which you had seen on that check?"

"Yes, sir."

"And how do you know *that* was genuine?"

"Because I saw her sign it, for one thing, and because the bank accepted it and okayed it, for another."

"You have that check with you?"

"Yes, sir."

"I want it marked for identification," Mason said. "I want to take a look at it."

"Oh, if the Court please," Hanover said, "that certainly is incompetent, irrelevant and immaterial."

"It's one of the documents relied upon by the witness in stating that this letter was signed by the decedent," Mason said.

"But she told him with her own mouth that she had written that letter," Hanover said.

"That's what this witness states," Mason said. "Unfortunately, Rose Keeling is not here to confirm or deny that testimony. This witness has now stated, if the Court please, that in testifying that a certain signature is genuine, he relied upon a comparison with the signature upon another document which he has in his possession. Certainly under the circumstances, on cross-examination, I'm entitled to inspect that document."

"I guess that's right," Hanover said with poor grace. "If you want to keep this thing running indefinitely, I suppose you have the right to prolong it by one excuse or another. Show him the check, Mr. Endicott."

Ralph Endicott opened his purse, took out the certified check he had previously shown Mason, said, "Be careful with this check. I don't want anything to happen to it. It's evidence."

"Indeed it is!" Mason said. "We'll have the clerk stamp it for identification right now."

The clerk made a stamp of identification on the check.

"What time did you leave Rose Keeling's flat?"

"I've already gone into that with you and Lieutenant Tragg. I left there around eight-thirty. I can account for every minute of my whereabouts during the day."

Mason said, "That's all for the moment. I may want to ask you a question or two later on. Your Honor, I would like to have this check photographed."

"Very well," Judge Osborn said.

"Well, I'm going to stay right here until I get that check back," Endicott declared truculently. "I don't mind you taking a photograph of it, but I want it back."

"We can have a photostat made at the first recess of the court," the clerk said. "I can make a photostat within ten minutes."

"Very well. I think Mr. Endicott wants to remain in court anyway," the judge said, smiling at Endicott.

"It's all right. I'll stay right here," Endicott said, and marched back to seat himself with his brother and sister in the rear of the courtroom.

"Lieutenant Tragg, back on the stand," Hanover said.

Tragg resumed the stand.

"Now then, Lieutenant, I show you this carbon copy of a letter to Marilyn Marlow and ask you where you secured that letter."

"Mr. Ralph Endicott gave it to me."

"What did you do with it after that?"

"I showed it to the defendant."

"And what did she say with reference to that letter?"

"She admitted that she had received the original in the mail and had destroyed it."

"You may cross-examine," Hanover said.

Mason said, "Lieutenant Tragg, you stated in effect that you had asked the defendant repeatedly whether or not she had placed the tennis things as shown in that photograph near the closet door for the purpose of bolstering her story, but that she had refused to admit it."

"That's right."

"Isn't that rather a prejudicial way of presenting a fact in the case, Lieutenant?"

"How do you mean?"

"In other words, you didn't have one scintilla of evidence that would indicate that she had placed those tennis things near the door, did you?"

"Well, I felt pretty certain she had. If Rose Keeling had written her this letter the day before, and was packing her things to get out of town on the seventeenth, and taking a bath, just ready to travel, she certainly didn't intend to go out and play tennis."

"But, Lieutenant, how do you know she was packing her things?"

"Because she was packing two suitcases. One of them was fully packed and the other was about half packed."

"You mean the other one was half *unpacked*, don't you?"

"I mean it was packed! She was packing."

"How do you know she wasn't *unpacking*?"

"How do I know anything?" Lieutenant Tragg said. "The evidence was there. You could see it. The woman was packing."

"Lieutenant, I show you this photograph of the bedroom and call your attention to a pile of clothes which were folded and placed on the bureau."

"Yes, sir."

"You saw those clothes?"

"Yes, sir."

"What were they?"

"Clothes that she'd been folding and getting ready to put in the suitcase."

"Did you examine that pile of clothes?" Mason asked.

"Yes, sir."

"You didn't disturb it but you looked through it?"

"I took a peek here and there to see what was in there."

"And what was in there?"

Some underwear, a nightgown, some handkerchiefs, stockings, various things."

"And they were folded to various dimensions, Lieutenant, but the external dimensions of the entire pile were just as shown here in the photograph?"

"That's right. Some of the things were small, like handkerchiefs and underwear, but the outside dimensions of the whole pile just fitted the suitcase."

"And, therefore, you assumed that she was getting ready to put them in the suitcase."

"That's right. She'd folded them so they'd just fit in the suitcase."

"Do you think it is possible for a person to do that?"

"Of course it's possible. The evidence is right there."

"Isn't the evidence equally amenable to the interpretation that the things had been packed in the suitcase and then were lifted out of the suitcase and placed on the bureau?"

"No."

"After all," Hanover said to the judge, "this is calling for a conclusion from the witness."

"He's qualified himself as an expert," Mason said, "by swearing on his oath that the decedent was packing at the time of her death. I want to prove to him that he's wrong."

"Go ahead and try to prove it!" Hanover challenged.

Mason smilingly pushed back his chair, got to his feet, said, "Please give me that package, Della."

Della Street handed him a large shopping bag.

Mason took a suitcase from beneath the counsel table, walked over to Lieutenant Tragg, said, "Lieutenant Tragg, you say it's possible for a person to fold garments so they'll fit into a suitcase without actually fitting them into the suitcase at the time they're folded. Here are some feminine undergarments and other wearing apparel. Now, go ahead and fold those so they will exactly fit into this suitcase. Do it without putting them into the suitcase itself."

Lieutenant Tragg said, "That's easy," and dove into the bag of garments, emerging with a pair of silk panties, much to his own embarrassment and the amusement of the courtroom.

"After all this isn't a fair test," Hanover objected.

"Why isn't it a fair test?" Mason asked. "The Lieutenant says it can be done. Let's see him do it."

"It's a cinch," Lieutenant Tragg said. "Just give me a table or something to pile these on, and I'll show Mr. Mason how it's done."

He cocked an eye at the suitcase, then spread the panties on the table. He next pulled a blouse from the shopping bag.

"Of course," Tragg said, "I haven't had too much experience in getting these things folded so they don't wrinkle."

"I understand," Mason said. "You're not supposed to be making a job of expert packing such as a woman would do. You're simply showing the Court how it's possible to put these clothes in a pile so that the external dimensions of the pile will exactly fit the suitcase."

Lieutenant Tragg started folding the blouse, then observed the edges of the fold with a certain amount of disquiet. However, he bravely delved into the shopping bag, brought out more garments and arranged them in the form of a rough square.

"I think this will about do it," he said.

Mason looked at the pile of garments and lowered them into the suitcase. "You have fully an inch and a half clearance here, Lieutenant."

"Well, I'll try it over again and make it bigger," Tragg said impatiently.

He rearranged the garments.

Once more Mason fitted them and said, "And this is three-quarters of an inch too wide. I'll have to bend up the edges of this pile in order to get it into the suitcase."

"Well, look here," Lieutenant Tragg said, "let me just put one garment down there so I can get the dimensions of the suitcase and then I'll . . ."

"But you can't do it that way," Mason said, "because the pile must contain several garments. There are only a few garments here that would be big enough to give you an exact pattern."

"Well, let me put in two or three and then I'll . . ."

"But the minute you do that," Mason said, "you're *unpacking* the suitcase, Lieutenant."

Tragg became awkwardly embarrassed as the extent of his dilemma suddenly dawned on him.

"So," Mason said, "it would now appear that these garments which you saw on the bureau had been folded as they were put into the suitcase and then removed and placed on the bureau. Isn't that right?"

"Well, I don't know that they just *exactly* fitted into the suitcase."

"But you said they did."

"Well, it looked to me as though they did."

"And the edges were exactly even and uniform? In the form of a rectangle?"

"On three sides, yes."

Mason said, "Try and fold that pile of garments so the edges are in the form of an exact rectangle without having some box or a suitcase to act as a pattern."

Tragg said wearily, "All right, you win. She was unpacking. That is, she'd taken some garments out of the suitcase and put them on top of the bureau."

"Exactly," Mason said. "So you were mistaken when you said she was *packing* at the time she was killed. What you meant was that she was *unpacking*. Is that right?"

"I still don't think she was unpacking," Tragg said.

"But you can't explain the evidence any other way?"

"All right. I withdraw what I said about her packing at the time of her death."

"Thank you, Lieutenant," Mason said. "So it now appears that the defendant's story is not so inherently improbable. Miss Keeling could have suggested that they play tennis."

"Well, she wouldn't have taken a bath just before going to play tennis."

"But in the bathroom, in the soiled clothes hamper, you found a playsuit that was torn and on which there were spots of ink, did you not?"

"That's right."

"And if some person had entered the flat after Miss Keeling had dressed herself in a playsuit for the purpose of going to the tennis court, had thrown ink on her, and had also torn that suit, and Miss Keeling had located herself in the bathroom and waited there until her assailant had departed, it then would have been only reasonable to expect that she would have divested herself of the torn playsuit and taken a bath to wash off any stains of ink that were on her skin. Isn't that right?"

"Oh, sure," Tragg said sarcastically, "go ahead. You can make an explanation that will fit anything, provided, of course, you concede those impossibilities. Go ahead and prove that some person called on her and threw ink on her."

"Thank you," Mason said. "I think I will, Lieutenant. That, I believe, is all."

"That's all, Lieutenant," Hanover said.

Judge Osborn said, "At this time, in view of the fact that Mr. Endicott wishes to have his check back, I think that it will be in order for the Court to take a twenty-minute recess while the clerk makes a photostat of that check. The photostat can then be received in evidence as an exemplar of the handwriting of the decedent."

Judge Osborn retired to his chambers. The newspaper reporters, gleefully sensing a dramatic picture which would attract the interest of their readers, thronged around the embarrassed Lieutenant Tragg, snapping a series of flashlight photographs showing the police officer pulling feminine lingerie from the shopping bag and trying to assemble it on the table in the form of a rectangle.

Mason caught the eye of Paul Drake as the tall detective arose from the spectator's seat where he had been taking in the proceedings.

Drake came forward, grinning. "You've sure got the boys on the run, Perry," he said.

Mason's features showed the extreme nervous tension under which he was laboring.

"Quick, Paul," he said in a low voice, "I want you to pull a job for me."

"What is it?"

Mason said, "We've got to consider the plain simple facts in this case. Rose Keeling had packed up to go somewhere. She suddenly started to unpack for no apparent reason. She gave Ralph Endicott a check for a thousand dollars. After having written Marilyn Marlow that Marilyn's mother was a crook and that the will was invalid, she suddenly became friendly and wanted to play tennis with Marilyn. Does that give you any ideas?"

"What do you mean?" Drake asked.

"There's only one logical explanation. Paul, there's no question but what Ralph Endicott has an iron-clad alibi?"

"No question. I've checked it and double-checked it."

"All right," Mason said, "then there's only one other explanation. I want you to go and stand at the door of the courtroom and continue to stand there."

"Why?" Drake asked.

"Just stand there," Mason said, "that's all. You don't need to do it until court reconvenes, but the minute Judge Osborn gets on the bench, I want you to go and take up a position just outside the door of this courtroom, where you can hear what's going on. And I want you to stand there."

"That's all?"

"No. One more thing. You've got some men here to help you?"

"A couple of my best boys."

"All right. I want you to give one of them this subpoena. It calls for the attendance of the cashier of the bank where Rose Keeling had her account and on which this check is drawn. The cashier is the one who certified that check and accepted Rose Keeling's signature on it. I want that man brought here and I want the records of Rose Keeling's account for the last sixty days brought along with him. Get one of your men in a cab, rush him to the bank, grab the cashier and bring him up here pronto. Tell him it's a forthwith subpoena and he has to appear at once."

"Okay. Anything else?"

"That," Mason said, "is all. But be sure that when court reconvenes you're standing in the door of the courtroom."

CHAPTER 21

Before the clerk returned with the photostat of the certified check, some thirty minutes had elapsed. Judge Osborn, apprised of the delay, waited in chambers, automatically extending the recess.

At the end of the thirty minutes, Judge Osborn, reconvening court, said, "The clerk was unfortunately detained. However, we now have a photostatic copy of the certified check which, I believe, you want to offer in evidence, Mr. Mason?"

"That is right, Your Honor."

"Very well. That photostat will be received in evidence as Defendant's Exhibit One. It will be stipulated, gentlemen, that so far as this entire case is concerned, the photostat may be considered as the original and the original check may now be returned to Mr. Ralph Endicott?"

"So stipulated," Hanover said.

"That is my understanding, Your Honor," Mason agreed.

"The clerk will deliver the original certified check to Mr. Ralph Endicott," Judge Osborn said. "Come forward, Mr. Endicott, and receive the check."

At that moment, Mason, who had been watching the door of the courtroom, saw Drake's operative come in with the cashier of the Central Security Bank.

While the clerk was delivering the certified check to Endicott, Mason walked out through the gate of the railed-off enclosure to greet the cashier.

"Mr. Stewart Alvin?" he asked in a whisper.

"That's right."

Mason said, "I want to put you on the stand. You have the bank's records with you?"

"Yes, sir."

"Just a moment," Mason said. "Wait right there, please."

He walked back to the railed-off enclosure, bent over Marilyn Marlow and said, "Marilyn, I'm going to take a gamble. I *think* I know what happened. I haven't any time to try and verify it." Then he straightened, said to Judge Osborn, "Your Honor, I have a witness whom I would like to put on out of order. I feel that the Deputy District Attorney will have no objection because I think he will also wish to use this same witness."

"Who is it?" Hanover asked, instantly suspicious.

"Mr. Stewart Alvin, Cashier of the Central Security Bank. It is his signature which appears on that certification of the check drawn by Rose Keeling. I wish to ask him about the certification and assume that the Deputy District Attorney will welcome an opportunity to have him identify the signature of Rose Keeling."

"Very well," Hanover said, "go ahead and put him on," and then added with something of a smirk, "If you don't, I will."

Mason said, "Take the stand, Mr. Alvin."

Alvin was duly sworn, answered the preliminary questions and then turned to Mason expectantly.

Mason said, "For the purposes of this examination, Your Honor, it might be better to show the witness the original certified check rather than the photostat. If Mr. Ralph Endicott will stand up beside the witness, he can show the witness the check as I ask him the question."

Ralph Endicott moved over toward the witness stand.

"You certified a check purporting to have been drawn by Rose Keeling, dated the seventeenth of the month and payable to Ralph Endicott, and being in the sum of one thousand dollars?" Mason asked.

"I believe I did, yes, sir."

"Please show him the check, Mr. Endicott."

Endicott handed the check to the cashier.

"That's right. Yes, sir. That's the check and that's my signature. It was certified at ten minutes past ten on the morning of the seventeenth."

"Go ahead and ask him about Rose Keeling's signature," Hanover said tauntingly.

Mason bowed. "And that's Rose Keeling's signature?"

"That's correct."

"You were acquainted with Rose Keeling personally?"

"I knew her signature."

"And were acquainted with her personally?"

"Yes, I knew her when I saw her."

"You knew that she was a nurse?"

"Yes."

"Now, can you tell us exactly what happened when Mr. Endicott appeared and asked you to certify that check?"

"Why, yes, I took the check, felt positive that it was the genuine signature of Rose Keeling, but knew I had to check her balance, and decided to check her signature at the same time."

"Why did you do that?"

"She didn't usually carry a very large balance, and I remember thinking that a thousand dollars was rather a large check for her to issue in one amount. I wanted to make certain that she had that amount on deposit. While I was checking the balance I decided that I'd check her signature just to make sure."

"So you compared the signature on the check with her signature on the records of the account?"

"Yes, sir."

"And found she had a thousand dollars on deposit?"

"Yes, sir."

"Do you remember the exact amount of her balance?"

"I can refresh my recollection."

"Do so."

The cashier looked at his records, said, "The exact balance was eleven hundred and sixty-two dollars and forty-eight cents."

"If that check had been presented the week before, would it have been good?" Mason asked.

The cashier smiled and shook his head.

"How did it happen that it was good on that particular day?"

"She had deposited one thousand dollars in cash on the afternoon of the sixteenth, shortly before closing hours."

Mason said, "Thank you, Mr. Alvin! That's all."

"No questions on cross-examination," Hanover said.

The cashier picked up his brief case and left the witness stand.

Mason said, "Just a moment. I'd like to have Mr. Ralph Endicott answer another question. He's already been sworn. You might just return to the witness stand, Mr. Endicott."

"This is further cross-examination?" Judge Osborn asked.

"Further cross-examination," Mason said. "Just a question or two."

Endicott slid into the witness chair.

"You've already been sworn," Mason said. "You've heard the testimony of the cashier of the Central Security Bank?"

"Yes, sir."

"You did present that check to him for certification?"

"Yes, sir."

"Do you know anything about the ink smear which appears on the back of the check? The smear of a thumbprint?"

"Yes, sir. I explained that to you a few days ago when you first asked me about it."

"And what was the explanation?"

"When I presented the check at the bank I started to endorse it. I got some ink on my finger from the fountain pen and that ink left the imprint of my thumb on the back of the check."

"Exactly," Mason said. "Now, I notice that that is a different type of ink, a different quality of ink from that which appears on the face of the check."

"That's right."

"And that," Mason said, "is because you use a ball-point fountain pen which writes with ink which is inserted into the pen under pressure and is a different type of ink from that used in the fountain pen with which Rose Keeling customarily signed her name."

"I don't know about what kind of a pen she uses," Endicott said suspiciously.

"You will notice the shading in the lines of the signature on that check which you have, Mr. Endicott. That was written by Rose Keeling."

"Yes, sir."

"And you notice the shading?"

"Yes, sir. I do, now that you call my attention to it"

"And it is impossible to shade with a ball-point fountain pen. No matter how much pressure is exerted, the width of the line remains the same?"

"I guess so. Yes."

"But you use a ball-point fountain pen and Rose Keeling customarily used a conventional fountain pen?"

"Apparently that's right."

"But this letter which she sent Marilyn Marlow, and a carbon copy of which was sent to you, must have been written with a ball-point pen?"

"Apparently it was. Yes, sir."

"Your pen?" Mason asked.

"What makes you ask that?"

Mason smiled and said, "Because, Mr. Endicott, the evidence would now indicate that you had called on Rose Keeling on the sixteenth, that you had bribed her by giving her a thousand dollars in cash and got her to write this letter at your dictation and send it to Marilyn Marlow. You had taken a carbon copy for your own protection."

"That's not true!" Endicott said savagely.

"And the next day," Mason went on smoothly, "Rose Keeling had a change of heart. She called you and told you she wasn't going to go through with it, that she was going to tell Marilyn the whole story and that she was going to give you the thousand dollars back. You called on her and tried to persuade her not to do this, but nevertheless she gave you the thousand-dollar check. Isn't that right?"

Endicott moistened his lips with his tongue. "No, sir," he said, "that's *not* right!"

Mason smiled and said, "No, Mr. Endicott, *I* don't think it's right."

"I'm glad you don't, because that's un unwarranted accusation."

"But the reason I don't think it's right," Mason said, "is because I don't think *you* were the one who called on her the next day."

"What do you mean?"

"Let me see that fountain pen you're carrying in your pocket," Mason said.

Endicott handed him the pen, then suddenly thinking over the situation, made a grab for it, trying to get it back.

Mason avoided the grasping hand, unscrewed the cap and said, "But *this* isn't a pen with a ball-point. And it has your name stamped on it. It is a conventional stub-point, rubber sack fountain pen."

"It's an old one," Endicott said. "My ball-point is my new one. I loaned it to someone and haven't got it back—never did get it back—or if I did, I lost it. I haven't been able to find it for some few days now."

Mason said, "You say that's your thumbprint on the back of the check. Suppose you just make your thumbprint here so we can see if it matches."

"But, Your Honor," Hanover protested, "that's incompetent, irrelevant and immaterial. It's not proper cross-examination. It has no bearing on the case."

Mason said, "It has a bearing on it now. The man has sworn that's his thumbprint. I submit, Your Honor, that it's not. And this man can be prosecuted for perjury. Go ahead and make your thumbprint, Mr. Endicott. I challenge you to do so!"

"You know that's my thumbprint," Endicott shouted.

Mason smiled and said, "It's not your thumbprint, Mr. Endicott. That thumbprint is the thumbprint of your brother, Mr. Palmer E. Endicott. And I'm going to ask Mr. Palmer Endicott to come forward. Come right forward and be sworn, Mr. Endicott, you . . . Stop him!"

Palmer Endicott, who had been edging toward the door, suddenly bolted from the courtroom.

Paul Drake, standing in the door, stepped forward and tackled the running man. The pair of them crashed to the floor of the corridor, with Paul Drake holding Endicott in a firm grip, the little man kicking and squirming, throwing his arms around in an attempt to pummel Drake's face.

Pandemonium broke loose in the courtroom.

CHAPTER 22

Mason, seated in his office, grinned across at Della Street, said, "Della, I think this calls for a celebration. The Ice Follies are here this week. Get four of the best seats available, and make arrangements for a table at our favorite night club."

Della Street moved toward the telephone.

She had just completed the call when Paul Drake's code knock sounded on the door.

Della Street opened the door.

Drake came into the office, assumed his favorite position in the big leather chair, scratched his head, and said, "How the hell you do it is beyond me!"

Mason grinned. "A murder case is simply a jigsaw puzzle, a lot of things to be put together. If you have the right solution, all of the parts fit into the picture. If some of the parts don't seem to fit, it's a pretty good indication you haven't the right solution."

Della Street said, "You're stepping out tonight, Paul. You and Marilyn Marlow, the Chief and I are going to see the Ice Follies and then make a little whoopee at a nitery."

"Okay by me," Drake said. "She's a pretty good-looking kid, that girl!"

"Unfortunately, Della," Mason said, "you're jumping at conclusions."

"You told me a table for four," Della Street said, puzzled.

"It isn't Paul Drake we're taking. Kenneth Barstow will be the fourth in the party."

"Well, I like that!" Drake exclaimed.

"I *really* like it," Della said. "I was becoming somewhat concerned over the turn events were taking. You should have seen the Chief's face when Judge Osborn announced that the case against Marilyn Marlow was dismissed."

"What about his face?" Drake asked. "An expression of relief?"

"Expression of relief, fiddlesticks!" Della Street exclaimed. "An expression of lipstick! You'd have thought he was Marilyn Marlow's Prince Charming."

"Beating Kenneth Barstow's time?" Drake asked.

"It begins to look like it," Della said, smiling. "Of course, the poor girl was hysterical. And then again, when you come right down to it, the affection between Marilyn Marlow and Kenneth Barstow has so far been one-sided."

"Don't kid yourself," Drake said. "Barstow fell for her like a ton of bricks. He was biting his fingernails clear down to the knuckles when it looked as though they had her booked for a one-way trip to San Quentin."

"Anyway," Della Street told him, "you should be willing to forego an evening at the Ice Follies in order to give one of your operatives a break."

"It might mollify me," Drake said, "if Perry would tell me how he knew what happened."

Mason said, "The thumbprint was the payoff."

"How did you know it was Palmer Endicott's fingerprint? I thought Ralph had pretty well established that it was his print."

Mason said, "Palmer Endicott is clever, don't make any mistake about that. Apparently he was the one who engineered the whole thing. Let's just look at the evidence for a second:

"Rose Keeling's fountain pen had a soft point. She shaded the lines in her signature and she shaded the lines in the writing on the check. But Ralph Endicott was able to show me a clear carbon copy of a letter she had written in pen and ink to Marilyn Marlow.

Her soft-pointed fountain pen couldn't possibly have made such a carbon copy. That letter had been written with a ball-point pen. You realize, of course, that these ball-point pens use a different type of ink from that used by the fountain pen. The fingerprint on the back of the check was one which had been made with ink from a ball-point pen.

"Ralph Endicott said it was his fingerprint. Apparently Ralph Endicott had had the only contact with Marilyn Marlow. Palmer wasn't supposed to know her at all. Ralph Endicott had a perfect alibi. Palmer Endicott apparently had none. Therefore, once it appeared that Palmer Endicott had left a thumbprint on the check, the whole case was cracked wide open.

"The significance of that fingerprint hadn't occurred to any of them until I went out to the Endicott house and Ralph Endicott told me his story of what had happened, a purely synthetic concoction of fact and fiction blended into the story the Endicotts had decided to tell. Then I called attention to the fingerprint on the check, and, of course, Ralph Endicott had to insist it was his.

"I asked him to verify that statement.

"Ralph Endicott wasn't a fast thinker. He didn't see any way out of that predicament. Probably he would have tried to become indignant at the thought of my doubting his word and asked me to leave the house. That, however, would have been rather a transparent subterfuge.

"Palmer Endicott *was* a fast thinker. He realized instantly that the fingerprint on the check must have been the fingerprint of his right thumb, so he gave Ralph Endicott the cue right under my nose, and did it so cleverly that for the moment he fooled me.

"Palmer Endicott insisted that Ralph stamp his fingerprints on a piece of paper and give the paper to me, and Palmer Endicott went into the next room to get a sheet of paper and an ink pad. He brought the sheet of paper back and showed it to us casually, so that we could see that it was blank, But, of course, when he held the sheet of paper, he was holding it with his right thumb and forefinger, and he had inked his right thumb before he picked up the piece of paper. Therefore, when he laid it down, the imprint of his right thumb was on the paper.

"I don't think Ralph Endicott understood what was up, but in order to stall along, he went over to the table to go through the motions of making his fingerprints, hoping that before he gave them to me some idea would occur to him and to one of the others, so that they wouldn't have to submit to fingerprints for my examination.

"When Ralph Endicott got over to the table, he found not a blank piece of paper, but a piece of paper with Palmer Endicott's right thumbprint on it and immediately realized what had happened. He knew then that he was safe, so he made the imprints of the four fingers of his right hand and of all five fingers of his left hand, and then brought the paper over to me. I compared the fingerprints with those on the check and saw that the print on the check was a right thumbprint which coincided with the right thumbprint on the sheet of paper which had been handed me, and naturally assumed it was Ralph Endicott's print. In the meantime, Palmer, under the guise of mixing a drink for us, had gone out toward the kitchen, where he had a chance to wash all trace of ink from his right thumb."

"My God," Drake said, "that was clever!"

"You bet it was clever," Mason agreed. "Palmer Endicott is clever. He had to ad lib that whole performance, and he did some mighty fast, accurate thinking.

"Once I figured out the riddle of that thumbprint," Mason went on, "the rest of it was easy. Rose Keeling was a nurse. One would hardly expect her to carry a bank account that had an idle balance of over a thousand dollars. But if the statements contained in that letter she wrote Marilyn Marlow and those made by the Endicotts had been true, her bank account would have shown a rather substantial balance for some time prior to the time the letter had been written."

"You don't mean the letter was a forgery, do you?" Drake asked.

"No, the Endicotts bribed her to write that letter. They gave her a thousand dollars in cash, and she wrote the letter in her own handwriting. The Endicotts naturally assumed Marilyn Marlow wouldn't make the letter public, so they had Rose Keeling use a ball-pointed fountain pen that would make a clear carbon copy, and kept the carbon copy for their own protection.

"Rose Keeling took the thousand dollars, wrote and signed the letter, mailed it, gave the Endicotts a carbon copy and then went to the bank to deposit the thousand dollars. After she'd slept on it, she became repentant. She telephoned the Endicotts and told them she wasn't going to go through with it, and that they could come and get the thousand dollars back. When she told them that, she signed her death warrant.

"Ralph Endicott proceeded to build himself an alibi. Palmer Endicott went up to meet Rose Keeling. He doubtless would have preferred to have had the thousand dollars returned to him in cash, but Rose Keeling insisted that it be in the form of a check because she had deposited the money in her bank the day before."

"But why didn't Palmer Endicott simply destroy the check?" Drake asked.

"Because the Endicotts weren't sufficiently affluent to enable him to do so. They simply couldn't afford to kiss that thousand good-by. Palmer Endicott's ingenious mind concocted a story that would account for everything. Under that story, the check, in place of being evidence that would incriminate the Endicotts, would become evidence that would incriminate Marilyn Marlow. But a check is no good after the person who issues it is dead, and Palmer Endicott wanted to be sure that they got that thousand dollars back. So he left Rose Keeling's apartment with the check, went to Ralph Endicott and told Ralph to cash the check. After the check had been cashed, Palmer planned to return and murder Rose Keeling before Rose had an opportunity to communicate with Marilyn Marlow and confess that the letter she had written Marilyn was the result of a bribe.

"You see, it became necessary for Palmer to get in touch with Ralph, and for Ralph to have an alibi, because they all intended to swear that Ralph had been the one who had called on Rose Keeling.

So Palmer had Rose make the check payable to Ralph. Therefore, it was necessary for Ralph to endorse the check personally and present it at the bank. In fact, when Palmer met Ralph, he probably went so far as to take out his fountain pen and hand it to Ralph so that the check could be properly endorsed, and it was then he got his thumbprint on the check.

"But Ralph said why not simply get the check certified? Then they could use it as evidence, and the fact that the check had been certified before Rose Keeling's death would make it as good as gold.

"So Ralph went to the bank and had the check certified, and after it had been safely certified, Palmer Endicott went out to murder Rose Keeling. That was where Palmer had a break. In place of ringing the doorbell and persuading Rose Keeling that she should admit him, he found the door open."

"Left open by Dolores Caddo?" Drake asked.

"That's right. Dolores had been there. She'd made a scene. She'd thrown ink from her fountain pen on Rose Keeling. Rose had dashed into the bathroom and locked herself in, but not before the ink had got on the playsuit she was intending to wear while she was playing tennis with Marilyn; and not before Dolores had ripped the playsuit half off of her.

"Then Dolores Caddo, feeling she had done enough damage, went out and left the door open. Rose Keeling, locked in the bathroom, decided her unwelcome visitor had gone, so she stripped off the torn, ink-stained playsuit, put it in the soiled clothes hamper and climbed into the bathtub to wash off whatever ink stains had been on her body.

"Palmer found the outer door open. He closed it, slipped up the stairs and found Rose Keeling in the bathroom. He ambushed himself so that he could stab her as soon as she emerged from the bath. At about that time the phone started ringing. It was the call Della Street was putting through for me. It didn't suit Palmer's purpose to have the phone continue to ring, because Rose Keeling might dash out of the bathroom on the run to pick up the receiver. She would find Palmer Endicott ambushed in her apartment and start screaming. And if she came out of the bathroom on the run, Palmer wouldn't be able to tap her on the head before she knew he was there.

"So Palmer stepped into the other room, lifted the telephone receiver off the cradle, then went back to wait for Rose Keeling. When Rose emerged from the bathroom with a towel wrapped around her, Palmer stepped forward. She probably dropped the towel and gave one jump, but Palmer smashed her over the head with a blackjack. Then he stabbed her, withdrew the knife, and left the flat, taking care to leave the outer door just as he had found it when he entered."

"What about the cigarette burn?" Drake asked.

"When Dolores Caddo called on Rose Keeling, Rose was smoking a cigarette. She had probably just lit it. It dropped from her lips when Dolores grabbed at Rose Keeling's playsuit and tore it. The cigarette lay there unnoticed and burned a place in the floor. Later on, when Palmer Endicott entered the place, he was smoking a cigar. An inveterate cigar smoker invariably wants to quiet his nerves with a good cigar when he's about to engage in some particularly desperate undertaking. But when Palmer found Rose Keeling was in the bath, and realized he had an opportunity to ambush her, he felt that the odor of cigar smoke in the apartment might betray him, so he ground out the cigar by pressing the end against the sole of his shoe, and probably tossed the unsmoked portion out of the window so it wouldn't betray him."

Drake, who had been listening carefully, nodded thoughtfully.

"So you see," Mason said, "once you get the correct solution, all of the evidence fits into place. Or, looking at it the other way, once you fit all the evidence into place, you have the correct solution."

"What about Marilyn Marlow's ad?" Drake asked.

Mason chuckled, and said, "You can see what happened there. Marilyn Marlow had a pretty good idea that the Endicotts were bribing Rose Keeling. She wanted to get the evidence. She thought the way to do it was to get Rose Keeling to fall for some young man who would, however, be loyal to Marilyn. It was an amateurish way of going about it. She should have hired a professional private detective to do her snooping."

"That's right," Drake said.

Mason went on, "She'll probably make arrangements for one tonight. Tell Kenneth Barstow he has to go out on a job. Don't tell him what the assignment is."

"You're a hell of a cupid," Drake said. "You get these two young people together and then provide them with a couple of chaperons."

Mason said, "That shows all you know about it, Paul. Tonight Della and I are going to forget all about business and business relationships. We're going to be completely carefree and romantic."

Drake heaved himself out of the big chair.

"Okay," he said. "Go to it, you youngsters. While you're doing that, I'll be sitting in my office, slaving my fingers to the bone."

"Doing what?" Mason asked.

"Making up a fat expense account in the Marilyn Marlow case," Drake said. "With the whole evening at my command, I'll think of a lot of things to put in it. After all, the gal's an heiress, isn't she?"

"She sure as hell is now," Mason said.

ABOUT THE AUTHOR

Erle Stanley Gardner (1889–1970) was the top selling American author of the twentieth century, primarily due to the enormous success of his Perry Mason Mysteries, which numbered more than eighty and inspired a half-dozen motion pictures and radio programs, as well as a long-running television series starring Raymond Burr. Having begun his career as a pulp writer, Gardner brought a hard-boiled style and sensibility to his early Mason books, but he gradually developed into a more classic detective novelist, providing clues to allow astute readers to solve his many mysteries. For over a quarter of a century, he wrote more than a million words a year under his own name as well as numerous pseudonyms, the most famous being A. A. Fair.

THE PERRY MASON MYSTERIES

MYSTERIOUSPRESS.COM

Otto Penzler, owner of the Mysterious Bookshop in Manhattan, founded the Mysterious Press in 1975. Penzler quickly became known for his outstanding selection of mystery, crime, and suspense books, both from his imprint and in his store. The imprint was devoted to printing the best books in these genres, using fine paper and top dust-jacket artists, as well as offering many limited, signed editions.

Now the Mysterious Press has gone digital, publishing ebooks through **MysteriousPress.com**.

MysteriousPress.com offers readers essential noir and suspense fiction, hard-boiled crime novels, and the latest thrillers from both debut authors and mystery masters. Discover classics and new voices, all from one legendary source.

THE MYSTERIOUS BOOKSHOP, founded in 1979, is located in Manhattan's Tribeca neighborhood. It is the oldest and largest mystery-specialty bookstore in America.

The shop stocks the finest selection of new mystery hardcovers, paperbacks, and periodicals. It also features a superb collection of signed modern first editions, rare and collectable works, and Sherlock Holmes titles. The bookshop issues a free monthly newsletter highlighting its book clubs, new releases, events, and recently acquired books.

58 Warren Street
info@mysteriousbookshop.com
(212) 587-1011
Monday through Saturday
11:00 a.m. to 7:00 p.m.

FIND OUT MORE AT:

www.mysteriousbookshop.com

FOLLOW US:

@TheMysterious and Facebook.com/MysteriousBookshop

INTEGRATED MEDIA

Find a full list of our authors and
titles at www.openroadmedia.com

FOLLOW US
@OpenRoadMedia